LILLIAN WHITE'S JOURNEY

KAREN KELLY

KLK Publishing
Published by KLK Publishing
KLK Publishing, Brookfield, Crewe, Cheshire
First published by KLK Publishing in the UK 2019
Copyright ©Karen Linda Kelly 2018

Karen Kelly asserts the moral rights to be
identified as the author of this work
ISBN: 978-1-9161018-0-7

Printed and bound in the UK by Ingram Spark

Cover illustrations by Mark Wilcox
Copy-Editor Sian-Elin Flint-Freel

To my Husband Dave for all your support, encouraging and believing. For my amazing children, Charlie and Maggie, who never complained about the lack of my *being* whilst writing this book.

I love you

LILLIAN WHITE'S JOURNEY

PROLOGUE

Rob and I are due to be married at 1400hrs today. It's 10.48am, I'm not showered, I'm not dressed, I'm not even out of bed yet, but there's signs that I should be as I hear the hotel awakening outside my Bridal Suite. As I stare into space wondering if it's too late to back out, I try to be optimistic, searching for reasons why this wedding is a good idea: he's loaded, my dress is gorgeous, breakfast is included and it's not raining. Also, since I was named around the time a new tampon was introduced, Lilly White's Tampons, it would be great to lose this association, along with the teenage name calling, and be known as Mrs Robert Lomax, which I think sounds more like a high-flying newspaper tycoon than a tampon.

They say if in doubt, don't do it, but I haven't the courage to turn back and should have addressed my uncertainties months ago. But I didn't (my bad), so it's here, my wedding day is here, and I don't know what to do. Shall I go for the traditional I do and have a fabulous day, or shall I grab my coat and run whilst there's still a chance?

Rob and I met in a hotel whilst working in Florida. I was a senior crew member with a leading airline and

Rob was a pilot for the same company. We sat opposite each other on our respective sun loungers bordering the hotel pool and, although I'd clocked him peripherally, it wasn't until he spoke with his well-educated British accent that he got my full attention. I don't recall those first words; they didn't register as I was too distracted by his Mediterranean good looks and piercing blue eyes, which completely took my breath away. He was heading my way. Dozens of other beauties lined the pool, ready, posing, groomed and, although I hadn't prepared for the occasion, only just managing to tuck my unshaven hair into my bikini bottoms as he approached, he chose me! He was incredibly handsome, too handsome, the kind that makes you think *why are you still single* handsome. But as his sexy, bronzed, lean body soaked up the sun as he sipped his Italian vino, the thought soon passed, and it wasn't long before we both finished the rich Bordeaux.

I smile at the memory of that day. He had a very gentle nature, calming, reassuring. I felt drawn to his silent confidence and surrendered to his need to take care of me. I'd had a challenging year and knew I'd fall at any moment. Although I was constantly told there were plenty more fish in the sea, I was exhausted from swimming, so when I met Rob, I allowed him his catch.

Six months later, it seemed right to accept his hand in marriage. Yes, there were some reservations committing to a man I hardly knew, but my argument was this: I *knew* he was decent, I *knew* he was fair, *I knew* he cared for me, so my thoughts were, why not? We were in the moment, enjoying life, happy, secure and both in need of solid ground beneath us. He was my saviour then, but now, I don't know if I need saving any more.

It's now 11.03am. I really don't feel well and there's an uncertainty puzzling me that I can't quite grasp. Did I sleep? Maybe I tossed and turned, nervous of the forthcoming event. I don't remember. I can barely open my eyes, the horrendous pain pulsing through my brain, the severity, the agony begins to worry me – why do I feel so ill? This must be the worst headache I have ever experienced. In fact, maybe I have a brain tumour, which would be a pretty good excuse to get out of a wedding! The room is spinning, I'm dizzy and feel incredibly nauseous. Why am I so tired and why do I feel as if I'm hungover when we only had a few drinks last night? I'd already had my official hen party weeks ago, so we'd decided on a petite night-before-the-wedding kind of girls gathering, but I'm struggling to remember what we did. It's all a bit fuzzy and my headache is torture.

My feet are cold, I'm freezing, and goosebumps coat my skin. I'm puzzled to discover I'm naked. Why am I naked? I'm normally zipped right to the top in my koala onesie with cute little ears sticking out of the hood. I know I'd packed it. No wonder I'm cold! I rub my feet together to aid circulation and snuggle down into the Hungarian goose down quilt when, to my shock horror, I realise I'm not alone! I feel another being also snuggling down into the duvet, and a heavy, muscular leg envelopes mine with a certain familiarity. I jolt upright, letting out a slight scream. *WTF? Who the hell is that?* Did one of the girls sleep over? Which one goes to the gym? How strange! They wouldn't sleep in my bed on the night before my wedding, surely, and, if so, I wouldn't have slept naked... unless... no way! Did I sleep with a girl? No! Nope, this did *not* happen, although the thought soon sobers me. Whoever it is, why haven't they moved? Didn't they hear me scream? Wake up! For a second, I think I'm dreaming, until the naked being turns over and rests its hand on my thigh. *Oh my god! Shit!* I try to move but a weakness overrules, and a bolt of electricity runs through my veins, attacking my brain, cashing in the reality cheque as I remember exactly why I feel so hung-over. Oh, dear god, what have I done?

V & Ms, Vodka Martinis, they always get me into trouble! My head's throbbing worse than before as the awareness, mixed with a lack of hydration, hits me in a tornado of guilt. I take a peek under the covers just to be sure. Shit, I'm sure! There's a naked, curly blond surfer guy lying next to me, bearing no resemblance to my forthcoming husband. He's tanned, he's toned and he's gorgeous. I'm dead! My hands grasp my mouth and I gasp as bits of the previous night pop into my head, although I don't recall bumping into any surfers or why this blond dude would be in my room. As his hand rests on my thigh, I fall into a state of shock as my memory slowly returns, visualising the events of the evening: I remember his fingers stroking my thigh and it was electrifying (omg); I remember my nerve endings awakening and my nipples standing to attention, hoping for more (OMG!); I remember his tongue teasing and every cell, every vein, every single hair on my body vibrating until I could take no more, finally erupting in intense pleasure. (Oh my god, what have I done?) I remember him holding my arms above my head with the strength of one of his, leaving the other free to caress my body. I didn't resist or put up a fight. I remember his blue eyes piercing mine and his thick, blond curly surf hair grazing my groin. (I'm a horrid person). I remember his hands travelling down my body and a dramatic rush of excitement as his teeth tugged on my PJs. (I knew I had that onesie on!) I remember he grabbed my hips, wrenching them upwards, then I remember... just letting go... arghhh... FUCK!!!!!!!!!!!!

I cover my face with my hands, hoping it will go away, but it doesn't.

I'm in deep, deep shit.

ONE

I was sure I was no different to any other sad singleton at my age, but I often wondered if there was something wrong with me and why my relationships never lasted. I must have dated every available man on the planet, even the ugly buggers, but I was still collecting dust on the shelf.

It was Friday, 13th June 1980 when I entered this world at six minutes past ten in the evening. No wonder my life never ran smoothly – you'd think my mother would have crossed her legs or something, at least for a few more hours. I was born into the millennium generation in the midst of the technology revolution, not that it rubbed off on me. And being a Gemini, I was supposed to be known for my positive energy and expressive feelings, albeit playful and mischievous. I wasn't going to argue with that, but as I shared the same birth month as my father, he used these whimsical traits in a more flirtatious manner.

My father was a popular man back then: tall, dark, incredibly handsome, sociable, funny and rather addictive, even I wanted to marry him. All women loved him, including my mother, so when he uprooted us to a little railway village in Cheshire, leaving the Cumbrian mountains behind, we didn't complain. However, within weeks of arriving, he had an affair, so my mother dragged her young daughters and mini zoo (Ginger the cat, Jaws the goldfish, and Harry the Hamster) back to the train station. But, of course, it didn't take long for Dad's charm to kick in and, after begging forgiveness, we'd be hoarded back home on the two o'clock train. He had other affairs, many of them, each one resulting in the same tedious journey, until one day, Mum also had an affair – with a train driver, no word of a lie! It didn't last long but the effects withstood and, although it devastated him, it was just the wake-up call Dad needed. He never so much as looked at another woman or left Mum's side after then, falling in love with her all over again. Surprisingly, I secretly missed those train rides.

Maybe my father was responsible for my bad relationships with men, not directly, but somewhere deep in my subconscious. I knew he was the reason why I was easily irritated and fussy with the male species.

My very first date was with John, a punk rocker, gangly, spotty, with a hint of petunia oil, gel lifting the spikes in his hair. He called on foot (because he'd failed his driving test) and we walked hand in hand to the local pub. He drank four pints to my four sips, then forced his lips upon me, smudging my Maybelline. I was mortified. Despite making my excuses, he escorted me home, only to find my distressed mother's legs dangling from the ceiling. He rushed to her aid, heaving her out so, of course, he became Mum's punk hero. I couldn't get rid of him after that but, a million sloppy kisses later, he had to go!

Then there was Phillip, an attractive boy with a long, extended forehead. I thought he'd be brainy so gave him a chance, but no matter how many caps or bobble hats he donned, one couldn't escape his pale, freaky frons.

Another chap wore tank tops on *every* date (wtf?), one held his knife and fork in the wrong hand, and there was one guy who shouted 'CHEESEBALLS' every other sentence at the top of his voice until I realised he had Tourette's. I tell you, I had no luck with men!

Dad wasn't all bad, though; after all, he employed me. He owned a small handbag factory, Wytes Handbags, initially opened by Grandad Herb after Nana Lou died as he wanted somewhere to continue her love of bags and display each one he'd bought for her on his travels: Chanel, Yves Saint Laurent, Mary Quant, Burberry and many other beauties decorated the reception area from a large glass cabinet. Totes, clutch bags and vanity cases, each teasing female visitors and staff desperate to touch, hold and play. Wytes handbags, although not on such a grand scale, took design ideas from those bags and, while it was a small affair, practically running itself, it kept me and Lou in a job and gave Dad something to do.

Dad was an only child to Nana Lou and Grandad Herb, by all accounts a very glamorous couple. Granddad Herb was a tall, handsome man, very smart. In fact, Nana Lou became popular locally as Granddad Herb was a pilot with Pan Am American Airways! It was quite scandalous back then if a Pan Am pilot was seen with a wife and child, due to a reputation of exotic travel and wild parties, but they had a very happy marriage. When Nana Lou passed away, Dad and Granddad Herb became inseparable and I vaguely remembered him at birthdays and Christmas, telling many a story of his exotic trips, the gossip, famous passengers and TV appearances, but most of all, the excitement of the airport. I remembered hanging on to every word. He gave me a passion for travel and an ambition to fly and I quite fancied myself as a Pan Am flight attendant. So, from a young age, I set my goals high. It was a sad moment when Herb left this world and, not short of a bob or two, he left everything to Dad, including the factory.

Life was pretty good. I loved working at the factory and with Lou and had a fabulous set of mad girlfriends who frequently lead me astray on boozy, raucous nights out. But, although Sam, Jess and Sally were amazing company, filling those occasional lonely gaps, I couldn't help but feel that something was still missing.

TWO

Jess shared her tales of woe; it was clear she'd had yet another fall out with Tom. Sam, discreetly rolling her eyes, offered a reassuring squeeze with one hand whilst mimicking the world's smallest violin in the other, clearly bored with the same old story. That was until she discovered the severity of Tom's harsh words.

"He said what?" Sam demanded, suddenly alert, clearly not having heard correctly the first time.

"I missed that. What did he say?" Asked Sally, not wanting to miss out on the latest drama.

Busying her hands through her bright red locks, Jess repeated Tom's cruel words. "I'm FAT, lardy and my face looks bloated..." She was sobbing. "... and..." More sobbing. "...he said it's like sleeping with a beached whale!"

Silence. *What a twat!* Sam, feeling a little guilty, now secured both hands around Jess in a sincere hug. Poor Jess! It was pretty evident that she'd gained a few pounds, but what do you expect working for a large confectionery company? Who'd turn down free chocolate? Well, obviously Tom would as he'd made it clear that Jess' new voluptuous figure was becoming an issue. Through sobs and sniffles, an explosion of giggles escaped, "...and..." More giggles. "...it was my fault he couldn't get a hard on as I don't hold *it* right!" At least she was laughing.

There was silence for a few seconds as me, Sam and Sally used hand gestures to describe how best to hold a penis. Lou was in stitches, as were many of the punters in BJs. Our regular haunt had never seen so much action!

"So how do you hold it then, Jess?" Asked Sam, imitating badly how one should hold a willy.

"Hang on a minute!" I scrambled through my bag, finding a slender deodorant spray. "Try this!"

Sam grabbed it from my hands, offering her knowledge of cock-holding, then we each took turns showing Jess how we did it. As Jess took hold, we all fell about laughing.

"I can see his point, Jess, what are you doing?" Even prudish Sally could see it wasn't quite right. "You'll fail to please holding it there. Grip it here, firm, take control, then you've got space to move up and down!"

Hysteria charged the air, but Jess couldn't sustain it as more tears flowed. Maybe it was time for more drinks!

As Lou and I stood at the bar, she gave me some news about Tom; as it unfolded, he'd slept with lots of women to feed his apparent sex addiction (wtf!) and was described as an amazing sex beast by his so-called ex-girlfriend Angela!

"Oh no! Shit, shit, does Jess have any idea? Does she know about Angela? Is she pretty? How old is she?" Maybe *she* held his penis right!

"What? I don't know and frankly don't care; its none of my business, but I think you should tell her."

"Louise!" She gets her full name when I'm unhappy with her.

"I hate it when you call me that!"

"Fine… Lou! But why me? The messenger always gets shot." I supposed it was down to me to tell her. Maybe if I told Mr Lacking Libido himself that I knew what he was up to, he might confess. With that in mind, we returned to the party, where vodka Martinis lifted the mood. Jess at least cracked a smile. I was thinking about cracking a bottle over Tom's head next time I saw him.

I'd had a restless night worrying over my conversation with Lou and whether I should bring it up with Jess. I couldn't let her continue seeing Tom, knowing what he'd been up to, but I also didn't want to be the one to shatter her already clouded dreams. Jess had been dating Tom for years and, although we believed they were engaged, it had become rather a taboo subject; as their relationship was more off than on, the ring only made an appearance if the wind was blowing in the right direction. Listening to the constant problems in their relationship was a little tedious. However, Tom wasn't the only stress in her life. Her parents had recently separated after her mum's *alleged* affair, leaving her dad devastated, so she'd broken all ties with her mother. Her brother was recently divorced, so she took that burden too, although none of them really needed looking after. She'd also been diagnosed with diabetes. (violin!) However, shit aside, she was still a mug, allowing all males to trample her down.

Maybe Sally could be the one to break the news about Tom. She was good at that sort of thing, although I think even Sal was losing patience with it all. It's different when you live in *Smugsville*. I think she'd lost touch with life beyond her cosy kingdom, avoiding that hark back to life as a sad singleton, keeping your beady eye on your man as other women were ready to pounce. This didn't happen to Sally; Lloyd was devoted. I didn't think they'd had even one row in all their engagement. She was always telling me not to be so fussy otherwise I'd end up a lonely old spinster, but I think her memory failed her, as she was once just as fussy herself, thus moulding her man into her own unique cover boy. Lloyd was a self-employed I.T. Consultant and made lots of money which Sally enjoyed spending. There was always an exotic trip, designer clothes or some fancy gadget she was about to purchase. She was doing ok herself though, working as a personal assistant, frequently jet setting around the globe. They had set a date for the wedding and I was sure they were secretly trying for a baby. She had forgotten that I'd crashed in their spare room a few times over the last couple of years, stumbling upon neatly folded bundles of unisex baby clothes. As it hadn't happened for them, I respected her decision not to bring it up. I loved them dearly, but they lived in a rose-coloured, cosy-tastic, smugsville world, a life which was totally out of reach for me.

With a slight hangover, I was looking forward

to some 'me' time, spread out on the couch with my Horlicks and a big fat fuck off box of chocolates. My conversation with Lou about Tom was still playing on my mind but talking to Jess would just have to wait another day.

As the night drew closer, I could hear the rain tap dancing heavily on the window sill, my subconscious in tune with the notes and I was lost in dreams of the future. There I was, happily settled, living in the country with my husband and two point four. A small holding overflowing with vegetables and chickens, Range Rover parked outside. We were all huddled around the fire eating marshmallows when I was rudely interrupted by a knock at the door. It didn't quite register in my daydreaming state, but as it got louder and louder it was clear that whoever was thrashing my door was desperate to get in.

"Lilly, are you in? LILLY, LILLY, open the bloody door. I'm getting soaked!"

Drearily, I opened the door to a drowned Jess, who appeared to have kindly brought half the river with her. She was hiding in the hood of her sweater and I could just make out the dullness of her eyes, which were also drenched, but not with rain, with tears, real tears. It was obvious this time that Jess was broken and Tom was not about to put her back together again – clearly it was over for good.

"What am I going to do, Lil? It's all such a mess." She sounded so desperate that I didn't know what to say. When a sex addict tells you he can't get it up because he doesn't fancy you any more, no longer loves you and is hopelessly in love, not just *in love,* but hopelessly in love with someone else, then it really is time to jump off that cliff and splatter yourself over the next fast train. Isn't that just kick-you-in-the-ass fantastic?

"Jess, I am so sorry. I really don't know what to say. In time, you'll realise you're much better off without him. Surely you can see that after everything he has put you through?" We sat in silence for a while as Jess composed herself. "I've an idea," I offered, "let's get fit!"

Jess looked at me like I'd lost my mind! "What? Join a gym, you mean?" She sniffed.

"Maybe not that far, but we could go jogging? Power walking? It will be great!"

"Will it?" Asked Jess sarcastically.

"Yes! There's no point moping around, Jess, so come on. Let's do something positive. As from tomorrow we're on a mission. We're going to start a strict keep-fit regime: walking, running, lifting cans of baked beans, the whole works. Thomas with his limp cock and lacking libido can just go and swivel!"

After hours of tears and laughter, stories of my disastrous dates and agreeing that men were no longer in our vocabulary, Jess was on the road to recovery and heading towards squeezing back into her size ten jeans. I was actually quite excited about losing a few pounds myself, eating healthier and becoming the new me. We both decided that the next day was the first day of the rest of our lives and, as this was the last day of our old lives, it would be rude not to finish this big, fat fuck off box of chocolates.

Feeling groggy, already regretting that extra tipple at 1am, I could hear Jess's clumsy movements in the kitchen with the unfamiliarity caused when working another's domain, presumably concocting some break-fast delights. Knowing she felt obliged after passing out on my sofa, I would have been happy with just strong coffee, but I could smell FISH!

As I flicked on the morning news, it took all my efforts not to throw up as she presented sardines on toast with two poached eggs, clearly forgetting my weird phobia of eggs and that I could no longer stomach sardines. They used to be my favourite and if they were ever on the menu, they'd have been my first choice – that was until my horrific sardines and vodka hangover many moons ago. I would never forget waking to my violent sickness and, as I didn't quite reach the toilet in time, everything from my duvet to the bathroom floor was covered in the remnants of a sardine starter avec aroma de vodka, so I hadn't touched them since – although I did forgive the vodka some months later! Poor Jess, she must have made a special trip to the shop as there wasn't a cat in hell's chance of finding sardines or eggs in my cupboards.

I took one look at the plate as it suddenly dawned on Jess.

"Oh no! Sorry!" She cried, taking the tray away. "Don't throw up… it's gone, it's gone, chill, chill! See? This is why I'll never make a good wife!"

"Good job I don't need a wife then, isn't it?" I giggled. "Seriously, Jess, it doesn't matter. I'll shove some toast in. Do you want some?"

Half a loaf and several sobering coffees later, we thought it best to get out of our PJs – after all, it was the first day of the rest of our lives! I tried to keep her spirits high as I could sense her mood deteriorating as the day brought realisation that she was now truly a single woman.

"I don't know how I'm going to get over this, Lillian." Jess burst into tears. "There's just too much to cope with, knowing it's definitely over with Tom, the stuff with Mum and Dad, my brother and injecting myself every five minutes. I hate it!" She sobbed. "It must run in the family, now we've all been dumped! What's wrong with us?"

A vision of Sam mimicking the world's smallest violin popped into my head! It was going to be a struggle to grieve her own break-up if she had to nurture her dad and brother's too, but why should that burden be hers? I kept pestering Jess to make contact with her mum, but she was too quick to judge her mother and their relationship had broken down. "I think you need to put yourself first now, Jess, it's about time!" This subject frequently fuelled me. "They're grown men, let them look after themselves. You've made a rod for your own back by pandering to their every need and now they expect it."

I thought she'd jump to their defence, but instead, after an extended sigh, she responded.

"You're absolutely right. I think it all the time, but it's harder to walk away from them."

"I'm not suggesting for one minute that you *abandon* them, just be a little less available?"

"Yeah, I know."

"And there's one more thing, Jess." I think she knew what was coming. "You need to call your mum."

"Yeah, I know that too."

We had planned to meet later in the day to go jogging as part of our new fitness regime. Bad idea. I'd already had a busy day preparing a recruitment advert for an Events Planner/Manager at Wytes as the function room was becoming increasingly busy and muggins here was juggling both jobs. Bizarrely, when Grandad Herb bought the factory it was attached to an old and tired-looking pub which had been thrown in to sweeten the deal, and we'd grown rather attached to it, despite its quirky faults. It had only been used for our Christmas parties and meetings until local businesses got to hear about it and started enquiring about accommodation and conferences. So, after a brief refurbishment, its use was rapidly expanding. I'd agreed to have dinner with my parents so Dad could check over the advert (clearly not trusting me), so a jog was the last thing on my mind. But I'd promised Jess. To top things off, I had to find some fitness clothes to wear, which was becoming rather stressful as my figure had altered and nothing quite fitted. I settled on some old black leggings and a Pacha T-shirt from my memorable Ibiza holidays, which would surely suffice – although, just for fun, I couldn't resist stepping into an old electric blue Lycra leotard I'd found lurking in the depths of my drawers, a throwback to my days of trying to look like a belonged to a certain dance school. I wondered how the excess lumps and bumps managed to creep up unnoticed, now enhancing the very obvious camel toe. How on earth had my figure changed in such a short period of time? Disappointingly, although hilariously, I peeled myself out, returning to the leggings and donning a cap, before adding a dab of lippy and perfume; you never know, Mr Right may just be a keen jogger too.

Feeling energetic, I convinced myself I could easily jog the few short kilometres to Jess's house, but what a bad idea that was. By the time I arrived I was covered in sweat patches and in desperate need of oxygen. When Jess opened the door, I couldn't believe what she was wearing: an electric blue Lycra leotard (with camel toe), clearly from the same dance class. However, I had to tread carefully, bearing in mind what the poor lass has been through, so I didn't have the heart to tell her that it wasn't a good look. I kept quiet and didn't say a word. Anyway, I couldn't if I wanted to, I was still out of bloody breath!

We left the house jogging enthusiastically, which soon turned into a power walk, then a walk until, within minutes, it was more of a stroll. Mmm, not sure we were cut out for this jogging lark, but we kept the pattern for about half an hour. Jog, power walk, stroll, jog, power walk, stroll and each time we only managed to jog a few inches further, but at least we were trying! Jess complained of a stitch, so eventually we just kept to a slow walk, but after about 40 minutes of shuffling along she insisted on a rest.

"I need to sit down!" She said with a sense of urgency, plonking herself down on the curb. "Lil, I feel kind of weird." Jess held her head in her hands and placed it between her knees, not caring that traffic was speeding past us, a few hoots on the horn thrown in for good measure. She did look a little pale. "I really don't feel right, Lil, I think I'm going to..." Jess fell backwards, legs sprawled onto the road, body blocking the pavement. *ARGHHHHHH!* That was just bloody great! Why was no one stopping to help?

"Jess, Jess, JESSICA.'" I felt my own panic rise. "Shit, shit, shit! Oh, Jess, please don't do this to me, please don't do this to me!" I rummaged for my phone, which was stuffed in my sock, and dialled 999 in panic. I gave the details to the nice lady on the other end – name, address, location, description, inside leg measurement, the works – then sat waiting nervously for help to arrive. I didn't know what to do and felt quite helpless sat on the chewing gum-decorated curb watching her chest, clad in electric blue Lycra, rise and fall. Stroking her arm and holding her hand, I was praying she wouldn't die on me when something caught my eye in the distance. It was a busy road, so to see a young man with bare feet carrying a surfboard was surreal. Cheshire was not exactly known as a county with lots of waves.

"You alright? She passed out?" Said a very tanned, delicious body with an Australian accent. Ah, that explained the surfboard, but did he know he was in the wrong country?

"Yeah, she's out cold!" I replied with an embarrassing Aussie twang. I have an annoying tendency to do that, suddenly acquire the accent of whoever I'm talking to! Where the hell was my brain? (probably on his amazing body and come-to-bed eyes)

Placing his surfboard on the pavement, he knelt next to Jess, leaning in close to feel her breath on his cheek, his hand hovering above her chest, waiting for it to rise. I didn't know about Jess, but my heart was racing!

"Let's get her in the recovery position. Can you hold this for a sec?" *Yes, yes*, I thought, *I'll hold that for you* (picturing another part of his anatomy), as he handed me a small sports bag then manoeuvred Jess's body. I watched as his hands touched her neck and moved her legs into a more comfortable position. *Me next, me next!*

"Nice board!" Was I flirting with him as my friend lay unconscious?

"Yeah, I can imagine you don't see many in these parts. It's got a few small cracks so I'm taking it for repair." He continued to fiddle with Jess's limbs as I pictured him fiddling with mine. In the distance the blues and twos were approaching. "She's breathing ok, probably just passed out, but here's the cavalry anyway so I'll leave you to it. I hope she's alright."

As he stood to leave, the creases on his shorts tightened over his thick, muscular thighs. I swear we had a *moment*. He was checking me out! Wow, he was drop dead gorgeous and I wanted to jump him there and then. He was still staring. *OMG, should I get his number? Was that appropriate?* I mean, she hadn't died, she had just passed out! Too late, he'd slipped away, leaving me to grieve inside as another missed opportunity and bad timing hit me, but at least Jess had started to surface.

"Jess, hi chic, welcome back!" I said as the paramedics took over. Oh, I do like a man in uniform.

"What's your name, love, can you remember your name?"

Wow, what a dish! Fancy being rescued by a George Clooney lookalike. An Aussie surf dude and a hunky ambulance man in one day – this couldn't be happening! Jess may have been semi-conscious, but it didn't stop my secret hand signals indicating for her to check them out! She tried to sit but fell back down again, so they insisted she went to hospital, but not before placing her Lycra-clad body onto a stretcher.

To Jess's dismay, they insisted on keeping her in for observation as her blood glucose levels were low, so I waited with her until a bed became available.

"I was due a trip to the hospital, not been here in ages!" I said. "How dishy was that paramedic?"

"What paramedic?" Asked Jess.

"The George Clooney lookalike who helped lift you onto the bed?" How could she not have noticed him?

"He's not my type; he looked more like the gawky newsreader from Channel 5!" This was clearly not true; she must have had a bump to the head!

"You need to let your family know, Jess. Shall I call your dad?" She smirked at me. "No, but you can call my mum!" She replied sheepishly. "Yeah, call my mum!" I gave Jess a big hug, thrilled that she'd been in touch with her mum. "I called her the minute I got in my car this morning," she continued. "I felt dreadful; she just burst into tears."

"They're just tears of relief, that's all," I replied, hugging her reassuringly.

She began explaining what had happened, but she looked exhausted, so I stopped her mid-flow and told her to rest and tell me some other time. She took no notice and continued.

"It's all been blown out of proportion. She didn't have the affair. They were just friends. She's been on her own all this time but, as no one would give her the time of day, she's really suffered!"

"Jess, she will totally understand. Come on, let's give her a ring!" I said with another reassuring hug. I grabbed Jess's mobile and pressed the green phone symbol next to 'Mum' in her contacts. I felt a little nervous because none of the girls had seen or spoken to Jess's mum since the alleged affair and now I was feeling somewhat guilty.

"Hi Jess, twice in one day, how wonderful!"

"Actually, it's Lillian. Jess is fine, but she's fainted and we're at the hospital."

"HOSPITAL! Oh God, what's happened?" Jess's mum shrieked down the phone.

I could see Jess trying to get my attention but couldn't understand her frenzied hand signals so tried to calm her mother down.

"I think her sugar levels are low due to the diabetes..."

"DIABETES! What diabetes?" Jess obviously hadn't told her mother this tiny detail, and sat there panic-stricken, holding her head in her hands. "I'm on my way!"

After telling her where we were, she hung up and left me dangling. I'd put my foot right in it.

"You didn't tell her then?" I glared at Jess.

"Didn't get a chance. One thing at a time. Anyway, I don't need to now, as you just did!"

THREE

Surprisingly for me, my life had been ticking along nicely. Jess and I had kept up with our healthy eating and fitness regime and we were both starting to feel the benefits. Even so, I had started to think I lived on a manic treadmill. As work had been hectic, especially with the function room taking off and me working all hours god sent in the process, I'd taken some well overdue and deserved holidays. I loved working for my Dad but being in his company several days a week, living and breathing one's blood relative, I desperately required time out. So, I'd left my very grumpy sister interviewing for an Events/Pub Manager – which she only agreed to if I would train the lucky candidate on my return. I hoped I wouldn't live to regret it!

My days seemed to roll into one as I fell into my new holiday routine. I was woken each morning by my friend, Woody Woodpecker, prompting me to make my first coffee of the day. The great spotted beauty could be seen quite clearly from my bedroom window, with his proud black and white coat and his little red hat, making kissing sounds in the distance or tapping on my trees. How wonderful it was having such a beautiful creature as my alarm clock, no batteries required! I loved the early mornings; it was my time and the only time I could switch off completely. It was so peaceful, the only intrusion being the rustling leaves and song birds – you'd think they were auditioning for the X-Factor as each one fought for the higher note.

I hadn't realised how much I'd neglected my house. I'd treated it more like a hotel than a home over the past months and I'd forgotten just how stunning it was, practically falling in love with it all over again: pottering, cleaning and enjoying each nook and cranny that generally went unnoticed in day-to-day life. It was a great house. Set in the county of Cheshire, semi-suburbia on the edge of a beautiful village called Sedley, it was a cosy, picturesque two-bedroomed cottage, one of three. I had fallen in love with it instantly. A worn-out gate stood at the foot of a narrow path leading to a blue wooden panelled door with a central large brass knob. White distressed bricks smothered in climbing ivy, which fought with the eaves and golden shutters, completed the chocolate box look. It posed the charm and character of a 150-year-old residence with the added beauty of gas central heating and UPVC windows! The natural wooden floors and terracotta tiles had been restored and cast iron fires, although time consuming, heated the whole house. The views were spectacular, with scattered woodland and surrounding farmland playing host to lots of wildlife, friendly horses and plenty of cattle. Perfect! It was often the meeting point for the girls to gather, drink and party, either before or after most nights out, and I loved that my home was the major hub.

With a week at home, I'd also become addicted to a morning repeat of *Countdown*. I loved it and, although it was clearly designed for hungover students, my brain became alive and refreshingly exercised – although the girls repeatedly told me I'd need to watch it all day, every day for it to make a difference to my I.Q. Cheers!

Just as I was trying to make a non-smutty word out of the line of letters on the board, I was distracted by activity at the front door.

It was the postman, later than usual so I had started to think he wasn't coming. A jovial character with a smiley face, a great physique but very bald, not an odd hair or a comb over to be seen. I think he quite fancied his chances after catching me in my bikini during a hot spell the previous year, when he hovered around longer than he should have. I'd been desperate at times, but I could never go there!

"Morning!" He sang, knocking into mid-air as I opened the door a little too eagerly, probably giving him reason to think I was waiting for him. "You're not normally home. Are you sick?"

"Morning! No, just taking some well-earned time off. How are you today?" I replied, not really wanting an answer. Thank god Mrs Broome appeared, saving me from engaging in deep, unwanted conversation. Mr and Mrs Broome were my elderly neighbours, a little nosy but a lot of fun. They appreciated the idea of some young blood living next door and loved the noise and laughter which vibrated the walls, interrupting the clock ticking and the wireless playing. They never complained, often inviting me in for tea, cake and gossip.

"Morning, Lillian. Oh, and good morning to you too, Peter!" (Of course they'd be on first name terms.) "I'm just giving my steps the once over, what with Harold and his muddy boots and the dog in and out all day long..." She rambled out a few more sentences without taking breath, not unusual for Mrs Broome.

Once the postman had left, I gladly accepted my neighbour's invite for a cuppa. Leaving my door on the latch, I followed Mrs Broome into her front room. The walls were bright and chintzy, adorned with circular plaques of the royal family. The sideboards were covered in crochet doilies and crystal decanters, with a black and white wedding picture standing proud. Decades had clearly passed since they'd decorated but I always felt at ease with Mrs Broome in her cosy home. She ushered me over to sit in one of the tired floral chairs.

"Anything exciting?" She asked as she poured a strong sweet tea into my willow cup, eyes fixed on the post that I hadn't realised I'd brought with me.

"I forgot I still had these. Probably bills as usual. I've not even flicked through them yet." But as I did, I noticed a thick envelope with a gold crest logo of an aircraft imprinted on the top right-hand corner. "Oh, hang on a minute, what's this?" I flung the remaining envelopes onto the coffee table laden with biscuits and cakes and looked closely at the envelope.

Mrs Broome offered her gold-plated letter opener.

I felt very honoured! She waited patiently as I opened the envelope carefully.

"I have another interview!" I squealed. I'd forgotten that I'd applied, it seemed so long ago.

"Is it for those airlines again?" She asked, trying to sound all knowledgeable. "How exciting for you!"

Well, it would be if it was my first airline interview, but as it was, I'd had quite a few. Unfortunately, I had failed miserably in all the others, resulting in a handful of Dear John letters appearing on the doormat. I'd lost count how many I'd had, but always scanned for the words 'unfortunately' or 'unsuccessful'. My heart would sink but I convinced myself that next time would be my time. I could taste it, feel it, and hear Grandad Herb describing his world. It all sounded so glamorous. It probably wasn't quite like that now, but I wanted to see for myself.

My very first interview had been a real eye opener and I hadn't realised just how tough the competition was. I was totally unprepared and up against experienced crew and extremely glamorous girls who looked as though they'd just stepped off the cover of *Vogue*. I had felt instantly unattractive and totally under-dressed and should have had 'I know I'm wasting my time!' Tattooed on my forehead. I hadn't done any revision, certainly wasn't expecting any tests, and remember chuckling to myself during a maths test at just how completely ignorant I was. *6% of 100? Dead easy. Right, 6% of 100... right, might come back to this one. Next question – 7% of 45... err... Fuck! Shit! Shit. Move on to the next section, General Knowledge. What's the capital of Hungary? Err... fuck! Capital of Sweden? Mmm... Who is the deputy leader of the Conservative Party? Who? What? Who? Shit! Shit! Shit!* And so it continued. It dawned on me that not only was I the least attractive there, but also the least intelligent.

After a few more interviews following a similar pattern, I decided to prepare myself by swallowing a map, doing Mensa puzzles and sleeping with an encyclopaedia! I did improve and passed many an assessment day where I left thinking the job was mine, but Dear John would still make his usual appearance on my doormat.

Dipping yet another Bourbon biscuit into my second cup that Mrs Broome had insisted upon, we both agreed that maybe this interview was my last one and if Dear John appeared again, it was just not meant to be.

FOUR

What better way to end my week off than a night with the girls? We'd planned on meeting at BJs first then moving on to the opening of a new club, Jacksons, a dance music super-club with three floors of different music genres, guest DJs and, by all accounts, only *sophisticated* clientele. However, as BJs had a disco night, more drinks were ordered, so we missed our deadline for free entry.

"I thought we were going to Jacksons? Have I got all dressed up for nothing?" I asked.

"Jacksons is a young, trendy, sophisticated bar for young, trendy, sophisticated people, but unfortunately we no longer fit those criteria!" Said Sam.

"Speak for yourself!" I replied.

"Fair enough, but have you looked at yourself in the mirror in the last half hour? Your eyes have glazed over, your mouth is stained red and your hair looks like you've been dragged through a hedge backwards!" Stated Sam, winking and ruffling my hair, knowing full well she could get away with these harsh words.

We went back a long way and had first met at college through a mutual boyfriend who, unbeknown to us, we were both dating. I had only just met Mark, who was working as a YTS mechanic at the local Kwik-Fit and had agreed to meet him for coffee during my lunch break. I was studying Travel and Tourism at the time and Sam, who had been dating him for several months, was studying for her A-levels. I'd caught a glimpse of this blonde bombshell as she entered the café and boy, did she have a presence. She was clearly angry and, if looks could kill, my time was up right then and there as she headed over to our table and sat opposite Mark. I didn't know what to do with myself. Mark was clearly shitting himself. She took a can of Sprite from her bag, shaking it violently before spraying the contents over Mark's head. Then, from the same bag, as if a magician, she presented a smaller bag, adding the contents to the sticky mess. Sprite and feathers! He looked like a petrified chicken. Standing to leave, she offered her middle finger before making her cool exit from the café, clearly full of pride and dignity. I liked her instantly! As you can imagine, our first words after the event were rather heated until we managed to laugh at the whole scenario. We've been friends ever since.

Sam was a pharmacist at the local hospital and, as she spent all day dispensing, she knew all there was to know about drugs. If you were prescribed medication, she would reel off a list of side effects which would eventually put you off taking it, so if you had a terrible disease you basically had to live with it! She loved her job but obviously didn't believe in the products! I always thought Sam would marry first. I'd imagined her meeting a dishy doctor or a sexy surgeon. But she was just too picky.

I was so used to her tough exterior that her occasional harsh words never offended, knowing full well she'd be broken if they'd caused offence.

She continued throwing her light-hearted insults loudly over the music, then slapped a huge lipstick mark on my cheek. "You know I'm only joking!"

She was right, though. Waving her mirror in front of my face, I realised it did look slightly distorted. My lipstick had melted into the cracks of my lips so I looked like Zsa Zsa Gabor, one of my false eyelashes had stuck to my cheek and a few crisps had taken hold of my hair! How drunk was I?

"Ok, Ok, you have a point," I relented.

But she wasn't really listening, too busy yelling towards the bar. "Gavin! Gavin!" She indicated for the bar tender to come over. "Gavin, over here!"

In our drunken state, we both sang, "Gavin, Gavin!" Louder and louder

"Who the fuck is Gavin?" Screamed the rest of the drunken clan – because the lad's name was Craig.

"One more bottle and a jug of water please... then Lillian will give you a free blow job," Sam promised, eliciting more giggles from the girls. Luckily, 'Gavin' didn't hear.

"Sam!" I screamed, "I think it's time we left!"

The girls were hinting that our next stop should be Blues – the saddest club you'd ever come across – and each time we went I swore *never again*. But it was the cheapest option, with old fashion tunes, so it wasn't long before our heels hit the dance floor to the sound of ABBA (I could never resist a dancing queen) and

Saturday Night Fever. But after jigging a rhythm to Madonna and Kylie, the world was seriously beginning to spin. Stupidly, after copious amounts of red wine, I'd moved on to vodka Martinis and the mixture was fighting in my stomach. I felt incredibly nauseous and dizzy, the heat of the sweaty club overwhelmed me and panic set in, and I felt as if I was floating. The last thing I remembered was a Rod Stewart lookalike dragging me away. I must have looked like a raving lunatic, although pleased I still had an ounce of pulling power, even when freaking out.

"It's Lillian, isn't it? I've been watching you for the last ten minutes. I think you need some air..." He was very well spoken, tall and thin but not gawky thin, more of a *Rawhide* Clint Eastwood physique: blond hair and plenty to say for himself, clearly finding my situation amusing.

"Thanks." I smiled as he handed me some water. "Should I know you?" I'm not sure if it was the beer goggles but he wasn't bad looking.

"James," he said, offering a firm, controlled handshake, "I've seen you around a few times with your friends; you're a confident bunch, aren't you?"

"Confident?" Not sure if I was insulted by that. "Should we be offended?"

"No, not at all. No offence meant. I just find women a little daunting!" He did have a point. Most men weren't looking for attractive, independent career girls who can hold an intelligent conversation, and they certainly wouldn't marry one. They may be ok to fool around with, but they saved their commitment gene to the quiet, reserved type with a low mileage and not much to say. That definitely ruled me out, although I wasn't sure I could hold an intelligent conversation, especially not when this drunk.

"So, do you find me daunting right now?" Was I flirting?

He offered a cheeky smirk then leaned in for a kiss, gently holding my chin and sending shivers down my spine. *Wow, wasn't expecting that!*

"Not bad. Get your coat, you've pulled!" And with that, he grabbed my hand and led me out of the club. I pinched Sal's bottom on leaving, discreetly pointing at James holding my hand, then followed my man like a sheep. I was bursting for the loo but didn't want to spoil the moment and, even though I was more than happy to be led into the unknown, I still felt quite tipsy and for a nanosecond debated whether I should be going home with a complete stranger. His amicable face didn't resemble Jack the Ripper, so these thoughts soon passed, but I hoped my friends wouldn't have to report me missing in the morning!

I vaguely recall getting into a cab and entering his flat still desperate for the loo. But once inside we became instantly intimate, our bodies entwined, ripping off clothes and stumbling naked towards his bedroom. I told myself, 'Don't have sex, don't have sex,' but I didn't listen as desire raged inside. Just as our rhythm began to sync, the rest was a blur and seemed to end rather quickly for James. I wouldn't have put him down as a premature ejaculator.

We must have fallen asleep after that as my only

memory was waking semi-naked in a Blondie T-shirt, my clothes folded neatly on the floor. James was snoring away next to me, so I studied his face, checking for flaws, but there weren't any. He was actually very handsome, with strong features and I have to say that, in my sober state, he bore no resemblance to Rod Stewart. *Look at those guns! Had he held me in those last night?* I pondered about what to do next. Should I wake him? Make coffee? Make breakfast, or was that too presumptuous? I hated moments like this, and I'd had my fair share! Heading straight for my morning wee I was puzzled at why I hadn't previously noticed his loud toilet seat shaped like a pair of bright red lips. Surely it would have been a kiss-my-ass talking point. *Gosh, how much had I drunk?* But a further shock was seeing my pink poker dot knickers soaking in the sink. *What the fuck?* Mortified, wondering what kind of fetish he had, I quickly rinsed them through and crept across the bedroom, breathing in at James' every stir. I stood ogling him as I dressed quietly, undecided whether to cough loudly or just leave. Why did I find myself in these situations? I reassured myself that I wasn't that desperate, especially if he was a premature ejaculator and clearly did things with women's pants, so I slid out of the room with that sunken feeling that another encounter had come to an end. We hadn't exchanged numbers or made further plans, so I slipped away whilst I still had some dignity. I hadn't seen James around before, so chances were I'd probably never see him again. After his performance in the bedroom, I didn't think he'd be seeking me out. I jumped in a cab and headed home. Another one bites the dust!

After a few hours' kip, Jess and I still managed to keep our jogging engagement and, despite not being one for exercise, Sam didn't want to miss out on the gossip, so she came along too.

"Come on, Lil, spill the beans. Did you shag him?" Sam never held back and didn't need any encouragement from Jess.

"Did he have a huge...?"

"Ok, ok, you don't need to hear the gory details!" I insisted.

"Alright, keep your hat on!" Jess chuckled.

"I bet he couldn't wear a hat with all that hair!" Giggled Sam.

"What was wrong with his hair?" I asked defensively. "He had lovely blond hair."

"Oh god, it must be love if she never noticed his Rod Stewart hair," Sam shrieked. "And what the hell was he wearing? You'll have to take him shopping or just date him in the dark!"

"What was he wearing? I can't even remember. I was too drunk to care."

"Oh no, the girl's got it bad. Lil, you're the first to comment on some poor bastard's dress sense, so the fact you didn't notice his pointed steel toe cowboy boots means you got it bad, girlfriend!"

Mmm... I didn't recall those boots but, if the truth be known, I did like him. He made me laugh and I hated myself for running out on him. Should I have stayed? Had I ruined what might have been a beautiful relationship? Although I'd failed to see that, apparently, he was dressed like a ranch cowboy! I welcomed the comments as a reassurance that I'd done the right thing by leaving, even if the thought of him left a lingering want in the pit of my stomach. Anyway, what was there to miss about a premature ejaculating cowboy with a fetish for women's pants?

"Don't worry, girls, I'm not going to end up as Mrs John Wayne. We didn't get very far anyway; the guy was a P.E.!" I regretted the words the minute they left my lips.

"A Physical Educator? A Picky Eater?" Asked Jess. "What do you mean a P.E.?"

"Premature Ejaculator!" Offered Sam, who roared with laughter, followed by a naive Jess, followed by me. Why couldn't I keep my big mouth shut?

I was secretly disappointed about the cowboy. I could have easily woken him and asked for his number, but that would have been too keen, wouldn't it? I'd lost touch of the dating rules, they changed all the time, and if my jogging was anything to go by, I was clearly no good at chasing.

FIVE

On my return to work, I struggled to find the motivation because I was getting more and more excited about my looming airline interview. I hadn't told Dad this time as he wouldn't take me seriously anyway and thought that I'd never leave. "You have a good reputation and responsibilities," he would argue. Although I enjoyed working at Wytes, travel was just something I had to do.

"The new chap starts today, Lillian. Have you seen him? He's a bit of a dish, big feet, if you know what I mean?" Lou placed a tepid cup of coffee on my desk, followed by her leather-clad bottom, ready to engage in morning chatter. I knew she'd used the clapped-out machine in reception, even though we all knew it puked out disgusting coffee, but her desire to check out the new guy overruled my need for decent caffeine. "Oh, and just to keep you up to speed, the flat above the function room now comes with the job."

"Right, ok, I take it Dad's made that decision, has he?" I asked, rolling my eyes. "Has he kept Jim up to speed?" Jim was our new boss, after investing most of his hard-earned cash into the company, but Dad seemed to forget that he was supposed to be semi-retired and should really put his ideas past Jim first. Old habits, I guess. But if I knew Jim, a quiet, family man, passionate about his workforce, he'd trust Dad's decision and wouldn't even bat an eyelid. He initially put plans forward to sell off the function room anyway, so probably the less involvement he had with it, the better – he was also a pro at humouring our father!

"He's just left Dad to it," Lou responded, shrugging her shoulders. "Anyway, let's change the subject. How was your week off?" She asked eagerly. "It's been manic here. Can you believe eighteen people applied, mainly female, but Dad reckons he needs some *masculine* support?"

I told Lou about my up and coming interview and about my one-night stand at the weekend.

"You hussy! I'm only jealous as I'm stuck in half the time playing happy families!" She always played her smugsville world down, but we all knew she had a great marriage to Simon and a fabulous daughter, Sadie. I reluctantly took a sip of the contents of the plastic cup as she continued chatting. I wasn't really listening and, as I'd failed to engage in her morning babble, she flicked my shoulder with her index finger.

"Ouch, what was that for?" I squealed.

"You weren't listening! Where were you? Reliving your one-night stand?" She teased.

"Not worth my energy," I lied, tidying my desk, searching for the notes I'd pulled together at the very last minute. "What do you think to this?" As Lou absorbed herself in my squiggled blurb, my mind flashed to James' lean body, those eyes, and huge guns, but I was brought out of my reverie when Lou began nodding in agreement to my suggestions, making positive noises. I'd spent most of the previous night working on an event planning training programme for the next two weeks. "I think we need to come up with a brand name. We can't keep calling it 'The Function room'. What do you think?"

As we browsed through the new project for Wytes we were interrupted by Mona, our receptionist, to remind me that our new man was still waiting.

"Go on, get a shimmy on!" Laughed Lou as I trotted out of my office. "I've done my bit, he's all yours!"

On entering reception, I wasn't sure, but there was something familiar about the way the new recruit was standing, or it could have been the odd blond hair. I tried to get a closer look but his face was out of view, hidden by the fake dusty palm trees. No, it couldn't be, surely! But when Moana also whispered, "Look at the size of his feet. There's a woman out there with a big smile on her face," I wanted to turn around and run.

"Lillian, this is James Dickenson. James, this is my daughter, Lillian White, who's overseeing the new events programme and will be carrying out most of the training for the next few weeks."

Shit! Shit! You're kidding me! It was him, 'PE,' the premature ejaculating cowboy with a fetish for women's knickers! *Oh god, look at his feet!* Huge trainers! Huge at the end of skinny jeans! ENORMOUS FEET! I could feel my cheeks turn crimson and, although my mouth opened to speak, nothing came out. Dad continued talking about James' work, how qualified he was, blah, blah, blah, then conveniently disappeared. *Oh no, don't leave us alone!*

I began to ramble, on and on, telling him all about the event space and plans for the future, when he cut me off mid-sentence.

"Very impressive. But what happened to you, Miss Lillian White? I awoke and you'd gone, although I must admit it wasn't the best performance."

I couldn't believe he'd brought it up, although I could listen to his sexy voice all day. I was also relieved that my memory had failed me as there was no Rod Stewart lookalike here, he was definitely more of a rugged Indiana Jones and his arse looked fantastic in those jeans! Oh damn – Sam was right – I did like him!

"You didn't mention that you were starting a new job!" I cried.

"You didn't give me chance, too busy getting your kit off – and mine. Really, Miss White, you should play a little hard to get," he teased. "It was all rather daunting! Anyway, are you going to show me around this joint? Hopefully you perform better at work than you do in the bedroom!"

"What's that supposed to mean? You were all over and done with before we even got started, so don't blame my performance on your lack of control!"

"Lillian, there wasn't even a performance as you practically passed out during foreplay!" He was smiling, while I tried my best to fit my head discreetly up my arse. "I tried to hold you back, but you were up for it. I mean, I know I'm irresistible, but you practically forced yourself upon me!"

OMG, I just want to die right there. So, I'd forced myself upon the poor boy in a drunken state then lay there unconscious. The girls would have a field day with that. Oh god, I told them he was a premature ejaculator! I had to ask about my pants.

"Why were my knickers soaking in the sink?" I demanded.

"Do you really want to know?" He asked.

"Of course I do. I honestly don't remember!"

"Lillian, you weed yourself!"

Instant heat flooded my cheeks and my whole body fell rigid in a paralysing mix of mortification, horror, and shame. Come to think of it, I had been bursting for the loo in the club and was trying to hold it in, then forgot about it as we'd just pounced on each other. James had a sexy grin on his lips; he was obviously enjoying himself.

"It doesn't matter, Lillian. Honestly, it happens to the best of us!"

"Shush!" I silenced him then stared into space. I didn't want to discuss it. Poor James! He was a genuine bloke. He wasn't gloating or making a big deal out of it and probably wouldn't have mentioned it if I hadn't pushed for an explanation. What must he have thought taking a girl home only for her to wee herself? I ordered the ground to open up and swallow me, but nothing happened.

"Hey, you were hot before that!" He offered. "And you're still hot now. You're not going to let a little wee wee get between us, are you?"

I covered my face with my hands, trying to disguise the smile seeping out of the corners of my mouth. "Oh god, James, I'm so sorry and so embarrassed! I realised my voice had been rising in hysteria and looked around to check if anyone could hear. Luckily, Mona was just hanging up on a call. "Is that really what happened?" I whispered. "I only remember waking up with a horrendous hangover and just wanting my own bed!"

"You should have stayed; I make a mean breakfast. Maybe next time?" He raised his eyebrows, making this an invitation that needed a response.

"But I weed myself!" I laughed, realising how funny the whole thing was.

"Well, as long as you don't make a habit of it!"

"Ha, ha, very funny!" I broke out in a fit of giggles.

James fluffed my hair. He genuinely wasn't bothered. (Just for the record, if it had been him who weed on me, there would be no going back!)

"Ok, next time I will definitely stay for breakfast!" I had butterflies in my stomach at the very thought.

So, with the introductions out of the way, I switched to professional mode and showed James around the function room before a quick factory tour.

"Why do you call this a function room when it's clearly a fully blown public house?" Asked James.

"Yes, I know, which is why we need you! This building is so old I'm not sure if the factory came first or the pub, but as they're attached, we've just always referred to it as the function room. It does resemble a good old English pub and, although we hold a licence, we need you to take over and get things up and running before Christmas. There's no reason why we can't take bookings for parties and so on, and maybe small weddings!"

"Slow down, we've only just met!" He teased, getting a small shove in response.

Leaning on the bar, I explained to James that due to increased interest we couldn't keep up with demand, so the pub wasn't being used to its full capacity. I went on to explain the change in directorship to Jim, where my Dad fitted in, how it had been Dad's decision to proceed with the events planning but Jim hadn't the time as handbags were selling like hotcakes, so it was not high on his own list of priorities. *And breathe!* Maybe I'd rambled on too much, but James listened intently.

"So, what do handbags have to do with event planning?" He asked, genuinely interested.

"They don't, not at all!" I said. "However, when Grandad Herb…"

"Grandad Herb?" He did ask a lot of questions, but as I could never tire of talking about my grandfather, he received the full-blown history and why Herb went into the handbag trade,

"What a great story! I would have liked to have met this Grandad Herb!"

"He was incredible, a one of a kind. Dad did so well to build the company when he took over. Don't forget, Jim is really the big boss now as my Dad is semi-retired…" I hadn't realised that saying this out loud would have such an effect on me and could feel a lump in my throat. After all the hard work my Dad had put into the factory, of course it would be hard to just hand it over to someone else. I made a mental note to show a little more empathy. "...but Dad might hang around the function room from time to time, so try not to think of him as too much of a pest? Maybe give him something to do. I can only apologise if he gets in the way!"

"Gotcha," he said with a wink which did strange things to my tummy.

"Thank you!"

"Where to now?" Asked James. I wasn't sure if I could trust myself as the next obvious stop would be to show him the flat above, seeing as it was being thrown into the deal for good measure, but James had found another place to investigate. "Where does this lead?" He pushed a solid double wooden door with descending stone steps on the other side. "The cellar?"

"Cellar?" I asked. "I didn't know we even had a cellar!"

"Who's training who here?" He winked again. "Come on then, down you come." He led me into a dark, chilly space which, unbeknown to me, was stocked to the brim with booze! It was an alcoholic's haven: barrels, crates and huge bottles of spirits lined the walls... if only I'd known as on a bad day (or a good day) I'd have sat in the middle and drank my way outwards!

"I'm trying to think of anything else I need to show you." I contemplated areas I needed to cover whilst trying not to look at his groin in those skinny jeans. James clearly noticed, raising his eyebrows as if he knew what I was thinking. "Kitchen!" I insisted author-itatively. So back up the stairs we climbed, heading for the fully stocked kitchen.

"So, I take it you're my boss then?" He asked flirta-tiously.

I was a little excited at the thought of being able to order him about, but found myself saying, "Not really, you'll be your own boss. Once everything is up and running it will be down to you."

He looked perplexed.

"You do realise you'll be finding your own staff? Recruiting? Interviewing and the like. We'll fund initially, then the plan is, well, hopefully the revenue will feed the rest!" I offered. "I suppose it's a bit like a franchise for you. Your own little business, just pay us some rent!"

"Yes, yes, I'm aware, but in the hour of need, who do I call?" He asked.

"Ghostbusters!" I smiled, unable to resist.

"Funny!" He continued, his face telling me it was anything but.

"I suppose if you have any questions, you should come to me," I admitted, feeling slightly chastised.

"Wasn't there an apartment included? Can I have a look?"

"I wasn't sure you'd be taking it, seeing as you have your own place?" I started to feel uneasy again.

"I'll be keeping both, for convenience. Shall we take a look?" He took the keys from my hand and indicated for me to lead the way. I reminisced in my head about our last encounter when I followed him out of the club.

Although I wouldn't have minded a quick smooch, I didn't quite trust myself not to jump on him so was a little relieved when Moana's voice screeched my name, so I left James to explore.

SIX

James settled quickly into the rhythm of working at the function room, finding staff, cooks and cleaners in no time and soon had things running in shipshape order. I was very impressed. We saw quite a bit of each other, and I'm pleased to say I managed not to wee myself, which is always a bonus. Both our work and personal relationships moved on swimmingly, resulting in a swift transition from dating to courtship in a short space of time. We stayed at one another's residence frequently, being comfortable leaving the odd overnight item here and there until it became too hard to leave each other, so more and more items were brought each time. Thankfully, he left his cowboy boots back at the ranch, along with his humongous trainers, replacing them with a more subtle shoe, although they were still size thirteen and a half (yes, that *is* me you can hear screaming from the rooftops), but at least he was trying. There was just no getting away from it, he had BIG feet! Although there was one dumpable offence that really irritated me about him – he was always late. Very late. Not just ten or fifteen minutes late, more like two to three hours! Imagine! I'd spend hours of excitement getting ready, plucking those eyebrows, thickening those lashes and carefully lining those lips to perfection then watched the clock tick past 8pm, then 9pm, tick tock, then just as Big Ben chimed along to my mounting temper, you'd hear the screech of his wheels flying up my quaint little road, coming to a halt at the very last minute outside my door. I'd be furious and miserable, only offering a fake smile in greeting at the door. VERY frustrating! What are you supposed to say to your date who turns up past your bedtime?

For one of our early dates he asked me to escort him to the evening reception of an old friend's wedding. I was thrilled as this clearly meant he wanted to introduce me to his acquaintances. He'd booked a room at the wedding venue, a very exquisite hotel, where we planned to meet, stroll around the grounds and get ready together. I was very excited, although a little concerned as to what far-out attire he might wear, especially on his feet! The cowboy boots were no longer an issue, but he did make some weird choices in the wardrobe department and, due to the logistics, I had no control over what he'd bring to wear. Anyway, pondering over his outfit only took the space of a small brain cell but it took a whole colony to decide what I was to wear. Knowing how indecisive I could be or how big my bum looked in a certain wind direction, I had taken practically the entire contents of my wardrobe. However, what needed my attention most of all was the preparation of my birthday suit.

The hotel was stunning, placed within some of Cheshire's most beautiful countryside, and a few famous faces had also taken their vows right there at the same venue. It was, as one might say, 'the dog's bollocks!'

Our room was also fabulous: traditional, spacious and ready for some action! I was so excited that James was meeting me there and soon set to work on transforming myself into an utter beauty. Never mind the blushing bride, I was going to be the belle of the ball!

A steaming hot Jacuzzi big enough for two scented the room with effervescent bubbles of sweet mint and camomile, and I hoped that both of us would be foaming in those bubbles later. I lathered my face in luxurious creams and replaced the blade in my razor. Where should I start? Legs, nips, toes or moustache? Amongst the choice of clothes was one almost transparent number which left nothing to the imagination, so all hair had to go! Tweezers first! Mole on left lip? Done. Nose hair? Done. Nipple hair? Done. Legs? You can't just stop at the knees, not in this instance, so it was all the way to the top. Left leg? Done. Right leg? OUCH! Shit, shit, shit! I always catch my ankle. The tub turned pink as tiny droplets of rhesus negative coloured the water. Why does the tiniest cut bleed and bleed and sting like crazy? Shit! It was so bad I had to pluck the layer of skin out of the razor. Bollocks! Plasters weren't supposed to be worn with this dress. Thank god for tissue paper, which wasn't a bad substitute. Ok, bleeding under control. What next? Bikini line? Mmmm... I didn't want to risk any more accidents so dug deep into my toilet bag and hoped to find some hair removing cream. Sure enough, there was an unused tube and, although it did state clearly to 'test a small area first', as there wasn't enough time, I just slapped it on nice and thick, covering the whole area from bush to beaver. What the hell, live dangerously! Seemed simple enough... or so I thought. The instructions stated to leave on for no more than six minutes, but what seemed like only seconds had gone by when I was overcome by an awful burning sensation and the desperate need to scratch. I tried to leave it for a little longer but as I scoured the small print – 'do not use on sensitive areas, blah, blah, blah' – it was obvious I was having a reaction, so I lowered myself back into the tub. There was a slight sizzling sound as my beaver hit the water – it was truly cooking and had bloomed to twice its size... shit, shit, shit! Bad idea. BAD idea! I reached for the shower head and drenched the area in ice-cold water – Argh, relief – but was interrupted by my phone melody coming from the far end of the foggy bathroom. Sod it. I couldn't bear to be separated from the soothing cold just yet. When I eventually relaxed back into the bath, I was appalled to see a red, blotchy, bald, swollen fanny, which was unbearable to touch, looked far from eye candy and, most certainly couldn't be covered by my new diamanté G-string knickers. What else could go wrong?

I sat in absolute agony until the water was tepid. As the room cleared, I could see my mobile dancing on the bathroom stool to tell me I had a voice message. "Hi, it's me. Sorry, babe, but running a little late so will get ready at home and meet you in the bar. Will be as quick as I can, see you later"

Nooooo! I couldn't go on my own to a wedding

reception of a bride and groom I'd never met. I could bloody kill him. I'd known this would happen, I bloody knew it. His voice may have sounded as charming as ever in his message, light and breezy, leading me to think everything was fine, but knowing his late record, I should have known. I was starting to think that the whole evening was doomed. I hung up with a sigh, annoyed at my presumption that things would run smoothly. I had planned the whole evening. We would get ready together while downing half the mini-bar, having lots of sex, and he would tell me how gorgeous and sexy I was and 'Oh, do we have to go down to the wedding?' type of thing as we'd fill the room with laughter, fooling around and swapping underwear which we'd later wear down to the reception. At this rate, neither of us would be getting any action, never mind swapping underwear, as my previously bushy beaver was becoming increasingly sore by the minute and was beginning to resemble more of a sunburnt, baldish hedgehog.

I was so disappointed and tried to call him back to see exactly how long he would be only to be greeted by his usual answer phone message to the tune of: "Hey, how you doing? Sorry you can't get through. Why don't you leave your name and number and I'll get back to you!" Arghh!

I wrapped myself in the 'Hers' hotel robe, leaving 'His' to hang alone, as I soaked up the blood still oozing from my stinging ankle. I kept the robe loose as I couldn't bare the towelling rubbing against my monstrous looking pubic area. I was so pissed off that

I attacked the mini bar; it would all feel better with a bourbon or two to numb the pain. No bourbon? NO BOURBON! Vodka would have to do.

I was going to attempt to pluck my eyebrows, which were beginning to meet for the caterpillar's convention, but thought better of it and, after the first few mouthfuls of Vladivar, I could hardly see them anyway. I lay on the bed and rang Sal.

"Sal, help. I've got the fattest, reddest, baldest fanny on the planet..." As I continued to ramble on about my sore genitals I was stopped in mid flow.

"Lillian, is that you? It's Josephine. What have you done with the planet?" Sal's mum was on the other end of the phone. They sounded so alike!

"Hi Josephine, is Sal about?" I tried to pretend that the conversation hadn't happened, which wasn't that difficult as Sal's mum was totally away with the fairies. I found out that Sal had left her mobile at her mum's by mistake. Making my excuses, I hung up.

Oh well, I would just have to suffer in silence. I returned to the mini-bar and softened the pain with more vodka and a bag of Maltesers. I rang all the girls, one by one, but as they all had plans of their own, I just got their greeting messages, so I decided to carry on regardless and not let the events so far spoil my evening.

Within an hour I was ready – in pain and uncomfortable with a plaster on my ankle, but ready nevertheless, so decided to make my way down to the hotel bar. It was full of wedding guests and cute loved-up couples. All eyes were on me, obviously, as I was the alien single guest with no partner, causing every female to cling tightly to their man just in case I'd steal him. Honestly, what was wrong with these women? To be fair, I would probably be one of those women if I was there with James – sad, insecure and threatened. I was quite self-conscious of being alone and felt my confidence slip even further. Instead of feeling sorry for myself, I drank further measures of vodka and decided to add a little cheeky Martini. As it travelled through my veins, it soon became clear(ish) that maybe all eyes were on me because of my sheer utter beauty and stunning attire! Get in!

My eyes constantly searched for James. No sign. Three more vodkas later (with another cheeky Martini) and there was still no trace of him. However, I was aware of someone heading towards me through the crowd. Although mortified to be approached by an older, bald, uneasy-on-the-eye chap, I was glad of the company.

"Are you alone?" Not giving me chance to respond, he continued, "Oh thank god, I thought I was the only sad singleton here. Just look at everyone, not one single male or female in the room!"

"Oh no, sorry, I'm waiting for someone, he's just running bit late!" I replied, embarrassed.

"A bit? If he doesn't hurry up it's going to be over! Where is he then, this *someone*?"

I fought the truth that I didn't know where he was. I was drunk, sad, sore and bald in unmentionable places, and paranoid that people were staring and questioning

'Who is that sad person over there? Is she with the bride or the groom?' "He's been held up at work," I lied. "He won't be long." *He better not be.* I sipped my seventh vodka and checked my watch – 9.40pm. Suddenly, my eyes were covered by long, cold, manly fingers with a faint smell of oil. James!

"Guess who!" He said, without a care in the world.

"Where have you been? I thought you weren't coming." I tried not to sound desperate or express my anger.

"Would have been here sooner but the bloody car broke down. Sorry, babe, let me get you a drink." His blue eyes were convincingly honest and, as the alcohol had numbed me anyway, I was past caring.

"Have you met the happy couple?"

No, I hadn't and had lost interest in doing so, but at least my man had arrived and we could enjoy the rest of the evening. I could relax now that I wasn't a husband-stealing singleton drinking herself into oblivion at the bar!

James seemed genuinely pleased to see me and we were soon chatting intimately, holding on to each other as young lovers do. The room was beginning to spin just a little, which was probably an indication to stop drinking, but as James had just bought another round, I felt obliged to drink it.

"Let's get you on the dance floor!" There was no time to argue as James dragged me onto the polished wood, not realising that I could barely stand as I wobbled unsteadily in his arms "How many have you had?" He asked, a smirk playing on his lips.

"Including the mini-bar? Probably a whole bottle of vodka, oh and don't forget the cheeky Martinis." I could feel my jelly-like legs buckle beneath me as James took my weight.

"Gracious, Lillian, are you drunk?" Which was a stupid question. I'd been at the bar on my own for almost two hours. Of course I was bloody drunk! I didn't have the strength to argue.

"I don't feel too good. I think I'm going to be sick..." I felt myself being half carried, half dragged until the cold fresh air hit me like a brick wall. Whoa, just what I needed, and in the nick of time too.

"How do you feel now?" He asked, rubbing my back. Such a cutie. As I absorbed the winter air offering fresh oxygen to my lungs, the sickness subsided and I began to sober up, not completely but enough to take in my partner's outfit. He was wearing a 'Squire of the county' type outfit, not something that I would have chosen but he looked handsome all the same. He obviously thought separates were ok for his young years, combining a brown hacking jacket with mustard coloured chinos, and his size thirteen and a half feet were poured into Timberland type shoes. Normally I would run for the hills but 1) I couldn't run anywhere in my present state, and 2) it's true what they say about big feet!

"Where are you taking me?"

James led me towards the back of the car park and, although I was freezing, I was a little excited as he had that look in his baby blue eyes. Oh well, no matter how mad I was that he kept me waiting, it was nothing a quick shag couldn't cure. Before I knew it, I was stark naked across the bonnet of his car. One thing for sure, the cool air was most welcoming on my lower bald region and my thumping head – couldn't say the same for my nipples though!

After our little *rendezvous,* he grabbed a blanket from his boot to keep us warm, which made me think he'd done this before, but I wasn't going to complain. It was so romantic making love on the bonnet of his motor under the stars. I was a little intrigued, though, as the car seemed fine, so I wasn't falling for the car breaking down scenario. Was he lying? Yes, his hands stank of petrol, but surely he would call for help, a lift or a taxi, to make sure he got to the wedding on time – after all, we did plan it weeks ago – so something didn't add up. Was he with someone else? The alcohol got the better of me and, as I'm no different to all the other insecure women out there, I just had to approach the subject.

"James, where were you tonight, really? Were you with another woman?" Great, now I sounded desperate and needy!

"Don't be silly! Why on earth would I want anyone else when I'm holding the most gorgeous girl in the world?" He soothed, kissing my neck and sending goose pimples down my spine. However, one look at my face told him that his answer wouldn't suffice and further explanations were needed. He sighed as he dropped his hands to his sides. "If you really want to know where I've been, I will tell you, but you can't tell anyone else. It's confidential and I could be in big trouble if anyone knew."

What had he been up to? Not sure I was ready for what he was going to tell me, I assured him that I wouldn't tell anyone and I would rather know the truth. So, my boyfriend then confessed to his second job... setting fire to cars for a living – oh, my parents would be so proud! He explained that his colleagues (Colleagues? Really?) stole them most of the time. (oh, that was ok then!) *He* only torched them! I didn't think the police would see it like that, he only stole the odd few. He was still a thief! A sexy thief, but still a thief! As he continued to tell me, it kind of wasn't as bad as it sounded, as the owners of the cars requested this service so they could claim on their insurance. OMG! A thief, arsonist and a fraudster. This did not look good. I felt sick.... but also a little turned on! I suppose that was the petrol aroma explained, and I had wondered how he managed his money so well and how he was never short of a bob or two. Setting fire to cars was obviously a good little earner.

Suddenly, I felt as if I was the guilty one and glanced over my naked shoulder in search of a police-man. I swung back and looked straight at him. Wow, my boyfriend was a villain – how exciting! The hotel was probably paid for with illicit earnings. Why I wasn't annoyed or disappointed by this news, god only knows, but being starkers with his willy growing between my thighs, I asked myself, could I really turn my back on the biggest sausage I had ever had? The only thing that had made me scream in a very long time? If I was completely honest with myself, I actually found it all rather exciting! God, I was not normal. He could go to prison for this. I could. The thought sent a shiver down my spine – again a turn on. I needed help; I was dating a complete rebel: Rod Stewart during the day and Charlie Croker by night (not a lot of people know that) – cool!

The night felt cold, so we dressed quickly and walked back across the busy car park hand in hand. We were soon faced with what seemed like a million eyes peering through the window and it became clear they were focused on us! Oh shit, they had seen us! I was mortified as they must have seen the whole performance. What I would have done for a sink hole just then. I wanted to crawl up my big fat bottom and never come out. The bride must have been horrified that I had stolen her thunder as the guests surely had been more interested in the two naked bodies humping outside than her wedding disco! How could I face any of them again? I put my head down and made a humiliating dash through reception back up to our room.

The following morning, I just about managed to crawl back out of my arse so we could go down for breakfast. Once again, all eyes were on me as they realised we were the dirty couple who had been shagging on the car bonnet. My cheeks were burning with embarrassment, but I kept it together and tried not to look so disgusted with myself. James, on the other hand, had a smile from ear to ear. He was obviously proud that everyone knew what we'd done and would have shouted it from the roof tops if I'd have let him.

"Morning everyone, great evening, wasn't it?"

OMG, did he feel no shame? I crawled back up my

bottom once again and didn't come out until we hit the M6!

As you can imagine, at our next gathering, the girls had a field day when they heard about my night at the wedding and I couldn't get a word in edgeways for their laughter, but at least I could see the funny side of it.

"Listen, listen, there's more. I couldn't find my knickers and when we returned to the car the following morning they were hanging from the aerial. Someone had obviously spotted them and hung them up for all and sundry!"

They howled as I sat with my head in my hands, planning my move to Australia.

"So, Lil, what about the car stealing thing? What are you going to do? Has it not put you off?" Jess was the innocent one out of the lot of us and was quite rightly concerned for me. "I mean surely you'll have to sack him; he might take the handbags next, or set fire to them, or you'll notice the beer barrels missing in the cellar. I'd watch him if I was you!"

"He's not that kind of thief, Jess!" I responded defensively, although she did have a point. "Still, it's best to keep this information as far from my family as possible!" *Maybe I should watch him closely!*

True to form, Sam was open to any opportunity. "Will you ask him if he will take my car? It's a nail and I could do with a new one!"

The truth was I wasn't going to do anything about the car stealing as, quite frankly, it didn't put me off. James and I carried on just the way we were. I didn't give him a hard time as long as he learnt to light those matches that little bit quicker and try to be on time in the future.

SEVEN

My airline interview was nigh and, as discussed with Mrs Broome, this was the very last time. I couldn't go through it any more. However, I'd swotted like crazy and knew every capital of every country. I knew all the relevant party leaders, what was happening around the globe and everything you needed to know about the company. Basically, I was even attempting crosswords, hoping to increase my brain power and awaken those sleepy cells. No-one could accuse me of being unprepared.

I travelled to the airport well in advance, leaving plenty of time to gather my thoughts over a skinny 'chino at one of the trendy airport coffee bars where I could sit and watch other interviewees arrive and fidget in their nervous state. I felt silently confident, not that I would get the job, but just reassured that I had done all I could do to present myself well. I wasn't as hungry or desperate for the role as I had been in the past so felt far more relaxed than I had during previous assessments.

The day flew by. I held my own and even quite enjoyed myself. I passed the first section and was invited for a one-on-one interview in the afternoon. I had reached this far before, so I didn't get too excited, but gave myself a pat on the back, nevertheless. Drinking coffee with the other candidates relaxed me as we exchanged stories of our past interview disasters. All too soon it was my turn, so I took a deep breath, walked into the stark room and sat with sweaty palms and pits. A handsome, jovial chap led the interview and a quiet blonde female took notes. I wondered what she was writing about me. Big nose? Spot on forehead? Anyway, a few handshakes later and I was on my way home, content that if it hadn't gone my way this time I could quite happily stay as I was.

A few days later I had a phone call offering me the job.

EIGHT

I was enjoying life. Contrary to the plan, I seemed to be working less and less in the office but 'helping out' more in the pub and loved working with my 'boyfriend'. I was very excited about my job offer as cabin crew, and was waiting patiently for my start date, although I was advised it could take up to twelve months for a position to become available.

Before I knew it, the function room/pub – or should I say The Wyte Shed – had been up and running for almost six months, which meant so had my relationship with James. He practically lived at the pub, so I ended up working many shifts myself as it was the only time I got to see him – admittedly, I thoroughly enjoyed it. We had new bar staff, chef and cleaners and, although I was juggling my office role, I found myself more of a landlady than an admin queen. I was meeting new people, got to know some of the regulars and was pleased to say that James and I worked well together. We had lots of fun flirting behind the scenes, catching the odd kiss – it was great!

Things were progressing at a steady rate until Dad and Jim dropped one hell of a bombshell which changed everything. Jim was more surprised than anyone that this little venture had grown so rapidly and only began to show interest when there were shiny gold pounds to be made. Dad got more involved and they'd both agreed the venue now needed more solid management. Jim planned on opening a bed and breakfast as there were 'plenty of rooms on the top floor that won't make any money empty' – in his words. Basically, they wanted a live-in couple to run the business, so either James would be out of a job or we would have to move forward with the business (and our relationship) and take on this audacious move! Dad obviously didn't take my airline job seriously – he had probably forgotten I had a start date looming! I loved that I could juggle my office and pub jobs, but the new responsibilities would be too much of a commitment – in more ways than one! As Dad explained the situation to us both, James raised his eyebrows in my direction; surely this was a shock to him too.

"The only snag is, guys," said Jim, "we need to get going on this and need a decision soon – maybe in a few days?"

After providing a few more details and a pat on the back, they left us flabbergasted! WTF? A few days? Was he kidding? James was quiet too and obviously didn't know what to make of it. We hadn't been together that long and were still growing as a couple, but this role would intensify the rate at which we were still learning about one another. Living together so quickly would certainly speed things up and we were happy taking things slow. I needed to speak to the girls – though they'd probably love it if there was free booze on drip.

"Well that's a lot to take in on a quiet Wednesday morning!" James interrupted my thoughts, clearly trying to lighten the heavy news. "There is one consolation, though..." He grabbed my hand and held it to his bulging crotch. "...this little baby would be on tap... and I get to look at you every morning!"

I jerked my hand away from his hardness, still blushing, as an elderly couple entered the bar. "Yes, what can I get for you?" I smiled as I took their order and pondered on the news. I didn't know if I was ready to take on such a big project and I didn't want to ruin things with James. Were we ready for this? What about my new job? I was thrilled one minute and totally unsure the next. What about my beautiful house? I liked my own space and I wasn't sure if James was ready to see me picking my feet, or my nose for that matter. We were just not ready!

James and I stood on the landing on the top floor, having examined all the possible bedrooms, which I'd already decorated in shabby chic in my mind – I couldn't help myself! Pondering over the busy street below as I leant against the filthy window – another job to do – I let out a sigh.

"I'm sure you've got your reservations, Lil, as have I, but it probably won't be that different, only on paper," offered James. "This is a great opportunity and think of the experience. Who wrote the sodding rulebook anyway? Yes, we haven't been together that long and yes, only fools rush in, but if we do it properly, try and carry on the way we are, then I'm sure it will all work out ok."

"Well yes, I do have my reservations, James, to be honest. I'm still in shock and not sure if I want the responsibility just yet! I haven't been in my house that long and I really don't want to give it up."

"Maybe you wouldn't have to, maybe you could live at home and drive to work daily just as you do now with maybe the odd night here and there. We could have separate rooms, there's plenty of them?" He looked at the rooms surrounding us and, although he was half joking, it wasn't a bad idea.

"I could probably live with that, if you're ok with that?" I replied.

"I'm ok with that... so... are you saying that you're willing to give it a go?" He obviously wanted me to say yes.

"Maybe. Can we sleep on it and see how we feel in the morning? I mean, I still have a job offer, remember, and a start date coming through at any moment, which I still intend on taking. What happens then?"

"I don't have all the answers. Maybe we just take each day and see how it goes." He pulled me close in his arms, kissing the side of my head reassuringly. "Look, I like you... a lot! I wasn't planning on moving in or settling with a family right now, but it feels kind of ok to do this." He made total sense.

Instead of dining out, we agreed to go our separate ways for the evening. There wasn't much more to say on the subject apart from repeating our thoughts over and over again, so we decided to talk it through with our respective families and friends and meet for breakfast the following morning to make our final decision. Despite my doubts, I was rather excited.

Sam was the first person I called as I knew she'd give me her honest opinion and would avoid beating around the bush.

"What? Move in together already? Bloody hell, Lillian, you don't waste time, do you?" Mmmm, not quite the response I was hoping for. "Living together and working together spells disaster with a capital 'D', so don't come crying to me when it all goes tits up!"

"Cheers!" I sniffed. What else did I expect?

"Of course, you can come running to me, you idiot!"

Next on my list was Jess.

"Oh Lillian, you're joking, right? You're wanting to move in together already? Do you love him? I mean, are you 'in love' with him... Are you pregnant?" I didn't think she had listened to the reason why we were considering living together.

"No, of course I'm not pregnant, but living in the pub is a requirement of us both taking over the premises as managers." I repeated myself several times before she absorbed what I was saying. "And I'm not going to really live in. James will be on site most of the time, I will still live here and stay over a few nights a..."

"Week? Month?" She didn't let me finish.

"Month? Maybe every two weeks? I'm not really sure yet."

"Well, you really need to think it through, Lillian, or you'll end up regretting the whole thing!"

Great, two supportive friends down, one more to

go! Actually, I decided not to go through with the same conversation, especially with Sally. As much as I loved her dearly, her life was pretty perfect, and this would definitely not come under the set criteria: meet boy, date boy for several years, save for a house, get married, move into house, have lots of babies. Sally's world was a million miles away from mine and my two-bit pub proposal and cock-on-tap cowboy!

Instead, I called Lou to see what her thoughts were and where she fitted into all this. Surely it would mean more work for her if I wasn't in the office as much. Then I called my parents and gave my dad the third degree for putting me on the spot. How dare he! It was probably his secret plan to stop me leaving. It was no secret that he had a soft spot for James. They seemed to muddle along quite nicely. James knew how to wrap him around his little finger though, frequently involving him in The Wyte Shed as much as he could. I had a feeling Dad would quite like him as a future son-in-law!

Curled up on my sofa, I immersed yet another chocolate digestive into my coffee, retrieving it just before it dissolved into a sugary putty. I thought I'd trained my brain to take just a few to prevent demolishing the whole packet. I hadn't. I found myself returning to the biscuit barrel in the kitchen to take *just one more*. I reassured myself that this was fine as I'd be burning off the biscuit calories just from the act of heaving my quads off the sofa to walk back to the kitchen. However, I calculated that at 75 calories per biscuit multiplied by the 12 in the packet, I'd have to burn off 900 calories in kitchen runs. As the kitchen was just a 20-step round trip, I was only burning off approximately 1 calorie per 75 calories worth of biscuit. I'd literally have to do the same act about 900 times to burn off a packet – which would probably result in my coffee going cold. In the end, I just kept the packet with me and devoured the lot. I accepted that a packet of biscuits per mug of coffee was acceptable. At least I'd tried! I was still exercising with Jess occasionally, so I was monitoring my waistline... and yes, it was clearly expanding.

Despite being slightly lifted with my sugar rush, it hadn't distracted me from my decision. Should I move into hospitality with Mr Bigfeet or should just continue at Wytes Handbags and wait for my airline start date? I didn't know why I was getting so bloody worked up over it all. Like Lou said, it was only a small decision in the scheme of things, just part of life's journey – 'just take it and go with it' were pretty much her words. I replayed the conversations with Mum, Dad (who laughed off his grilling) and Sally (who had heard the news from Jess). My head was spinning with all their advice, but it didn't make my decision any easier.

James called just before I fell into bed. We both agreed to give it a go, we would be running The Wyte Shed as managers in two weeks' time and would just have to review the situation when I heard from the airline.

NINE

I'd survived almost a year working at The Wyte Shed, thoroughly enjoying myself. I even managed a slight taste of what life would be like in *cosy-tastic smugsville* – but it didn't last long. Although I ran a pretty tight ship, there was no avoiding a few rogue waves: tills were frequently down as staff were pilfering and no-shows for shifts became the norm, drunken customers, fights, damage to furniture and broken windows. It was unsettling, this was our home, and after a few groundhog weekends it just became tedious. Also, despite my best intentions, I found myself living more at The Wyte Shed and less at home, as had been the plan. The odd night became two, then half the week, until eventually I was there the whole time.

James often disappeared, unannounced, which I challenged frequently and, although he wriggled around the truth, I knew that he was still up to no good stealing cars – it didn't help the situation. He wasn't being truthful and was becoming unreliable, so eventually the chemistry altered between us, leaving the honeymoon period behind. To top it off, there was no time to appreciate what we had anyway. We worked considerably long hours and were exhausted and drained. Our relationship was dwindling.

The only thing was, I still loved him and believed he still loved me, but I truly felt that the relationship was breaking down. Dad noticed the chilly atmosphere between us, but I habitually shrugged it off, although I knew I had to be honest with myself if there was any chance of the relationship being saved. However, my heart sank further when James failed to return home on several occasions. I had my suspicions that maybe there was someone else. He denied this of course, blatantly, but once those doubts are embedded in your brain the trust is challenged and your imagination runs away with you. It was eating away at me and, although we tried to continue our relationship, it just wasn't the same.

James, clearly not a morning person, would occasionally need reminding that, as I'd seen to the B&B guests and served breakfast (amongst a zillion other things), it was *his* responsibility to open the bar at 11.00am, so the daily discussion would go along the lines of:

"JAMES!!!!" I'd shout. "ARE YOU GETTING UP? WE'RE OPENING IN FIVE!"

No response.

"JAMES? JAMES!" I'd bellow.

No response.

"JAMES, GET UP! NOW!" I'd be practically screaming at this point.

No response.

"JAMES! PEOPLE ARE WAITING OUTSIDE!"

They weren't.

"JAMES, YOU LAZY BASTARD, GET UP NOW!"
No response.
"I'M JUST GOING TO OPEN UP... AGAIN!!!"
I wouldn't.
"YOU LAZY BASTARD, WE'RE OPEN!'
We weren't!
Grabbing the soda siphon, I'd run upstairs and spray the fizzy contents all over him.
"Sorry, did I wake you?"
At which point, he'd snatch the damn thing from me and chase me back down the stairs! Sometimes I'd dare the waitress to siphon him instead; it was hilarious.

Needless to say, our days were numbered at The Wyte Shed. If the truth be known, we were inches away from killing each other, so it was a welcome twist of fate when I returned home one evening to find a large, thick envelope covered in aeroplanes. Inside, there finally, highlighted in bold, was my start date. Thank god!

I spoke with Dad first, who was of course disappointed but not totally surprised. I unofficially resigned from The Wyte Shed, agreeing to help out in my previous role when I could. In return, Dad promised that he'd happily keep James on for a while *just in case*! I think he secretly hoped I would change my mind and things would return to normal. In fact, I'd go as far as saying that I swear he'd had an ulterior motive throwing us in the deep end like that. Was it his way of keeping me around? Could I blame my Dad again for another failed relationship? I couldn't dwell on it, but I wasn't going back.

James was disappointed too but knew how desperate I was to fly and how long I'd been waiting for the letter. I was touched when I arrived for work the following day, because it was obvious he was genuinely pleased and making an effort.

"Congratulations, Lillian, well deserved, well done!" He fidgeted with the hole puncher and moved papers around the desk. "Look, I'm sorry things didn't work out here, but if it's any consolation, I do still really care for you. It's just all been a bit crazy." He tucked a piece of hair behind my ear then brought his hand down to squeeze my shoulders. "I sincerely wish you all the best."

I was moved by his unexpected display of emotion; it was the closest we'd been for ages.

"I'm sorry too. I've been running around like a headless chicken but there didn't seem any other way. Trying to keep a hand in with Dad with handbags, being here, dealing with the change in our relationship, the to-ing and fro-ing. I'm secretly relieved it's coming to an end." He looked hurt. "…with the pub, I mean… we were thrown in at the deep end!" I wasn't sure what I meant. Was it the end for our relationship or just the business part of it? I could sense his cogs turning. Had I said the wrong thing? What was he thinking? Did I really want this to come to an end? We were at ease in the moment, like we used to be, relaxed, loving, normal. I still loved him – I thought. He had said he cared for me, was that the same as love? Or did that mean that he didn't love me anymore? A part of me just wanted to hold him, be held, turn back the clock, but the other part of me was eager to close the doors on this place and move forward.

"What about us, James?" Oh god, I didn't know where that came from, but an inner confidence surfaced. "...is there still an *us*?"

James didn't answer immediately, which pretty much *was* my answer. He took my hands and held them in his. "Maybe this isn't the right time for us, Lil. This all happened so fast..." He stopped me with a squeeze of my hand before I interrupted with 'well why did we do it then blah, blah....' and smiled. "Yeah, we knew what we were getting into and it was right at the time... but now..." My heart sank to that familiar place at the pit of my stomach. We held each other's gaze. "...now maybe... maybe we need to take a break..."

Was this a question? Would my answer make a difference now that *that* word was mentioned? I had words waiting at the end of my tongue: 'I'll stay,' 'It will still work, we'll make it work,' but they would just sound desperate. I swallowed the pleas, hiding my disappointment, because deep down I knew this is the right thing for us. A long silence prevailed.

"I don't know what else to say," offered James.

Neither did I.

We sat in silence for a while until our bedraggled cleaner arrived, banging on the door, overloaded with buckets and bags. James offered a smile whilst opening the door then proceeded to the cellar for a stock check. Oh, was that it then? Was that the end for us? What happens now? I was a little bewildered. I thought he'd have more to say. I thought I was worth more than that, deserving at least a 'Please don't go, Lillian,' or a 'Stay, I love you.' But... nothing. I sighed heavily, holding back the bile that hovered at the base of my throat, seeping into my stomach, trapping the anxiety within. That must be it, then. Over. Kaput. I guessed as tough as it was, my life was changing paths again and it was time to head off on a different journey.

As my final shift drew to an end, I took one last tour of the bar, noticing for the first time the amazing display of prints decorating the walls, unappreciated until that very moment. I was drawn to one particular painting, a stunning watercolour of The Wyte Shed many moons ago. It depicted a hot summer's day with plenty of punters inside and out, sleeveless T-shirts and bare little legs dangling from old fashioned pushchairs. Flower-boxes rested on the shiny black trims of the rickety old sash windows, each filled with colourful pansies and roses. The words printed at the bottom were 'Beaumont Jockey'. I wondered what that meant. There was a ginger cat sleeping on the ledge of the very top window, looking as if it might fall at any moment, yet relaxed, dreaming. I wondered how old this painting was and who that cat belonged to. The pub had history. I had never stopped to look at the painting and had not noticed its beauty, even though I'd probably walked past the same image daily.

"Quite magnificent, isn't it!" James appeared, offering a chilled cocktail in a silver Martini glass, an unused gift from when we first met. I knew the contents

– vodka Martini. I took the glass, smiling at the gesture. Was he making peace?

"Do you know where the name 'Beaumont Jockey' comes from on this painting?" I asked.

"Well, yes I do, actually. I found it in the storage. Unmistakably it's this place, so I researched the artist. Turns out that one of the owners many moons ago was a wealthy chap called Eric Beaumont. He kept horses, thoroughbreds, designed for flat racing. He loved his horses probably more than his wife and was a decent jockey himself in his time. He named his favourite flat horse, which he'd owned since it was about two years old, after himself, Beaumont. Anyway, he adored it and won many competitions. But during a training session, something startled Beaumont and he fell, taking Eric with him. As a result, he broke his leg and had to be put down!"

"Who? Eric or the horse?" I asked stupidly.

"The horse!" He grinned.

"That's really sad!"

"I know, but it is a fabulous painting. Anyway, cheers!" He raised his glass. "To the Beaumont Jockey!"

"To the Beaumont Jockey!" I whispered.

We exchanged a glance for several seconds. We still had that spark between us. Had it just lost its way? Leaning against the solid oak bar sipping cocktails, I took a moment to look at James. He was a good guy really, one of the best, and I would probably always love him. My heart sank with the uncertainty of what lay ahead for us. When our glasses were empty, I watched James take the vodka and Martini bottles from their dispensers, indicating for me to follow him, eyebrows raised as if to ask if I was coming. Willingly, I followed. Was it the vodka warming my veins or the Martini freeing my spirit? Either way, at that moment in time it felt right, and I began to relax for the first time in ages. My throat was on fire from the raw mix of spirits, leaving my taste buds wanting for more. He led me into our living area, now *his* living area, which should probably have felt weird but for some reason it didn't. Soon, my female touch would no longer decorate the mantelpiece, Laura Ashley throws would no longer warm the chairs when I was no longer a resident. James would be running the place single-handed for a while – my dad adored him too much to just kick him out. I had no doubt that James would transform our home into a cold, unattended bachelor pad as soon as I left.

He poured a second large cocktail and within seconds the contents of the glasses had gone. We held each other's gaze as James mixed a third, but my legs gave way and I sank into the sofa. What was this? The finale to our relationship or the beginning of something else? I wasn't sure, but my heart was racing and knew it would welcome whatever came next. Raising my third cocktail, I downed it in one. The glass slipped through my fingers to the floor. James placed his empty glass on the table. No words were spoken; they weren't appropriate as we were both on the same page. Want... need... sex... now! He took my hand, raising me from the couch and leading me into the bedroom, now *his* bedroom, then we kissed like we'd never kissed before. He meant it, he needed it, he needed me. I kissed him back and, before I knew it, I was naked under the duvet. There was no time to hesitate or to think what I was about to do.

We shagged.

Like Rabbits.

Repeat.

Six weeks had passed since I had left The Wyte Shed, and although I was still making an appearance in the offices at the handbag factory, it took some getting used to being back in my little house, *alone*. I loved my house, but in comparison to the chaos and constant activity of the pub it was exceptionally quiet and, unbeknown to me, I'd lost the admiration for my little abode.

A small part of me wished I was still with James. I missed the regular laughter, his mischievousness and the air of excitement. I longed for him and my heart was suffering. I couldn't eat, I couldn't sleep. There was a grey dullness hanging over me that just wouldn't shift: grief, emptiness, helplessness. I couldn't accept the lack of fight for our relationship. The sense of fun, love and togetherness was replaced with a feeling of worthlessness. I needed to know how he was feeling. Was he sad? Distraught? Angry? The *not* knowing was hard to bear and the lack of control created waves of depression. We'd had such a wonderful last night together which played over and over in my head, so why hadn't he called me? I was far too proud to call him, maybe he felt the same? I cried buckets over James and, although they dried eventually, the waves of emotion took longer to fade. But as time passed, my strength returned and I finally accepted that we were done. Although neither of us had actually said *those words,* I believed my gut feeling that maybe this chapter had come to a close.

"Look, if he was going to get in the way of you and your dream job then he had to be ditched! Take him out of your vocabulary and get over him!" Sam was right. "Move on, biatch!"

Jess, on the other hand, would say, "Well if you miss him that much, why don't you ring him. I'm sure you'd get your old job back!" But Sam would come back with, "Oh Jess is a wimp, full of shit. What have I told you, Lillian, get a bloody grip?" Then hang up.

She was right. So, I brushed myself down and told myself to get a grip, biatch!

TEN

So, this was the first day of the rest of my life. The day I started my new job. I was an Air Hostess, Dolly with a Trolley, Tart with a Cart, Dragon with a Wagon. Very exciting! Although, due to the lack of sleep and my broken mental state over James, I wasn't really functioning on all four cylinders.

My usual OCD had failed me slightly and I'd fallen into some disorganised black hole. I'd misplaced an information pack I should have studied ready for day one. I'd casually browsed through it the day it arrived, but hadn't thought about it again since. It was nowhere to be seen. Like a mad woman, I searched the kitchen as though my life depended on it. Bedroom, bathroom, spare room, car – nothing. Eventually, it was located lying gracefully on the breakfast bar. My pulse increased when I realised there were approximately 50 multiple choice questions to complete in addition to a 20-page glossary we had to learn. Oh dear, I was cutting it fine as it was. I decided to squeeze in a quick study session before setting off but would have to break the speed limit getting there. What I'd do for a photographic memory. This was not a good start.

I flicked through the booklet quickly, hoping to

memorise everything in it. It didn't work, as pages and pages of airline jargon faced me:

`Complete the missing words of the phonetic alphabet.`

The what? Er...Airplane, Bottle, Chocks away, Die, Elephant, Fannies, Grannies? I had no idea. What was wrong with the normal alphabet? EVERYONE knew it! I continued turning the pages and landed on another section:

`You will be tested on the following Airport Abbreviations:`

Why abbreviate them?

`Birmingham BHX, Manchester MAN, Heathrow LHR, Tenerife TFE, Corfu CFU, Zekinthos ZTH, Thessaloniki JSI.`

I was now very hot under the armpits and the switch in my brain was hovering between 'stress alert' and 'meltdown', but as long as 'over the edge' mode wasn't hit I'd be ok. I rushed through several forms which were with the booklet but had to skip most questions:

`How many endorsements do you have on you driving licence?`

Mmmm... I had nine points (NINE!!!) Should I lie? Would they check this?

`Do you have a Full clean licence?`

Well, there's no coffee stains on it!

I admitted defeat and began my journey into the unknown.

It could have been a lack of breakfast, lack of sleep over previous weeks, the worry of the day ahead, I wasn't quite sure, but I was suddenly overwhelmed with an instant sickness and almost had to pull over. I was so tired and emotionally exhausted, and the consequences of the lack of shut eye over previous weeks had decided to rise to the surface. Perfect timing. I could feel the bile rising and my already flustered brain got the better of me. For the third time that morning I reached for my Rescue Remedy, but with one hand on the steering wheel it was proving quite difficult. My free hand turned my handbag upside down, the contents splaying all over the foot well of the passenger seat. I couldn't stretch that far. I didn't recall relying on this little bottle as much ever before, but since leaving James and becoming a singleton again, I was almost at the end of my fourth decanter. GET A BLOODY GRIP!

I convinced myself it was only a little relapse, but I had been driving around the same roundabout for what seemed like an hour. Terminal one, two and three were clearly signposted, but when I took the exit for T3 there was no sign afterwards! I returned to the roundabout and decided on the first exit for T1 and soon arrived at a second roundabout, where I was faced with more irrelevant signs which did not help: short stay, long stay, staff, staff north, south, east and west with zones 1-50 to choose from! My instructions said to locate a large yellow Portakabin and take the first left onto the car park. I could not see anything yellow and wanted to scream at the top of my voice, 'Fuck off everyone!' I had no choice but to pull over on double yellow lines.

Fighting the tears, I finished the contents of the Rescue Remedy, bringing my fourth bottle to an end.

Cars were hurtling past, horns blazing because I'd caused an obstruction. Great, so now I'd probably get towed and awarded three more points, giving me the maximum twelve, so I'd probably get banned from driving. My dream job was fading before I've even set foot on the tarmac.

Staring mindlessly at the directions, I spotted a traffic warden approaching in my rear view mirror. Fantastic! I took deep breaths and accepted defeat. As she approached, already scribbling in her important little notepad, I noticed a big hairy brown blob on her chin. Shit, she'd seen me staring, her pen had paused.

"My god, Lilly, is that you? What the hell are you doing here?" Screeched a voice I didn't recognise, although the wart looked vaguely familiar. If I was not mistaken, this woman used to threaten me at school, putting me right off my lunch. Hopefully I'd get her name right. I put on my best fake smile.

"Maisy Mole?" Oh shit, I was sure it was Molen! "Oh my god, I didn't recognise you. Long time, no see. How great to see you!" I lied. We used to call her 'Moley Maisy'. Thank god I didn't slip up! Reminiscing over our school days, I pretended to agree what fun we had together (we didn't), but who cared, she jumped in, stumbling over the debris underfoot, and directed me to where I should be. Maisie Mole was officially my new BFF!

Lime swirl wallpaper furnished the walls and a lilac check lined the floor. That in itself was a challenge for my thumping head and sensitive nervous system. The designer, clearly on a budget, should have definitely sought out an alternative vocation.

With seconds to spare and desperate for coffee (I'd missed the opportunity for complimentary refreshments.), I just managed to slip in line unnoticed. Although, listening to the friendship groups that had already formed, it was clear I was too late. I felt a little intimidated. This was a whole new world for me, but I'd arrived stressed, hungry and tired. As I absorbed the air of beauty surrounding me I also regretted my choice of attire. The room was filled with catwalk models. Was I in the right place? Pristine suits, slender ankles, perfect lips and L'Oréal hair (they were so worth it) were all around. I sensed that I stood out from the crowd for all the wrong reasons.

I sat alone, observing, singling out the leader of the pack and those who aspired to be. With thick, dark locks in a subtle beehive creation, navy blue trouser suit, crisp white shirt and Jimmy Choos, it was obvious to me who the pack leader was. She glanced in my direction, but just as I was about to engage, her frown struck me down, clearly not inviting me to join the *tête-à-tête*.

Fortunately, I noticed a timid little mouse clutching her handbag, clearly petrified. Thrilled there was someone more anxious than me, I moved closer and seized my chance. She began to relax, as did I, as we exchanged stories of our fraught journeys here. A non-driver, it had taken her three bus rides to get there exceptionally early with time to kill before realising she was in the wrong waiting zone and ending up having to run like the clappers to arrive by the skin of her teeth. I wasn't the only dippy newbie.

We were eventually greeted by two Airline Trainers: Debbie, a tall, slender, smart, smiley female, and Angela, the total opposite, shorter, fuller and poker faced. As the day unfolded, it became apparent that Angela didn't take any shit, treating us new recruits as if it was our first day at an army base – regimented, strict, with no room for mistakes.

I took my seat behind my name card 'LILLIAN WHITE' and noticed all the completed work booklets placed neatly, awaiting collection. Even the timid mouse had completed hers. I tried to fight off the panic as it sank in just how important those notes were. I really should have looked at mine. As Poker Face drew close, she looked at me questioningly, so I offered an excuse apologetically that I'd left it at home. I sensed her disappointment, my card was already marked. Was she going to order that I do ten press-ups? If only she had, as what followed was a question and answer session on what we had learnt. *Shit!* The questions began and I started to sweat as I knew fuck all.

"Can you turn your name card around... Lillian, isn't it?" Poker Face pounced on me like a Canadian bear on an open wound. "So, where are we? Let's start with the phonetic alphabet, shall we?"

All eyes were on me. I froze and couldn't find any words. I opened my mouth, but nothing came out.

"No? Cat got your tongue? Anyone else?"

To which the whole group sang, "Alpha, Bravo, Charlie, Delta..." Great! Now I looked completely stupid. She didn't leave it there.

"Ok, so Lillian, can you tell me which airport has the abbreviation JSI?"

Nope! Oh god, this was terrible. *How THICK am I?* Why hadn't I learnt this stuff? Heat overcame me and hunger, stress and paranoia took over. I was going to be sick. I suddenly felt a little light-headed and became aware that my skirt was way too tight. I had to unfasten it. All eyes were on me, again. I felt hot, very hot, very hot indeed. In fact, that's all I can remember as I flumped to the floor in one big heap. I could imagine Poker Face stepped over me and moved on to the next person to continue the phonetic alphabet.

I'd fainted and when I came around, I came face to face with Debbie, the nicer instructor, standing over me, so I almost passed out again. However, she was sweet. To the point, but sweet.

"So, Lillian, you fainted. You're my third fainter this month but at least you're not hurt!" She escorted me to the common area and offered a glass of water. "What's the matter? Oh god, you're not pregnant, are you?" What a weird question to ask!

"Honestly? I haven't looked at the booklet." Her smile was comforting so I thought it be best to come clean. "I ran a pub up until last night (one little white lie wouldn't hurt) with my boyfriend... ex-boyfriend... so I literally haven't had the chance. And no, I'm pretty sure I'm not pregnant!" Then I burst into tears. Uncontrollable tears. I sobbed and sobbed, quivering lip and everything. The saga over the pub, James, the booklet, my dream job, the journey here, the traffic warden, my hair, sickness, too-tight skirt, Rescue Remedy, the whole caboodle came bursting out in one big blob of words.

"Ok, so you've had a shit time of it, I get that, and yes, you can be forgiven a little, but to be honest, you have been lucky today. If you'd have got Angela coming to check on you, she would probably send you home."

"Really?" I wept. "You're not going to send me home?"

"I don't really bite! It could be worse." I took a breath as she smiled at me and placed a clump of tissues into my hand. "Many moons ago I managed to get through the training course *without sobbing* but I was grounded after my first flight!"

"Grounded?"

"Basically, I hadn't reached the safety requirements, so had to resit part of the course and exams before I could fly again."

"No way!"

"Yes way." Debbie told me the story of her first ever flight as cabin crew. It was on an inbound flight which had been diverted due to bad weather. "It was obvious that the purser took an instant dislike to me from the word go. She was a complete bitch and I couldn't do anything right!" I couldn't believe she's telling me this, I was practically a stranger. "It was October and we had been diverted to Athens from Corfu due to an horrendous thunder storm so ended up spending the night in Athens. The crew all headed for a night out and were warned not to drink too much as we weren't sure what time the flight would be heading back to Manchester. However, crew being crew, that meant only having one bottle each instead of ten!" *Maybe I would fit in well after all!* "I didn't feel too well and if it wasn't for the fact that I was the 'new girl' I would have probably gone to bed, but instead I went down to meet the rest of the crew. They were already tiddled when I arrived, but as I felt rotten, I just drank water. As the night drew to a close, I felt considerably worse, lost all my colour and began vomiting – everywhere. I couldn't hold it in, and by the time I'd reached the toilet I had covered several sun loungers, one holiday maker and the steps to the pool!"

"You poor thing!"

"Unbeknown to me, I had salmonella, resulting in being sent home rather than actually working the flight home."

"So, why were you grounded?" I asked, starting to feel a bit better about my situation.

"The hotel put a complaint in to the company, obviously mentioning the vomit everywhere, stating that the crew were all drunk and sick with alcohol. But I hadn't touched a drop! The purser had to offer her side of events and, in her statement, quite clearly noted that it was I who had been sick. As it was my first ever flight, I was grounded immediately for bad behaviour."

"OMG!"

"I know!" She continued. "When I got home that night after the flight, I was so ill my mum took me to hospital where I remained for several days. Luckily for me, they took blood samples and examined my watery sick, neither of which contained any alcohol. My mum complained to the airline, sending in all the results from the hospital. I was reinstated. Anyway, it was years ago, but I think my story beats yours!"

My tears had dried as I was engrossed in her tale. "So, what happened about the hotel in Athens and the purser?"

"Believe it or not, she had to rewrite her statement, apologise to me and was temporary demoted as she didn't put the safety of her crew first!" Debbie giggled. "Ironically, I am now above her in the ranking!"

"She still works here?"

"Yes, she's in there with me now, training!" Debbie held her finger to her mouth to hush me before I spoke another word. "It's our secret. Now get to the loo, sort your face out and grab yourself a coffee!"

I have no idea what she told Poker Face, but no further questions were fired my way and I promised to have all relevant papers completed for the following day.

Debbie and I really hit it off! God knows why she warmed to an erratic weirdo crying like a baby within half an hour of her first day, but she did and, after that, the following six weeks were a hoot.

The course was hard, full on and demanding. From day two, hair and make-up had to be immaculate. From day nine, we all had our uniforms, so everything had to be 'just so' and there was no excuse for sloppiness. I secretly enjoyed the strictness: no stray hairs, no pony tails measuring beyond 12 inches, shoes cleaned, nails manicured and kilt pin positioned in the exact spot. I loved it and found myself scrutinising others, observing their errors. Was I becoming the new leader of the pack?

I felt much better after my outburst that day. I hadn't realised I'd held back such emotion in the months after James and I had split, but once all the tears had drifted away, most of my fears had disappeared with them. I felt lighter, brighter and ready to take on the world.

By the end of the second week my vision was clearer, and I had truly taken stock. I'd hardly touched my fifth bottle of Rescue Remedy. James was becoming a distant memory. He had texted to see how the course was going and I was surprised by how little it had affected me. I didn't read into it or reply immediately. I was getting on with my life, my new exciting life as cabin crew, and I couldn't wait for my fabulous career to begin.

I studied hard at night, blossomed in class and was always first to raise my hand with all the correct answers. It was like being back at school, only my answers then were rarely right. I'd become the girly swot that I initially set out to be; it helped that I was thoroughly interested in all the subjects. There was just no stopping me.

My neighbouring trainee was a very attractive male named Lyndon, who had Ashton Kutcher good looks and a lean physique. It was hard to make eye contact without flirting, so I was relieved when it emerged that he played for a different team. He was a real fun character, bringing great humour to the course. Clearly wealthy, speaking the Queen's la-de-dah English, it didn't stop him swearing like a trooper. There was no doubt he was clever, having trained as a barrister. He simply admitted that there was more chance of him getting laid on a plane than in court – or less chance of him being arrested on a plane than in court!

In a short space of time we became partners in crime. As the course progressed, an unexpected trio emerged as Debbie (Debs), Lyndon and I were drawn to each other, forming a natural friendship, and they soon became an extension of my fabulous girlfriends.

The exams came and went, so did the wings ceremony, which I passed with flying colours, and before I knew it I was back in BJs celebrating with the girls and my two new friends, Debs and Lyndon. For the first time in a while, I felt free and happy and had found my true vocation.

ELEVEN

I woke a little nauseous, feeling sick to my stomach, but I wasn't going to be ill today of all days as I had my first operational/shadow flight, so I tried to push it aside. As I was the extra crew member for take-off and landing, I would sit in the cockpit, although it wasn't a '*Cockpit*' as the pilots looked about 110! But geriatrics aside, it was an amazing experience.

Although I'd flown many times as a passenger, being in the flight deck with a clear view of the airport, fields and buildings was a reminder that from this height, the world was tiny, insignificant. It was very exciting being up front, and I had to stop myself screaming as my stomach flipped and adrenaline forced through my veins when we hurtled down the runway and up into the clouds... WOW! My brain tried to focus on the weird g-force pull and it took all my strength to refrain the "Ye-ha" in my throat. It was such an amazing feeling – all in a day's work too! I loved my job!

However, my co-workers didn't make my first day easy. On the inbound sector, as I carried out the manual safety briefing, I discovered that the crew had set me up. Upon donning the dummy life jacket and pulling down on the cord, I was thrown backwards as it inflated, sending me flying into the galley. The whole cabin was in stitches, including the crew.

There were a few hiccups and my feet were killing me, but I survived and thoroughly enjoyed myself. I was loving my maiden flight and was excited at the prospect of being a travelling career girl with a million new friends. We checked out the hot guys in row 21, compared rosters and exchanged disastrous boyfriend tales, generally having a great flight, so were completely taken by surprise by what happened next. One minute we were laughing and joking, and the next there wasn't a pearly white to be seen.

"WILL THE SENIOR CABIN CREW MEMBER REPORT TO THE FLIGHT DECK IMMEDIATELY?" I heard the words but didn't absorb them, looking at the crew for reassurance that I'd misunderstood.

"What did he say?" I asked my colleague, Jane, an attendant with ten years' experience.

"Just pull the cart back to the galley!" Her voice was firm.

I was nearest the galley and the bar cart couldn't move until I did, but my brain was still trying to make sense of the words. Last time I'd heard them was in the training room only weeks ago and, if I remembered correctly, they also appeared in one of the exams:

In a planned emergency landing, what would be the P.A. from the captain?

Fuck, fuck, fuck, fuck, fuck, fuck, fuck, fuck, fuck, fuck, fuck!!! Shit, we're going to die! A planned emergency landing. A PLANNED EMERGENCY LANDING! My legs went to jelly and my hands shook as the colour drained from my cheeks.

"Lillian, LILLIAN!" Jane's voice raised an octave as she tried to get my attention, but I was frozen in the aisle, clinging on to the double drinks cart and staring into space. The drill was to disengage quietly from your duties whenever you heard the emergency P.A., stow everything away and report to your stations. ("Excuse me, I just need to get past as the plane is going down and we're all going TO DIE. Excuse me, thank you, thank you!") Suddenly, her voice came into focus. "Now, Lillian, we need to stow the cart NOW!" She was almost shouting as, like all of us, was probably shitting herself. Because we didn't know the nature of the emergency, it was only natural to think the worst.

With a fake smile, I eventually made my way to the galley, observing the uneasy restlessness within the cabin with only a few stray passengers queuing for the toilet or messing with the overhead lockers, obviously unaware of the importance of the announcement but sensing something was not quite right.

When I finally got back to the galley, the reality of the situation hit me as the crew's training switched them into emergency mode and they stood by their stations awaiting further instruction. I secured the galley as best as I could and waited patiently to find out how death would become us. Belly flop? Nose dive? CRASH FUCKING LANDING? My heart was racing faster and faster and I could hardly get my breath.

"Is everything ok with the plane?" One woman asked, her brow knotted in concern. For a nanosecond, as I pictured Phoebe from *Friends*, I wanted to say we'd lost a *phalange*, but I refrained.

"Is there a problem?" Asked another, and more questions were fired my way as I was the only crew member without a station.

"It's fine, we're just waiting to hear more now!" I replied, a smile plastered on my face.

"What do you mean? So, there is a problem... oh my god! OH MY GOD!" Screeched a nervous-looking young male passenger, alarming everyone around him.

"It's fine, please remain calm, it's all under control!" *I hope it is!* I hovered in the galley, keeping busy, not daring to sit down, although my legs could collapse at any second. In fact, where would I sit for crashing? I wondered if I had more chance of survival sitting in the flight deck or should I sit in the cabin? Was there even a spare seat? The crew replaced their handsets and began stowing bags, taking glasses and heeled shoes from passengers, collecting rubbish, locking toilets and securing everything. Passengers were moved around so that exit doors could be opened by able-bodied people. The cabin had never looked so tidy and all passengers remained in their seats, facing forwards, listening to the senior crew member give instructions over the P.A. The hydraulics had gone, which would affect the landing gear, resulting in a possible belly flop on landing, so we had to divert to a safe landing area immediately and prepare for an emergency landing. Great... a belly flop! We all know how painful that can be when your dive goes wrong. I'd seen pictures of how bellies had split on hitting water. It's not pleasant. The water acts like a knife slicing the skin. Were we landing on water? Was this how I was going to die?

I grabbed my bag and rushed to the toilet. My mind had gone blank. I knew there should have been something I should have been doing but I just couldn't think straight, and I still hadn't got the feeling back in my legs. I sat on the toilet seat, rummaging in my bag. I knew I had some Rescue Remedy somewhere, but it had been such a long time since I'd used it, the stuff was probably out of date. I gulped the whole lot. It tasted marvellous and warmed straight to the bone. I felt a little tipsy, but my breath returned and I could feel my legs again. *Come on, Lilly, get a grip. So, we are going to crash land. Hey, it might even be fun, just like a fairground ride.* I hate fairground rides!

Even in my semi-conscious state I was amazed at how the crew worked together as a team and threw themselves into emergency duties. They were mainly experienced crew and, as I was the only ignorant sod amongst them, I took orders and got stuck in. Well, I didn't want to die so I did my bit to prevent the worst from happening!

Absolutely everything was stowed away. We took a wooden leg off a passenger, false teeth off several other passengers (including one of the handsome dudes in row 21 who wouldn't be getting my phone number), trouser pockets had to be emptied and people moved around so children and parents could crash and burn together! Fuck, this really was happening! How surreal.

I was told not to sit in the flight deck for the landing, but there were available seats in row 32 and I should sit down immediately and fasten my seatbelt securely.

"Remember the brace position, Lillian, listen to the P.A, ok?" God, we really were having this conversation!

"Yes, brace position, yes!" I couldn't think of the brace position! Did my legs fold behind under my seat or at a 90-degree angle? Did I interlock my fingers on my head or just stack one hand on top of the other? My chest heaved and I could hear my heart pounding through my ears. I couldn't remember, I didn't know, my head has gone... Argh, this could be the end of Lillian White's Journey!

The effects of the Rescue Remedy were wearing off and my bag was just above my head so I half stood, stretching my arm as high as I could, but it was too late.

"Lillian, sit down!" Jane instructed.

"But I just need to get something!" I replied desperately.

"No time, sit down!" Seeing the look of absolute panic on my face, she softened, touched my arm and whispered, "Good luck!"

Did she just say good luck? *She thinks we're going to die!* My throat was burning as bile travelled up my oesophagus. I was suddenly bombarded with questions. "Has the captain had a heart attack? Have we lost an engine?" I didn't respond, frozen in fear. I just smiled and focused ahead, transfixed on the back of the seat in front of me. It took all my concentration to control my breathing as I knew I could crumble at any moment. I heard the passengers whispering and questioning what was happening but I was in my own world of panic. We were going DOWN!

The plane shuddered as we fell into our descent.

Sounds of banging metal spread throughout the cabin and oxygen masks dropped, scraping our foreheads. Lockers burst open, spilling their contents as screams echoed down the cabin. This was real, and the end was nigh. I clung to the seat with an intense grip, preparing to brace. Should I brace now? I could feel a deeper sense of panic as I wanted to brace but couldn't move.

"Five minutes to landing!"

Oh god, that was the captain. Obvious things were racing through my mind, like my family, my friends, James. My mind drifted into thoughts of some poor guy pronouncing me dead but holding his nose at my fishy tights and probably questioning why one wouldn't be wearing knickers. Oddly, I then thought about my financial situation and a tiny smile appeared on my face; ha, ha, fuck the overdraft and fuck the repayments on my car!

I felt an acceptance that this was our fate. I looked around at the lovers holding hands and the families huddled close. A baby on a lap and a toddler huddled tight sent shivers down my spine. The cabin was full of families, mums, dads and children faced with this awful catastrophe, their lives over before they had even begun. A lake of tears flooded my cheeks. I had never felt such passion towards children and was suddenly aware of their soft cries and baby oil aroma. What was wrong with me? My heart was racing, suffocated by a hopeless responsibility for every child on board, as though they were my children. The sickness I'd brushed aside came flooding to the surface. All I could hear was children screaming.

The noise and vibrations were so severe you'd think we'd already crashed as lockers, cupboards and toilet doors burst open, throwing debris into a vigorous washing cycle.

Landing was imminent, but just as the g-force ripped at my skin, the plane roared upwards and began to climb. I had to question if this was real or whether I was dreaming. But yes, the plane was climbing, higher and higher, almost vertical. Was this normal? We waited as a sense of calm washed through the cabin, faces searching for reassurance that we might just be out of danger.

My brain registered pain in my fingertips and I glanced at my bloodless knuckles, my hands still clinging to the seat. The shudders and vibrations eased as we continued to climb. Relief and adrenaline teased my body, waiting to surface but not quite convinced.

The captain mumbled over the tannoy. I didn't quite catch what he said. Was it 'cabin crew sit down' or 'stand down'? He made a second announcement.

"Cabin crew, stand down and resume normal duties."

Immediately after this announcement, the senior crew member came over the P.A. "Ladies and gentlemen, please remain seated with your seatbelt securely fastened."

We were safe!

She continued, "No services will be running at this time. Cabin crew to forward galley please, cabin crew to forward galley!"

What? Who? Where? It took my brain some time

to focus and absorb this information, but my body was drowning in euphoria at the realisation that the plane wasn't going down and this wasn't my time to leave the world. It was apparent that the hydraulics and landing gear had decided to work again which meant, hey presto, we weren't going to die today.

It was a soft landing and the whole cabin cheered as we taxied off the runway. Totally out of character for me, I found myself with a baby on my lap, and was amusing it with silly sounds and inhaling the soft Johnson's baby bath hair. As I inhaled the aroma, I swear my nipples began to twitch! What the hell was wrong with me? I hated kids! Then it dawned on me. I hadn't had a period in quite some time, well before the training course, which must have started over two months previously. Noooooooo! My brain went into overdrive as I realised I could be with child. I tried to remember the last time James and I were 'together', and recalled that last night. How could I forget our last night that sent me into depression? Oh dear god, what would he think? Did he even want kids? Did I? What would I do? I was pregnant! PREGNANT!

"Are you ok, love?" Asked the lady sat next to me, who'd obviously noticed the change in my body language and eagerly offered to take her baby back, probably thinking I may drop it at any moment. I caressed its cheek but gladly returned the little bundle, allowing my brain to focus on my next catastrophe.

After a few minutes, I had another shock. It might not be James' baby. OMG! SLUT! TART! It could be someone else's baby, but whose? I remembered one drunken night with the girls and vaguely recalled bringing some guy back home where we got naked and fumbled around, but I didn't think we did anything... or did we? I didn't even catch his name, couldn't pick him out in a line up! I couldn't remember! I didn't want a baby. I couldn't keep it. I couldn't change nappies on my own. Nappies, dummies, prams, cots, and the thought of single parenting spun in my mind. I needed my Rescue Remedy, but would it harm the baby? Did it matter? Was I keeping the baby? My head was truly battered and the lady sitting next to me had moved her baby away as she realised I was having some sort of mental breakdown. One of my hands was rubbing my stomach and my eyes must have looked wild.

The aircraft came to a complete stop away from the terminal and was met by an emergency tsunami of ambulances, fire engines and police cars. I got my bag and swigged my Remedy, regardless of child. I had to speak to the girls – IMMEDIATELY! I needed to get off – woman with child, woman with child!

TWELVE

I tried to ignore the fact that I could be 'with child'. I just couldn't face or accept it and had convinced myself that it was just nerves about starting a new job and the aftermath of the crash landing. These things happened to people, didn't they, when the chaos stops the shock kicks in? So I thought it was all part and parcel and that was why I'd not had a period.

However, I had been feeling sickness for several weeks, which just got worse and worse. Then I was sick, really sick, every morning! All I seemed to do was run up and down stairs to the loo. I'd never been so fit!

It was time to face it head on, so I grabbed my coat, jumped in my car and headed for the nearest chemist. I raced up and down the aisles, scanning for the dreaded product to no avail. Then suddenly came head on with millions of the damn things lying there on the counter, next to the throat lozenges and smokers' patches! There were loads of people in the vicinity so I'd have to come back. I might know someone! Shit, I did know someone – it was the cleaner from The Wyte Shed and she was heading right for me. Oh no, it was Sylvia – nosy, crazy Sylvia.

"Lillian, it is you, isn't it? Why, you look fantastic!

How's things? What are you doing hanging round the smoking patches? Are you trying to give up? I didn't know you smoked, Lillian. It's so bad for you, but good on you for giving up. Go on then, you can go first, go on, jump in before me." All in one sentence, not coming up for breath!

I felt sick. A different kind of sick, but all the same, I felt sick. I smiled at Sylvia, returned a polite sentence, then excused myself, paying for two packets of smoking patches and making a sharp exit! *Bollocks! Now what?* Did I take my chances and wait for her to leave or should I try somewhere else? I peered through the window and saw that she'd cornered someone else. She could be ages, so I'd have to try somewhere else.

I drove a few miles down the road until I came to another chemist on the corner of a tiny street – *Love Lane* – was it fate? I parked up and rushed through the chemist door, where I collided with a blond, sexy being. He looked familiar, but I couldn't place him until he spoke in that heavy Aussie twang.

"How's your friend?"

OMG, it was that bare-footed god who came to Jess' rescue. I'd forgotten about him. I'd not even mentioned him to the girls. Why, oh lord, would you send him my way now? Great timing!

"She's fine, thanks!" I replied, sounding cold and uninterested, which couldn't have been further from the truth, but what was I supposed to do?

He must have sensed my thoughts so wished me farewell and left. I watched his curls flow in the breeze as he disappeared out of reach. My heart sank. He was a god and that accent... lordy, lordy. I returned my thoughts to the mission at hand. *Please don't be pregnant, please don't be pregnant!* I scoured the shelves searching whilst in a quandary over the Aussie blond hunk that I'd just let go... again.

"Can I help you, Madam?" A friendly voice appeared from nowhere.

"No thank you, just looking," I replied, although it was obvious I needed some help as I couldn't think straight. The Aussie blond had thrown my brain into disarray.

"The digital ones are best, brilliant in fact. They're quick and easy to use with the most accurate results," the pharmacy assistant continued. "This is also good value for money; you get two together, which is probably not a bad thing as occasionally the test can show a false negative or positive." I think she saw the horror on my face: false negative, false positive? Well that would just lead me into a false sense of security, so what was the bloody point? She noticed my questioning frown. "Sorry, what I mean is if you don't pee on the stick properly and ruin the first one, you have the second one to fall back on and get a better reading."

At that point the doorbell went as someone else entered the shop, so I grabbed a couple of packs, threw my money on the counter and couldn't get out of there quick enough.

Back home, not quite believing my situation, I sat contemplating life with a child, a baby. I was trying to imagine my house full of high chairs and prams and other baby things but couldn't get my head around it. Of course I wasn't pregnant, it was just a bit of stress, shock combined with a sickness bug. I convinced myself it would be fine, of course it would be fine.

I sat on the toilet, eyes fixed on the thin blue positive line which stared back at me, strong and powerful and totally controlling my life. How could one long plastic tube hold the key to my future? My mind was racing, absorbing the news which sank my heart as a wave of disappointment smothered my gut. I heard the phone ringing downstairs, several times with a slight pause in between. I didn't answer but wondered who needed me so urgently. It rang off but then began again, and again and again. Go away! Eventually, I practically fell down the stairs and grabbed the loud plastic receiver.

"WHAT?" I shouted, maybe a little too aggressively.

"Oh my god, Lilly, how are you? I just found out about the emergency landing and the fact that you were on it. Shit, babe, what happened? How are you? Shall I come over?" Lyndon was so enthusiastic, which seemed at odds with how I was feeling, but I could do with his loving gay ways, the safeness of his love, no threat, just buckets and buckets of innocent attention.

Within forty minutes we were sat side by side on my leather sofa drinking Chardonnay. After four huge mouthfuls, I suddenly realised that maybe I shouldn't be drinking alcohol and put the glass down. Had I made my decision to keep the little dot growing inside me? I wasn't sure. I picked the glass back up and held it to my mouth, preparing myself to break the news to Lyndon, but the smell of strong white wine nearly knocked me out and I ran upstairs yet again to hug the toilet seat. Lyndon came running after me and held my hair back from my sweaty face and wiped my brow. What a doll!

"Babe, is everything alright? Are you suffering from shock? Shall I...?" Lyndon's voice broke off as he picked up the white plastic test from the bin. "Oh my god, Lillian, girlfriend, do you have a bun in the oven?" He has never sounded so camp, but gorgeous. "My god, girl, Mamma's going to have me a baby child!"

He saw my disappointment and held me close, and didn't let go as I broke down in floods of tears and cried an ocean. I felt warm and safe but a little alone. He wasn't straight and wasn't my boyfriend. He wasn't going to take care of me, even though his hugs were so convincing.

Some hours later we were lying on my bed chatting, laughing, crying and finishing off the last scrapes of the delivered pizza, popcorn and chocolate. Comfort food.

"So... whose is it?" He asked.

I went bright red, held my head in my hands, and after a long silence I breathed out, "It can only really be James..."

Lyndon raised an eyebrow as he sensed my uncertainty. We fell about in floods of tears, but tears of laughter at the thought that I wasn't 100% sure and the prospect of me being such a tart! Although deep down I knew exactly who the father was and yes, it was James.

We decided it would be great fun to do a little research into my situation and did a little surfing on Google. I was glad that Lyndon had taken control as I was far too scared to look. He brought up pictures of the different stages of my little dot, and I couldn't believe that something so tiny could have eyes, fingers and toes at such an early stage. From nowhere – absolutely nowhere – Niagara Falls as I collapsed in a soggy puddle of helplessness. Again, Lyndon held me, but for only a short time and then told me to get a grip.

"Bitch!" I snapped.

"Pleasure's all mine, honey. Just give me a minute." He calmly flicked through the pages and pages of endless information on birth, babies, breast feeding and latching (latching?) then turned towards me. "How far gone are you?"

I had no clue but explained to Lyndon that I knew it had been a while and normally Sal and I 'bled' together, probably because we spent so much time in each other's company so were in sync.

"Lillian, I'm not interested in Sal's bleeding cycles, I just want to know how far gone you are!"

"Ok, ok, keep your hair on, point taken!" I made a mental note to call Sal. "I must be three months, I think?"

"Three months? Shit, Lillian you're almost there!"

"Don't be daft, you carry a baby for nine months."

"It's almost ten actually!"

"Why do you know all this stuff?"

"I just do!" Lyndon confirmed I was nearing the end of my first trimester and that the feelings of sickness should subside at any time. It was at that stage a high percentage of women began to enjoy their pregnancy. "Hey, here we go, listen to this: *a healthy first trimester* is crucial to the normal development of the foetus. The mother-to-be may not be showing much on the outside, but inside her body all the major body organs and systems of the foetus are forming – Awww, Lillian, you're making a little being inside of you right now! Oh, look there's more." Did I want to hear more? "All major body systems continue to develop and function, including the circulatory, nervous, digestive, and urinary systems, the embryo is taking on a human shape, although the head is larger in proportion to the rest of the body, the mouth is developing tooth buds (which will become baby teeth), the eyes, nose, mouth, and ears are becoming more distinct and the arms and legs are clearly visible. Wow, Lillian, this is real, you can't get rid of it, it's already formed!"

OMG, he was stressing me out. I hadn't made any decisions. I also had my first flight after the 'incident' the next morning so would have to put it all to the back of my mind. It wasn't going to be easy.

"Right, Lyndon, honey, you're going to have to go. I've got an early start tomorrow, a night stop in Edinburgh and lots of safety revision to catch up on, so mum's the word, eh?" Lyndon looked at me, a smile playing on his lips as he was obviously dying to tell someone the news. "Lyndon? Answer me! Mum's the word, right?"

"Yes, ok. I won't tell anyone!" He didn't sound convincing.

"Lyndon, I could lose my job, be grounded or whatever, and I'm not even sure what I'm going to do yet. All I know is that I feel sick most of the time, like death actually. I'm exhausted but still have to work so can't face anyone about this yet!" I felt myself well up at the hopelessness of my situation.

"Mum's the word. Of course I won't say anything, girlfriend," he said sincerely, giving me a squeeze. "Listen, why don't you call in sick?"

"I can't do that. I don't want a bad name for myself. I've only had one flight!"

"Which was a catastrophe. You have the perfect excuse. Tell them you're not ready yet," he continued. He looked at me, questioning, and pressed my phone in my hand. "Ring Deb, she'll sort it!"

"Lyndon! I'm fine. It was nothing!" It clearly WAS something as my eyes filled with tears again.

He looked at me with puppy dog eyes, pleading.

"Fine!" I made the call.

After a long conversation with Deb, trying my hardest not to spill my news, I pulled a sickie, promising Lyndon that when I was ready he could be the first to spread the good/bad/indifferent/fucking terrifying news to whoever wanted to hear it.

"Right then, can I stay?" He asked.

"Yes, you can stay!"

Without any encouragement, Lyndon continued to read, "...the fingers and toes are still webbed but can be clearly distinguished, the main organs continue to develop, and you can hear the baby's heartbeat using an instrument called a Doppler, the bones begin to develop, and the nose and jaws are rapidly developing, the embryo is in constant motion but cannot be felt by the mother..."

"STOP! Please Lyndon, that's enough information for one day!" I couldn't believe that all this was going on inside my body, a tiny being was growing and developing and I was thinking of putting an end to its unappreciated existence. Could I really go through with it? "Can we just have a lazy day with no more talk about babies?"

"Ok, no more talk about babies," he replied, closing the laptop and squeezing my hand.

We had a lazy evening and following day. More pizza and chocolate was consumed, chick flicks were watched and the phone unplugged. I still hadn't spoken to the girls properly and, although initially desperate to do so, Lyndon took this pressure away. He was my rock, my saviour, my unavailable gay boyfriend, and I needed him and leant on him and took all he had to offer. Everyone needs a Lyndon!

When he eventually left, I felt alone. He was going to stay but I had to deal with this on my own with no guilt trips from anyone else, this had to be my decision. What a mess! I had just landed myself the job of my dreams so how had I let this happen? I was on the pill; wasn't it supposed to be 100% effective? I fumbled in my bathroom for my pill box and carefully read the information, scrutinising every word and not missing anything. I dropped the leaflet to the floor and sat back in astonishment, as apparently the pill is only 97.8% proof! So, 2.2% of the time it doesn't work. How typical that I should fall under that category. Well, I like to be different, I suppose. However, it was a bit of a bitch that I should get pregnant whilst taking contraception.

From out of nowhere, thoughts of the Aussie blond god flashed before me as I reminisced over our last two encounters. How was it that we kept bumping into each other when it was most inconvenient? Now I was pregnant, he was even more out of reach. He was absolutely gorgeous and I practically blew him out! I tried to brush him aside and focus on the present and what the hell I was going to do.

Sam would know what to do so I grabbed my phone and dialled her number, which rang and rang until the answerphone kicked in.

"Hello, this is Sam, leave a message!" *Oh shit, where are you?*

"It's me – I'm pregnant!" I blurted into the answerphone then hung up.

I sat holding my mobile for what seemed like a decade, thinking about the enormity of it all. Did I want a baby? I mean really? Should I get rid of it? I stared at the kitchen wallpaper, which caught my attention. It contained tiny dots dancing around in a 3D merry-go-round. I was hypnotised by them and imagined all those tiny dots growing inside my stomach, expanding by the second.

Thank god for the gentle tap on my window to break the image. It was Sam. She gave me a smile, a comforting smile which reassured me that I wasn't alone. Stupid maybe, but not alone! God, I couldn't live without this girl.

As I opened the door, she hugged me close. The dam gates opened and the tears gushed. She sat in silence for a few minutes until my sobs eased.

"So who knows? Have you told the girls, or work? Deb?" Sam asked gently.

"Only Lyndon... and you! I feel awful but I'm just not ready and I felt awful lying to Deb on the phone!"

"She'll understand so don't stress, right? Have you thought what your options are?"

"A little, ish, not really," I whispered.

"Are you going to keep it?" She asked. "Sorry, he, she, the baby!"

"No! I don't think so, no... no, I'm not keeping it. I feel gutted that I'm pregnant. I'm going to the surgery later to find out how far gone I am, and I guess we'll discuss my options then?"

"Right, well you don't sound too sure?" She'd hit the nail on the head. I didn't want a baby *now*, but I'd never *not* wanted children. "Shall I come with you?" She asked.

"Yes please, would be nice to have some company." "You got it!" She got up and switched the kettle on. "Anyway, how was your first flight?"

"It was a complete plane crash!"

"Very funny!"

"Seriously! We had an emergency landing, but it was aborted last minute, which was when I found out I was pregnant!"

"Bloody hell, that's a lot to happen to one person in one day!" Exclaimed Sam. "I take it the plane didn't actually crash then, unless you were the only survivor?" She was trying to be humorous, although I could see the concern in her eyes, which to my horror were beginning to well up. Was Sam about to cry? She caught the tears before they surfaced. "Sorry, Lil, are you ok?"

"Sam, I'm fine. Look, no harm done... well, apart from being pregnant, I mean!" I laughed, but it was slightly strained.

"Are you absolutely sure?" She asked.

I reassured Sam that I wasn't too traumatised, just a little shaken, but it was more the shock of the tiny cells growing inside me that had knocked me for six. I continued to explain what happened and how I'd called in sick for a few days. Sick of hearing my own voice, I badgered her to explain what happens during pregnancy.

"Are you sure you want to know?"

"Sock it to me!"

Over a cup of tea, Sam described in great detail all the possibilities ahead. Eventually, she got to what happens during labour. "Whatever you do, don't give birth naturally. In fact, don't surrender your body to pregnancy." She wasn't making me feel better. "Personally, I might just buy a baby, adopt or even borrow one. At least you could give it back! And some women have issues down *there* and have to have fanny physio, legs in stilts whilst your flaps are massaged."

"You are not helping!" I screeched.

"I know, I'm giving you the worst-case scenario. You have to know your choices. Have you thought about the alternative?" I looked at Sam. It had crossed my mind, but nothing had been clear until she'd explained what happened to my tiny dot if I chose this path. Sam could see I was in turmoil. "You don't have to make any decision yet, Lil..."

"I have already!" I interrupted. "I'm keeping it!"

"You'll be fine either way, Lillian, and you're not on your own, whatever you decide." She kissed my head then got to her feet and put the kettle on again, as this is the answer to everything – pop the kettle on and we'll all have tea!

We sat in the doctors' waiting room in complete silence. A lady came in heavily pregnant, walking like a penguin, with a small boy clinging to her swollen legs. Snot was running from his nose and into his mouth as he drank from a baby's bottle full of cola. I was horrified.

"Your face is a picture!" Sam giggled.

"My child will never have a snotty nose!"

"How do you know? All kids have snotty noses!"

"I shall have all possible green phlegm removed at birth so that *that* never happens to my child!"

"You are keeping it then?" She nudged me then picked out a baby magazine which we began to flick through. This was obviously a first for Sam and definitely a first for me.

"Where's the Hello! magazine?"

"Lillian White, room three!" It was my turn.

Sam smiled in encouragement. "Break a leg!"

Sam had to return to work, but not before a nurse grabbed her to console me as, when it was confirmed that I was almost ten weeks pregnant, I collapsed in tears! Poor chap! I don't think the doctor knew quite what to do with me! It was just hearing those words from him, so matter of fact: "Congratulations, you are most definitely pregnant!" Why he felt the need to congratulate me, I don't know. Surely, they should wait for a reaction from the patient? Clearly shocked at my response, he practically threw a wad of leaflets at me, one of which was the *alternative.*

I threw it away the second I got home, even forcing it towards the bottom of the bin. I still wasn't sure if I wanted to keep the baby but neither did I want *not to* keep the baby! I wondered if it would be a boy or a girl. Maybe I should think of names. Maybe not. Maybe I *should* read the leaflet. I scrambled to the bottom of the bin, past the dead teabags and stale crusts to locate it. I looked at the front cover then put it back in the bin.

The leaflet was still in the bin but asking me to read it.

The leaflet was by the bin – outside – ripped into tiny pieces.

I didn't read the leaflet. I lay on the sofa, holding my stomach, my index finger circling my belly button. I thought of James. I longed for James. It was stupid, really. I was getting over him not many months ago, but suddenly my brain had created some freak formula in my frontal lobe so that I couldn't concentrate on anything but James. I wondered how he'd feel at becoming a dad? I thought back to our last encounter when tiny dot was conceived. So how would I tell him? 'Congratulations, James, you're not firing blanks!' I'd just tell him straight, then he'd do the right thing and we'd run off into that sunset, when the clouds had lifted.

I grabbed my phone and dialled his number. Straight to answerphone. I didn't leave a message.

THIRTEEN

I didn't pull any more sickies. Although I was a little nervous about returning to work, I was glad to be back on the radar, fingers crossed the planes would stay on theirs.

As soon as I reached thirteen weeks the sickness disappeared, just like that. It was as if someone had turned the light switch back on; one day I felt dreadful and the very next I felt fantastic. I no longer felt sick every waking moment; I felt liberated, free, and hungry! So, for a while I ignored the fact that I was *with child* and carried on with my life, plane hopping around Europe and having a great time. I didn't mention my situation to anyone at work, even Deb, as I didn't want to compromise her position. Lyndon was sworn to secrecy not to let it slip. I wasn't showing, there were no obvious changes to my body, so I would tell them when I was good and ready, whenever that would be.

The girls came over a few times and it was great to take the focus off me.

"Mum's moved back in!" Jess was sparkling.

"Oh that's fantastic, I'm so pleased!" I enthused. Her mum had been seen with a male work colleague on several occasions *getting close,* but as it unfolded, she was consoling said male as he had lost his job. Her mum was very fond of this man, but only platonically. Because she had a few issues at home, she had offloaded onto said man, but that was as far as it got.

"My parents are working through a few things, but at least they're under one roof again!" Jess added, smiling.

This was great news, although it didn't justify the radiant glow.

"And... is there anything else you want to share with us?" I probed.

"Well, don't be mad, but Tom and I have been in touch." I could see she felt a huge weight had been lifted just by saying those words, and we knew what was coming next. "He told me everything, *everything,* admitting he's been a complete idiot and asked if we could give it another go."

I couldn't believe she'd forgiven the two-timing twat, but I'd not seen her look this happy in a very long time. She seemed in control, had lost weight and seemed like the old Jess again.

Sally was quiet, not her usual poised, elegant quiet, but something wasn't sitting well with her and I thought I knew what the elephant was in the room. How unfair life could be. Sally had been trying for a baby for a while, had a loving husband-to-be and a gorgeous home, probably with a baby room in development. I was in an unplanned pregnancy situation, no partner and no gloriously decorated baby room. Understandably, she'd feel a pull on her heartstrings. If only it was her instead of me, but fate doesn't operate that way, the cards aren't always dealt in the right order. I'd broken the news to the girls about my situation and independently to Sal and, although I'd felt a little uncomfortable doing so, we were fine. I just wished everyone else would stop rubbing her nose in it.

"Your tits are going to get huge," stated Lou, "and your body will never be the same again."

"Thanks!" I replied.

"Your ankles will swell up; your face will swell. In fact, you'll just get fat!"

"Again, thanks sis, very much appreciated!"

"And as for labour, whoa, it's not for the faint-hearted!" *For god's sake, be quiet.* "Your fanny gets ripped open and tears like a crusty baguette, blood and guts everywhere..."

"Stop, Lou, you're putting us all off!" Cried Jess, who held her hands over my ears to stop my imagination from running riot.

"Why do you think I stopped at one?" Lou continued, not put off by the evil eyes Jess was throwing her way. "Your fanny won't rip, Lil, it's plenty big enough!" *Why do people keep referring to the size of my fanny?* "Only kidding!"

Sally contributed to the conversation, leading us on to nappies and how Terry's were best as they were good for the environment. I wasn't ready for nappy talk, but as Sally was a recycling freak, she had a window to educate us.

I was keen to break away from baby and nappy talk, so I managed to steer them away with stories of my last few flights.

"I'm not kidding. I was busy trying to secure the cabin ready for take-off and she just handed me a wooden leg and asked me to put it in the overhead locker." Well, of course they were in stitches. "Wait, there's more! When I opened the cupboard looking for a space long enough for her leg, a pink straw hat fell out, landing on some bloke's head! I didn't know where to look or what to do first, it just landed perfectly as if he'd put it on himself!"

So the evening continued with our embarrassing work stories filling the house with tears of laughter and, if only for a short time at least, I could forget about all the worries which lay ahead.

At twenty-four weeks, things were considerably different. Work was manic, and I had quite a few luxury trips: 5-day Toronto, 4-day Orlando and an 8-day trip to Goa. However, my body was in conflict with my brain and I could no longer hide that a being was growing inside. Almost overnight I had fuller boobs, a more rounded waistline and, yes, Lou, my ankles were swollen most of the time. I tried to disguise my changing shape with baggy shorts and various sarongs on trips but I swear the crew were sniggering at my new fuller figure. Luckily, the weight was an even gain all over, although I was bursting out of my uniform as I'd also found an appetite I didn't know existed. However, I was still in denial and couldn't accept that my life was going to change.

At twenty-eight weeks, I was struggling, and could barely get my Kardashian bottom down the aisle of the plane. I also couldn't hide it any longer from Deb, who happened to be on one of my flights listening as I pleaded ignorance with the senior crew member who challenged the possibility. I wanted to scream 'How rude, I've just gained weight', but my cover was blown and I had to admit to my situation and start to accept that something was going to have to change.

Deb couldn't believe it, reminiscing about my first training day when she guessed that I might be, but she didn't give me too much of a hard time, as long as I made that flight my last one!

I didn't, but the next one was the game changer. A young girl, aged eight or nine, had fallen unconscious in her seat after eating a whole bag of lemon sherbets. The call bells were going crazy, urgently requiring attention as distressed passengers and family called for help. I was the only crew member in the vicinity and had to act fast. With my pulse racing and my heart pounding, I placed my fingers on the girl's neck to find her carotid pulse, but it was weak and irregular – she wasn't breathing. She was slumped forward in her seat, so without thinking I flew into action and pulled her back, preparing to give her the kiss of life. Her mother was pale with shock and an audience had gathered. All sorts of things were going through my mind: firstly, I didn't have the strength for this, I was seven months pregnant; and secondly, I shouldn't be giving anyone mouth to mouth as I might catch something and pass it on to my unborn baby! And there it was, my first proper concern for my unborn child. Luckily, just by the sheer reaction of pulling her back in her seat, she threw up, firing lemon sherbet sweets at my forehead like a machine gun. She was alive! Her mother sobbed as she took her child in her arms. Surrounding passengers were also sobbing. It dawned on me that this woman could have lost her child, which made me realise that I didn't want to lose mine.

Shock and adrenalin, combined with the regurgitated sweets, were just too much, so I ran to the toilet just in time. I retched and retched with nothing to show but fluid and bile, but my stomach was hurting and I began to worry. How foolish had I been? Not sure if I should be feeling this sort of pain, my worry turned into panic. I could hear the purser knocking on the door to see if I was ok, but then the noise seemed to fade away. All I remember was a gently tapping on my cheek; by all accounts, the purser had to practically carry me out of the toilet then strap me in my seat for landing!

I was still shaken after the flight and realised what a huge risk I was taking by continuing to work. When I got home, the pains in my stomach got gradually worse, so I called Sam.

"Lillian, you are joking. For god's sake, you should go straight to A&E!" She shouted after I had explained to her about my day. "Look, I'll come straight over and take you down there." Before I could reply and say no, she had hung up and was on her way.

En route to the hospital, Sam was telling me how she had seen Lyndon with a guy at the weekend, getting very cosy. I felt an urge of jealousy; bloody hell, these hormones were playing havoc with me! How the hell could I be jealous of my gay friend's squeeze? Had I relied on him that much? Sam was rambling on, but I couldn't hear as I wondered who was this man that Lyndon was with. I was an insecure basket case. *Get a grip, Lilly, get a bloody grip – he's gay!*

"Lillian? Lillian, hello? Are you listening?" Sam shouted, bringing me back from my thoughts.

"Sorry, what did you say?"

"I said have you thought of any names for the baby or, better still, have you told the bloody father yet?"

Luckily, I was saved from having to respond when a cyclist whizzed by, clipping the side mirror of the car, causing Sam to holler a stream of expletives out of the window. But no, I hadn't told the bloody father yet!

Minutes later, I found myself lying on a couch waiting to be examined.

"Ms White, Lillian, hello!"

God, I was in love. Standing before me was an Adonis of a man: tall, dark and handsome... Mmm... was he my doctor?

"What seems to be the problem? Overdoing it, eh?" He leant forwards to check my pulse, which of course raised further with his touch.

Oh god, my nipples were twitching. He was gorgeous! *Please don't leak, please don't leak... argh, too late.* I described my symptoms and, before I could say any more, he reached for the KY Jelly. *Dear lord, please tell me he's not going to put his fingers inside... phew... over my belly.* He moved his tools in circular motions.

I felt excitement in my lower region and couldn't look him in the eye. *I bet he's got a huge…*

"Right, Lillian, there's nothing to be alarmed about, but I think the baby is a little distressed. Have you been lifting heavy objects, or have you been under stress?"

"I have to confess that, yes, I have been a little stressed."

I told him the lemon sherbet story and about the retching and stomach pain, but he wasn't impressed. Not only was he shocked that I was still flying at such a delicate stage in my pregnancy, but he was concerned that I had come into contact with someone else's sick and proceeded to tell me how harmful this could be to the baby. I was ordered to take complete rest for at least two weeks and under no circumstances should I be flying or doing any sort of lifting whatsoever. He also wasn't impressed that I hadn't seen a doctor or midwife during the whole term and branded me totally irresponsible. God, he was bossy. I felt like a naughty schoolgirl. Why did that turn me on?

"You were ages. How did you get on?" Sam offered me her coffee and helped with my coat.

"He ordered lots of rest and…" I looked at my sick note. "…it would appear that I'm unfit to fly!"

She had that 'heavens above' look on her face. "You need to start taking care of yourself, seriously. And will you do me a favour, stop passing out? MAN UP, GIRL!"

"Ok, ok, I'll try!" I smirked.

"It will all work out, you'll see," Sam reassured me with a gentle nudge.

Will it?

FOURTEEN

I was grounded to office duties with only weeks to go until I was officially on maternity leave. Eight months pregnant, I was in the final trimester with approximately four weeks until due date. I'd been using the pregnancy as an excuse to eat and had become ginormous. I could no longer wear the standard maternity uniform, so they had one especially made, and I'd resigned to wearing flip flops as my feet were too swollen for shoes. I looked like a tank and moved like a duck, not like Jagger. Having gained four and a half stone, I was almost unrecognisable.

Everyone around me was going stir-crazy that I hadn't told James.

"Babies should come into this world with two parents, two!" My mother would declare.

This baby had two, the other just wasn't aware. I was going to tell him. I'd tried, it just hadn't happened. I'd rung several times and left numerous messages, but he'd never got back to me. I was secretly devastated but played it cool. Of course I wanted him involved, a day didn't go by when I didn't think about us running off into the sunset, but it didn't look likely. No-one had seen him for ages, even Lou hadn't heard from him.

He had moved on from The Wyte Shed some time ago when the new managers started. I'd made it clear to all involved that it had to come from me, so even if they did bump into him, they couldn't let it slip.

One afternoon, I dialled his number but was directed yet again to answerphone. I put down the phone and pondered whether I should leave a message, but what would I say? 'Oh hi, it's Lilly, remember me, Lilly White? Just a quick call to see how you are. Give me a call sometime, oh and by the way, I'm pregnant!' I didn't think that would go down too well. Pausing for a minute to come up with a better message, I took a deep breath then redialled. OH MY GOD, it was ringing. I put the phone down. *OMG!* I started panting, afraid that I may actually hear his voice again. I felt excited, afraid, exposed, and insecure all at the same time. Should I redial? The enormity of what lay ahead fell heavily on my shoulders. Why had I left it so late? I was eight months pregnant, he was going to go mental. I could feel my heart racing with every pulse pressing on my skin. I couldn't back out, especially as he was now ringing me!

Taking a few deep breaths to slow my galloping heart, I eventually answered.

"Hello!" I whispered softly, my whole body shaking.

"Lillian? Did you just call?" His voice was familiar, warm and sexy, offering a comfort I hadn't realised I'd missed. Butterflies. I took a very deep breath.

"Hi James, how's things?"

FIFTEEN

I replaced the receiver and broke down in tears, which were still present when the girls arrived later that evening for moral support.

"What's up? What did he say?" Jess asked.

"I didn't have the courage to tell him!"

"So? Ring him back!" Said Sam.

"She can't ring him back now, she'll appear too keen!" Replied Jess.

"Keen! She's already carrying his baby!" Sam quite rightly pointed out. "I think they're way past 'keen', don't you, Lillian? You *need* to tell him!"

All in all, the call hadn't been that bad. It was just the shock of hearing his voice. As it turned out, he was doing well and had met someone. It didn't sound serious; in fact, he seemed delighted to hear from me.

"Girls, he's met someone else!" They went silent.

"Well, she's not carrying his baby!" Demanded Sam. "I hope not, anyway!" She added quietly.

"Oh thanks! I hope not too!" I replied.

"Spill the beans then, who is she? Anyone we know?" Asked Sally.

"Jenny Ward. It's not serious, but he thought I might know her..." I was stopped mid-sentence.

"Jenny Ward! Jenny Ward! It can't be the same one, surely! The only Jenny Ward I know used to be an underwear model. She was pretty famous locally but dropped it to continue her studies," offered Sally as tears began to form in my eyes.

"You know her? Are you friends with her?" Nope, couldn't stop them, out they came.

Sally could see the effect of this news. "I used to know her but... I'm not her friend now, no definitely not!"

Too late – my tears came trickling down, weirdly turning into a fit of giggles. "So, not only does she have a body to die for..." I repeated, "...she has brains as well?" I felt sick with jealousy and wondered why I had never met this wonderful Jenny Ward! "She gave up the chance to be a famous model for her studies. What did she study?" I had to know.

Sally continued to put me out (in?) of my misery. "Well, last I heard she was still at university. I mean, she's already a qualified doctor, but she was in further training..."

I interrupted this time. "You mean she's a fucking doctor! What's she training to be? A bloody brain surgeon?" Not jealous, not jealous at all!

"Oh, Lil, I'm sorry! She could have done really well with her modelling too; god knows what she'd be doing with James!" Sam tried to comfort me.

"Well, thanks a bloody lot! That doesn't say much for me now, does it!" I could feel the depression setting in.

"Oh, don't be silly, Lil, it won't be her, and if it

didn't sound serious... anyway, how did you leave it with him?" Sam was trying her best to backtrack.

I stood in the middle of my lounge with my belly sticking out. My boobs were resting on my stomach and it wouldn't be long before my chin rested on my boobs. My feet were so swollen I could only wear flip-flops and my ankles were the same width as my calves. Cankles!

"Who do you think he'd choose, eh?" I waddled around the room like a duck. "Come on, it's close, isn't it? Really close – underwear model or this little beauty?"

I paraded around again until they all shouted, "You, of course, you!" ...and that's why they're my friends!

Although I was making light humour of the situation, my stomach had sunk, as I knew deep down that any girl in your prospective man's life was a threat. Fat, thin, pretty, ugly, dim or doctor, they're all a possible threat, and when you're pregnant by said man, your life may well and truly be over.

"We're meeting on Friday night. He's coming here for a catch-up," I offered.

"Some catch up – you'll have to catch him; he'll fall to the floor with the sight of you!"

"Sam!" Yelled Jess. "Zip it!"

Well, it was true, she had a point. I couldn't hide behind doors forever, but I was expanding by the second. At least the girls thought it was a good sign that he was putting himself out on a Friday night. Why would he do that if he wasn't keen on seeing me? I still hadn't planned on how I was going to tell him. Put it this way, once he saw me, he'd know the score, but while he was standing at the front door with my belly tucked behind the same door, he wouldn't know!

Thank god the girls were around to cushion my mood, lifting the ceiling with their usual laughter. For the rest of the evening we discussed how my 'poor child' would survive not only my cooking but many of my other fine attributes too.

"Remember when you boiled those potatoes in your cookery exam? Almost setting fire to the room because you forgot to put the water in?"

"What about serving frozen lasagne at The Wyte Shed as she'd not defrosted it!"

"Hey, that could happen to anyone!" I thought it was an easy mistake.

"The best one was the bread in the microwave. She thought it would take forty minutes to defrost. The kitchen was closed for days!"

"Ha, ha, ha, yes, very funny. I'm still in the room, you know! So we'll eat out all the time, people do!"

Although at my expense, I did see the funny side, especially when they discussed what James' child might look like. Sam said it was inevitable that the baby would be premature, because of my previous experience with him, and that it wouldn't be a bad thing because the massive hair would not have fully formed. They added that as long as I used my GHD's from the day it was born, it could easily be tamed.

We howled all evening until I couldn't keep my tired, sorry arse awake any more.

"Good luck Friday. Let me know how you get on,"

Jess said as she opened the door.

"Big kiss!" A hug from Sally.

"Ciao!" A quick squeeze from Sam before the door shut behind her, leaving me alone with my thoughts yet again.

I took myself off to bed with a glass of water and a bottle of Gaviscon in anticipation of the indigestion which appeared every evening. Really, there was no need for all these side effects!

Jenny Ward used to be an underwear model AND she was a fucking doctor. That's all I bloody needed! I stood in front of the full-length mirror naked, not recommended when you're heavily pregnant. However, my boobs could give anyone a run for their money! Never mind Jenny Ward, I could certainly model these babies – they were fantastic! Huge, round, firm and... Oh, the slightest knock as I got too close to the mirror caused them to leak – I was covered in milk. How attractive! I bet Jenny Ward's boobs didn't leak. I was so tired. To hell with Jenny Ward! He sounded casual about her, so it couldn't be serious. Anyway, I had convinced myself that James was fully available to bring up our child so closed my eyes and disappeared into the land of nod! It was 9.40pm – what a rebel!

SIXTEEN

It was Friday and I felt good. James was coming over. No specific time had been discussed and, from what I could remember, that could be anything up to midnight. I hoped I could stay awake until then! Once I got in from work, I began the process of transforming myself and trying to look as non-pregnant as I could, even though I was getting closer to the due date and resembled the largest breed of hippo!

I took a long soak in a very deep, warm bath. It was not a pretty sight, I have to say, but I couldn't bear to shower any more. I had an intolerable issue with water on my forehead, an horrendous sensitivity where the slightest trickle of water anywhere near it made me feel sick. So, I chose to bathe instead (despite the nightmare scenario of having to heave myself out at the end) and had shares in dry shampoo. I was aware there were parts of my body that I hadn't seen for a while, parts that I had difficulty reaching, but upon seeing a vision of my current self in the mirror as I stepped into the bath, I was mortified to notice the almighty jungle staring back from my pubic zone. What was normally a neatly pruned bush now resembled an overgrown hedge! I panicked a little as I wondered if James would get to see this – surely not. The thought made me quite nauseous. Did people have sex when they were heavily pregnant? Wouldn't they poke the baby? I hadn't planned on any action, but I wanted my man back, so I was open to anything! I couldn't see the full frontal image but decided to have a go anyway and began to hack away. I may as well have been blindfolded, so it truly was a guessing game and, being a delicate job, it did take a while.

By the time I'd finished, the water was tepid, but I was so exhausted I just lay back for a little longer. I began to feel cold so tried to get as much of my body under the water as I could, which was not an easy task. The weight of my body caused the water to rise and, although the level was high, my breasts and stomach still floated above it. I did look a bugger! Going back eight months or so, I thought I was fat. I wasn't fat, I looked amazing in comparison, but now I was fat! I was a proper hippo porker and there was nothing I could do about it! Things were happening that you'd never imagine. For instance, there was a long, thin brown line running from my belly button heading as far south as I could see. My nipples leaked at the slightest touch and the veins surrounding them resembled the spaghetti junction. My bottom was spotty. Not just a few spots, but absolutely covered in big red juicy spots. I wouldn't mind, but I couldn't even reach them to squeeze the buggers, not even do 'dot to dot'!

I lay still for a while daydreaming about how the evening might pan out. I hadn't seen James for ages, too long, but so much had happened that our past history seemed somewhat of a blur.

Lying in my tepid water in some sort of trance, trying to make some sense of it all, I noticed a large spider dangling from the far corner of the bathroom. This did not sit well with me so, feeling my heart rate rise just a tad, I calmly tried to manoeuvre myself for a sharp exit from the bath. It soon dawned on me that I was no longer in a position to carry out a sharp exit. So I remained still and watched my little scary friend from afar. At least, for now, he was at a comfortable distance away, hanging lazily in front of the bright, clinical wall. The bathroom suite was yellow when I first moved in, clearly in need of a revamp. And being one of the first rooms to decorate, I was quite proud of how it had turned out as I'd done all the work myself. I'd sanded and varnished the floors, and replaced the yellow for a lime green and purple colour scheme with long voile curtains draping the window. My towels were folded in a lime, purple, lime, purple order, resting neatly on a chrome shelf next to the shower. It was one of my favourite rooms in the house.

It was getting chilly and James would surely arrive soon. I checked the position of the spider. Convincing myself I was safe, I attempted to lift my body into a sitting position before I could heave myself into a standing position and get out of the bath. As I raised my body, my skin vacuumed my stomach area, leaving a taut outline of the baby which resembled that horrific scene from Alien – seriously, do not try this at home! The baby didn't like this arrangement and moved frantically, trying to get comfortable, with the odd hand and foot kicking my sides. It was horrendous really, so I put my hands over my tummy and hauled the hippo slowly up onto its wobbly legs! It was no good though, as I felt light-headed, so to stop myself fainting, it was safer to sit down again. Slowly, I lowered my weight back into the bath, taking deep breaths to prevent the sickness. I gawped at the ridiculous hump in front of me. Was this really me? Was this what it had come to? Was this what I wanted? Well, it was a bit late now!

I was shitting myself about the whole damn thing. What the hell was I thinking keeping a baby in my position? I had finally found the job of my dreams with the chance of travelling all over the world, yet I chose to be pregnant. What a fucking idiot! I'd probably be crap at it anyway. What if I didn't instantly bond with it or love it, then what? I couldn't exactly send it back! Maybe I should stop calling it 'it' for a start! The thought of seeing James again had emphasised my predicament and the panic was hard to control. I took deeper breaths, talking myself through the whole process. *Come on, Lilly, deep breaths.* Maybe it was normal for new mums to freak out once in a while. I was definitely FREAKING OUT! What if I dropped it? Say I took the wrong baby home by mistake? What about my job? My home? I was sitting in freezing cold water by this point, but my body was getting hot. I needed to get out of the bath!

Heaving myself up once again, I climbed gingerly out of the bath to the sound of someone banging on the door.

"Hello, hello, Lillian, are you there?"

Oh shit, that distinctive voice could only be James. What was he doing here so early? He was never early. Oh great, he picked this moment to improve on his timekeeping!

"Just a minute, be right with you." I moved as fast as my weight would allow, grabbing the biggest towel to haul around my huge waist. Rushing hadn't been in my vocabulary for the last few months, so if you can picture an overweight elephant in a relay, that would best describe me!

"Hellooooo, is anybody home?" James was now ringing the doorbell and banging the knocker. He obviously hadn't heard me shouting.

"I'm coming, just a minute!"

I wanted to make myself look as presentable as I could. As trying to look slim and beautiful was too big a mountain to climb, I did the best with what I had in the time allocated to me. I heard more banging from below and knew that if I didn't answer soon he would presume I wasn't in and leave. I couldn't take the risk so took each stair carefully whilst donning my dressing gown and towelling through my hair. I ran a comb through it quickly and pinched my cheeks en route to the door through the kitchen, catching a glimpse of my reflection in the oven. I didn't look my best and there was ample room for improvement, but what the hell, I just wanted to get this over and done with.

Opening the door, I saw James just about to climb back into his car when he noticed me.

"There you are! I thought you weren't in. I was just about to leave. How are you, Lil?" He closed the door to his brand-new Audi and began the short walk back towards me, but on his approach, I could see the colour drain from his face. He looked at my stomach area and started to speak but nothing came out of his mouth. I realised that in all the commotion, I had forgotten to hide my bump!

"James, are you ok?" I asked, but James didn't speak. Instead, he was indicating for me to get back into the house! "James? What's the matter? What are you doing?"

He closed the door behind us as his head fell into his hands. The silence was deafening, but it was clear that I shouldn't speak. As he focused on my middle spread, you could read his eyes acknowledging that maybe he had something to do with my situation.

"Oh my god, Lil, is it mine?" Thinking of the right words to reply, I took a deep breath to respond when he answered the question for me. "Of course it is! Why else would you call me out of the blue for no reason? I had convinced myself it was something to do with the pub, you know, to do with business... oh god, Lil, this is..."

I scrunched my face, thinking he was about to say 'awful' – or maybe great – as he started pointing towards the door, in the direction of his car.

"James, what an earth is the matter? I don't want anything from you, honest (I lied), I just thought you should know."

"You don't understand, Lil. Oh my god, what a mess, what a fucking mess! Jenny is in the car..." And again he pointed towards the door, then his hands reached for his face and he buried his head in them as he collapsed into one of the armchairs.

I looked through the window discreetly and noticed a girl sitting in the passenger seat. "You brought your girlfriend with you?" I gasped. Why would he bring her with him? It wasn't serious, after all, or was it? "Is that Jenny Ward?"

James didn't look up immediately, but when he did he stood up and hugged me. He hugged me so tight I had to pull away as he was blocking my oxygen flow and also the baby's (our baby's)! He pulled away and took my hands, knelt down and placed his head against my bump. This was all very strange and not what I had expected, but the natural thing to do was to put my hands on his head and comfort him. What was I doing? What was going on? He had a girlfriend, so what? I kind of knew, but we could sort something out, surely?

"James, it's ok. Don't worry, we will get through this!"

He was about to speak when there was an impatient bang on the door.

"Oh god!" Cried James. "Oh dear god, here goes, my life is about to fuck up big time! Time to ring the undertakers!" He got to his feet, touched my cheek with his hand (just like in the movies) and headed towards the door just as whoever it was knocked again rather aggressively.

James opened the door and there stood Jenny Ward. Yes, the underwear model. Yes, she was gorgeous, tall, thin with... wait a minute. There, stood in front of me, was a gorgeous, PREGNANT Jenny Ward.

SEVENTEEN

I could feel the bile burning my throat and had to swallow several times before it reared its ugly head. I couldn't believe what was happening to me! What did I do so wrong that this was how it ended for me, sharing my man with another, my unborn sharing their father with another. An overwhelming depression smothered my body and my legs weakened beneath me. I was still in my robe, looking huge and dishevelled; she was in a clingy white dress with her glossy hair falling perfectly around her shoulders. There was no competition here.

She looked at my bump then at her own. I looked at her bump then at mine, then we both looked at James. Were we both pregnant with James' child? How could this have happened? When did it happen?

Jenny Ward stared at my stomach, holding on to her own neat bump with a perfectly manicured hand. Without warning, she clenched the other into a tight and angry fist, punching James straight between the eyes! He went flying, blood pouring from his nose as she stormed out angrily, driving away in the Audi. She was a crazy woman but she had some spunk, I'd give her that. My legs were wobbling like jelly and my mouth stuck open, struggling to close. Now what? There was blood all over my floor. This was not how I planned my meeting with James!

"Oh Lillian!" Groaned James. "I'm so sorry to put you through that, but to be fair, I probably deserved it!"

Passing him a fistful of tissues, I led him into the kitchen. I didn't have anything, still in shock at the whole damn thing. Finally, my mouth relaxed and found something to say.

"Aren't you going to go after her?" I asked in disbelief.

"No! Would you?" He replied, mopping the blood from his nose, "She'd probably stab me!"

"Not if I stab you first!" I added. "Bloody hell, James, what a mess!"

"I know... Lillian, I'm so, so sorry. Look at you!" He went to touch my bulging stomach, but I took a step back. I didn't mean to, it was just a reflex action. "Sorry, Lil, but it is mine, isn't it?" He asked, his eyebrows raised in question.

I think so...

"Of course it's bloody yours, you idiot! Why else do you think I've just put myself through all of that!" I pointed angrily at the door then I burst into tears. "Why is everyone thinner than me?" The tears were flowing. "How come she (I pointed in the direction of the door again) looks like that and I look like this." I made a sweeping gesture across my entire body. "I'm so fat. I hate being pregnant!" More tears flowed. "Why are you with her? How can she be pregnant too, at the SAME TIME AS ME!" More tears. "You must have slept with her when we were still together! How could you do that to me? Just LOOK AT ME... LOOK AT THIS!" I was now screaming like a mad woman, sweaty faced with damp, scraggly hair – it seriously wasn't a good look. I finally stopped yelling and sniffed away snotty tears. "Are you going to go after her?" I asked again.

James turned to face me. "As if I would leave you like this!"

"I don't want the sympathy vote, I just asked you a simple question!"

"No, I'm not going after her. What's the point? What can I possibly say? I had no idea you were pregnant too. She won't believe me now, whatever I say to convince her, not after that."

He did have a point.

"Why didn't you contact me, Lil? I mean it is mine, the timing and everything, how far gone are you?"

"Of course, it's yours! What sort of girl do you take me for?" I shouted.

"Ok, ok, I just can't believe it!" He rubbed his face with his hands again, resting them over his mouth as though trying to stop himself from speaking. "Lillian, I didn't sleep with her whilst we were still together!" He continued. "But.."

I looked him straight in the eye. "But... but what?" I asked.

"Remember our last night *together?*" He asked. How could I forget? I nodded in response, indicating towards my stomach. "Well, after you'd finally gone, moved out, it really hit me hard so I turned to drink for a few days. I've known Jenny for years and she'd just split from her boyfriend. We used each other's shoulders to lean on and then... one thing led to another... and before we knew it, in a drunken state, we had... slept together." He looked down as if accepting his fate. However, one look at my disbelieving face got him on the defensive and he started to argue that we hadn't actually been *together* together at the time. I couldn't believe he was even admitting this – even though there was a niggle at the back of my mind, reminding me of my hypocrisy. "Jenny was in the right place at the right time. She was interested, that's all!"

"I'd only just moved out, James!" I cried. "I thought that after that night..."

"Thought what?" He interrupted.

"That you might have called? Asked me to come back? Declared your... undying love!" I fell to the sofa in ridiculous, loud sobs.

"I wanted to, Lillian, I really did, but I didn't want to get in the way of your dream job. It was all you ever spoke about. I wanted to run after you, stop you. I pictured myself begging you to stay but it wouldn't have been fair!"

My sobs turned into sniffles. "Is that what you wanted to do?" I whispered as James fell to his knees beside me, taking my hands in his.

"Yes! Yes, and I almost did, but I stopped myself and poured a drink instead. Then another. And another, and didn't stop for three days!" He wiped my snotty tears with his hands then continued, "You could have called me, told me how you felt?"

The sobs returned at what could have been. James

tried to comfort me.

"So how come *she's* still on the scene?" I sniffled.

"We'd hang out. It was just a casual thing, you know, she helped take my mind off you. It didn't really help, but I suppose after a while there was an attraction. She knew all about you and our situation. As far as she was concerned, we were over, and she wasn't treading on anyone's toes!" He stopped to take a breath! "But Lillian, if you had told me sooner about the baby, then maybe..."

"Maybe what, James? Things would have been different? Well, Jenny and I couldn't be more *different* if we tried!"

"Lillian, this *is* an awful situation." With a sigh, James rose to his feet, a long silence followed before a burst of uncomfortable words, "...Jenny's due next month!" He looked at me, sadness in his eyes. *Oh god, please tell me he's joking, she looks so great.* I was also very near my due date – talk about two for the price of one! "Lillian, when is your due date?" His eyes were fixed on me now, waiting for an answer.

"I'm due in about four weeks. Four weeks, James, stick that in your pipe and smoke it!" I shouted as more tears fell.

My beautiful fairy tale was spoiled; he had stamped on the book and torn out the pages. What the hell was I thinking and what was I to do? I couldn't help but think about Jenny Ward and what she must be thinking. I slumped, crying uncontrollably. To be honest, at that point I didn't care if I ever stopped! James knelt beside me and took me in his arms. He held me close, kissing my head, holding my hand and sending shivers down my spine. His head rested close to mine. We were like this once before and it felt good then too. Working together and living together had taken it all away from us, confusing resentment and anger with absent love and exhaustion. I suddenly felt horny, real horny, and I could feel tingling down below that I'd forgotten even existed. I realised in an instant that I still loved him, and my heart ached like never before at the thought that I had probably lost him. I couldn't stop the tears.

"I loved you, Lillian. I still do. It was always you but I couldn't turn her away when she told me she was pregnant. Coming here we both thought it was just innocent business stuff. God knows what must be going through her head now! To be honest, I'm not sure what's going through mine!" He gave a nervous giggle. "You've totally fucked up any future plans I had with Jenny!"

"What do you mean, future plans? What? Are you getting married?"

Silence.

"James?" I couldn't take my sodden eyes off him as the bile rose once again before I puked all over the kitchen floor and all over James!

"Lillian!" Grabbing a tea towel, he held back my hair and wiped my face.

I heaved myself up towards the sink, splashing cold water to my mouth as James leant against the sink, staring at the floor. Eventually he answered my question.

"I was going to, Lillian, do the right thing. I didn't

know what you were doing or with whom, where you were, let alone know you were pregnant. For all I knew you could have been engaged to be married yourself. It's a long time, Lillian, nine months, a lot can happen." His eyes were fixed on my stomach as mine glanced towards the sick splattered all over my floor!

"Salt, we need salt!" I demanded as James frantically opened all the kitchen units in a desperate search for salt.

I poured it over the 'vile bile', hearing the salt crystals absorbing the fluid, then threw up again! I broke down with more uncontrollable tears, shouting, screaming, ranting, crying. I couldn't stop. I couldn't believe what was happening. Salt was flying everywhere as James once again grabbed my limp body and led me into the lounge.

"Lillian, you're going to give birth at this rate! It's ok, it will be ok!" He was making shushing sounds into my hair.

"I can't do this on my own, I really can't. I'm scared, James, and now you're going to marry Jenny, and she's gorgeous, and I'm just fat and ugly and single and lonely..." I went on and on and on in a high-pitched voice, snot and tears falling in my mouth! I leant further into his chest, wiping my face on his shirt, his familiar odour offering some comfort.

We sat in silence for quite some time, taking in the car crash that lay before us.

"Look at me!" He said softly. "I haven't asked her yet, Lillian. It's not something we've discussed, so stop getting ahead of yourself, ok?"

I didn't move.

"Lillian?" James broke my chain of thought. "You ok?" He took a deep breath and sighed. "What a fucking mess!"

He squeezed my hand, patted my knee, and then rose to his feet. I felt a sickening loss in my heart as I thought he had got up to leave, then I heard a few cupboards open and close, followed by the old familiar sound of bottles and glasses, then the 'glug, glug, pour' (god, I'd missed that sound). He came back with two very small measures of sherry.

"I know you shouldn't, but go on, have a few sips. It will make you feel better!" James swigged his down and went back for a refill. In fact, he brought the deep blue Harveys Bristol Cream bottle into the living room, sat down and finished the lot! We sat for hours, familiar, comfortable, talking things over, tears, smiles and laughter, intimate, devoted, until mental and physical exhaustion took over. The fight to keep my eyes open was far stronger than the fear of him possibly leaving so I left him snoozing and crawled into bed.

A gentle knock on my bedroom door stirred me into consciousness. It was James holding two hot mugs and a huge plate of toast.

"You always knew the way to my heart!" I said, trying my best to sit up with as much elegance as I could muster. James busied himself around me, plumping my pillows, straightening my duvet and opening the curtains a little to let in the morning sun. "I'm not sick, you know, just pregnant!"

"I know! Cheers!" He offered.

"Cheers back!" I replied, exchanging mug clinks.

"What are we cheering to again?" I asked, puzzled.

"Lillian, we're having a baby!" He stated clearly.

I didn't know how to take this. Why was he suddenly excited? What did he mean by *we're* having a baby? Did that mean he wanted us to be together? Or did that mean he will share the load a little, even though he was marrying Jenny? My heart sank again, especially when my thoughts turned to Jenny Ward... pretty bitch!

"How did you sleep?" I asked, knowing that he couldn't have slept well on the sofa, especially with a bloody nose, bruised face, and of course a sherry headache!

"Not bad. My head's a bit delicate though!"

"I'm not surprised! She throws one hell of a punch! Anyway, is there any sherry left? That was my emergency supply!"

"Don't worry, I'll replace it!"

The anxiety returned as I thought about our conversations but at least he had been honest about Jenny. I suppose I had left with no promise of return and was equally to blame for the lack of contact. Why hadn't I let him know sooner? Why hadn't I tried harder to tell him? I was torn between being cross with myself, cross with him, and cross at how things could have been so different. But one thing I knew for sure, Jenny Ward may be gorgeous and clever, but he was with me, eating breakfast with me, with our little baby growing inside me, so he obviously cared! I loved him and he still loved me. His phone started ringing,

"Is that her?" I asked anxiously, my bubble bursting once again.

"No, Lil, it's not her," he replied patiently, staring at his mobile a little longer than necessary, "but I do need to speak to you about something."

Here we go, I thought, *this is where he's thought about it and realises that maybe if he had his children with Jenny Ward they'd have much better genes.* He must have read my mind, seeing my face drop into a depression.

"Lillian, it's fine, it's nothing bad," he said. "Look, we can't ignore the fact that I'm dating Jenny, or *was* dating Jenny, and the fact that she's also carrying my child. It's a shit awful mess which will probably require counselling for the rest of our lives! But I'm going to have to speak to Jenny. It's only fair. I'm not a bad bloke so I have to do the right thing. Now, I know you being pregnant changes everything, but I do need to get my head around things. I mean, shit, it's huge!"

"My stomach is huge, James!" My bubble was exploding over everything around me. "So, what am I supposed to do while you get your head around it?" I was going to be sick... again!

"I didn't mean it like that, Lillian, and you know it!" He replied. "Anyway, as huge as this is, and this shit is huge, there's one more thing I need to tell you!"

"Oh god, who else have you got pregnant?"

"Ha, ha, very funny! There's no-one else but... I'm going away..."

"GOING ON HOLIDAY!" I interrupted. "Bloody great timing!"

"No, Lillian, I'm NOT going on holiday, but I've got some work coming up in…" he hesitated, "…London. Great timing, I know."

I couldn't believe what I was hearing and, although he offered an explanation, something about helping out a friend, (did he say bar work? Waiting on?), I'd only heard blah, blah, blah, as my brain zoned out, already picturing myself doing this alone, I could feel anger and disappointment brewing.

"I'll try and make it back for both births!" This last sentence brought me back from my pondering.

"Both births? I don't want my baby to be one of 'both births', I want my baby to be the *only* baby, the 'one birth' with a daddy present!" I said unreasonably.

"I understand, but I can't let Jenny go it alone. As for the job, I'm sorry, I'm just so sorry, it's just I can't afford to turn it down."

He cleared the breakfast things and headed downstairs. I had to fight the tears otherwise the only memory he was going to have of me was as an ugly, fat, mad crying witch whose breath stank of sick. *Get a grip, Lillian, get a grip!* I got out of bed – slowly – found a huge king-size-quilt type dress, which just about covered my midriff, put a comb through my hair and pinched my cheeks, clearly my new beauty regime. I didn't look good, but under the circumstances I would just have to make do.

"I've got to go, Lillian, but I'll call you, ok?"

I wanted to ask, 'When, when will you call?' But, thank god, I restrained myself. I was better than that.

"I love you, Lillian, always have, always will. It

will be fine. We will work it out." He kissed my cheek, then my lips and, before we knew it, we were having a full-blown snog! Wow, I was not as numb down there as I thought! Neither was he – not bad considering I hadn't picked up a toothbrush!

"I'll call you!" He held his hands over our baby bump and turned to leave.

"Bye then!" I replied, watching until he'd disappeared out of sight. Little did I know then that James was deeply heartbroken. He'd seen my missed calls and all my messages, but having no idea of the situation at the time, chose not to respond. Jenny was pregnant so he'd made his bed and surrendered to lying in it. Now he was regretting his actions.

EIGHTEEN

"Oh my god, I can't believe he's with Jenny Ward and she's pregnant!" Exclaimed Sam. "Is she fat?"

"Sore subject!" I replied.

"I hope so, skinny bitch. I bet she's the only woman to have maternity wear in a size zero!" Continued Sam, on a roll now.

The girls couldn't help but laugh. In fact, neither could I, because as much as I tried to fight it, it was true. Sal, Deb, Lyndon and Sam had turned up on Sunday, keen to get the low down on what had happened with James. I had no idea where to start!

"Who's Jenny Ward?" Asked Deb, looking a little perplexed, clearly out of the local loop. "Is she pregnant or skinny?"

"Both!" We sang in unison.

I filled them in on the latest, ending in the tale of the punch fired by Jenny.

"She never did!" Sal was gob smacked that Jenny had given James a bloody nose.

"Hey, it wasn't funny, I almost gave birth!" I laughed. "I suppose it was a bit funny. Took me by surprise, I can tell you!" I continued to tell them what had happened afterwards and that he said he might miss the birth(s)!

"Waiter? Is he gay?" Asked Sam.

"I am here, you know!" Interrupted Lyndon jokingly as Deb ruffled his hair.

"No, he's not gay... clearly!" I said, indicating towards my tum. "What's killing me more than anything," I continued, "is that he's choosing to go when I need him most, missing the birth of his child..."

"Children!" Corrected Sam.

"OMG, what a mess!"

"So, have you heard from him since?" Asked Sally.

"Not really!" I replied.

"What does that mean? You either have or you haven't!" Asked Lyndon. "Maybe he's already started this *Gay* job and hasn't had chance."

"I've had a text!"

"And?" He encouraged.

"It just said 'thinking of you xx'," I replied.

"Well, that's good, isn't it? Bloody hell, Lillian what can you expect? You'll just have to be patient. The poor guy turns up with his gorgeous, pregnant girlfriend..."

"Hey!" I screamed.

"Sorry... but joking apart... he turns up with his *equally attractive as you* pregnant girlfriend to find a *stunning* pregnant Lillian. I mean, it would blow your head right off, wouldn't it?" Lyndon made explosion gestures around his head.

"You're bloody gay, so how would you know?" I asked.

"I'm still a bloke, Lillian, with a bloke's way of thinking, so trust me, he'll be freaked out!" He replied.

"The best thing you can do is leave him alone, give him all the time he needs to get his head around it!"

"I do get that, Lyndon, but he hasn't exactly got that much time to think…" I pointed at my stomach. "…and he's not got a great communication record, has he? How many times did I try and call him to no avail?"

"Not enough!" He argued.

"So, I have to play the waiting game again, *waiting* for *him* to contact me?" Looking at Lyndon's' face, it would appear so. "And in the meantime?" I asked.

"Don't approach it like that. Just get on with your life and look ahead. God, Lillian, you have an amazing creature in there, this is the start of a new chapter!"

"Yeah, there's some great books out there too, Lil," Sam cut in. "The Single Parent's Handbook, The Single Mother's survival kit…"

"Sam," scolded Sal, "you can't say that!"

"Oh, don't be daft. I'm just trying to make humour out of the situation!"

"Thanks!" I cried.

"You're totally welcome!" Replied Sam, who offered me a cheeky wink.

Sal gave me a bear hug. "You'll be fine," she said. "What will be, will be… and… you've got all of us!"

The girls (and Lyndon!) all cheered and raised their glasses.

"To Lillian!" They all screamed.

"To me!" I said sarcastically.

"And your family!" Added Deb, nodding to my expanding tummy.

Lyndon stayed over as often as he could and Deb was never too far away. They had both slept over to keep me company, for which I was truly grateful. As the due date loomed, the more nervous I became.

One night, the three of us were all huddled on the sofa after the gang had gone, drinking hot chocolate... with a kick! It tasted delightful and I had resigned myself that drinking a little bit of alcohol at this late stage could surely do no harm. I sat in the middle of my two musketeers, feeling safe and loved, if only for one night. It got me thinking that Sally was right, I was not alone and had great friends who would be there no matter what.

Lyndon was giving me a little pep talk, saying I should concentrate on my career and put a plan into place for when the baby was born. I hadn't even given it a thought and presumed that as I was only on a temporary contract, and especially as I was pregnant and 'no good to them', that they would just let me go, but Deb begged to differ.

"I swear, Lillian, that's what they said," she continued. "This is off the record, mind you. If I'm found to be blabbing then we'll both be out of a job, but you are definitely being invited back next summer."

"Well, bloody hell!" I was shocked. "I can't believe it!"

"Yep, so you'd better pop that baby out on time and concentrate on getting back into that uniform!" She smiled, squeezing my knee.

It was reassuring to hear that my pregnancy hadn't affected my flying career. If anything, regardless of me trying to squeeze down the aisle at such a late stage of the pregnancy (not that kind of aisle, no shotguns in sight as yet!), it had been obvious what I was willing to sacrifice for my career and had displayed true dedication. I'd had great reports and, as soon as I was ready to start flying again, Deb didn't think it would be long before I was promoted!

For a moment, I forgot all about James and his 'both births' and reminded myself how truly brilliant I was. I was good at it, you know, the flying. I was a quick learner, excellent timekeeper (skin of teeth), had excellent social skills and, of course, had survived an 'emergency landing' – although I had completely and utterly shit myself and thought I was a goner! But this was my path and I had every intention of striding back down it as soon as it was feasible.

"What about the baby? Who will look after it when I go back to work?" I asked, having no clue.

"Ever heard of nurseries or child minders or Daddies?" Replied Debs.

"Daddies might have to be crossed off the list for the time being," I sighed. "I can't rely on James, not from his past record. Maybe I could wear one of those 'papoose' things with the baby hanging in front of me."

They both looked at me as though I was mad.

"On that note, I'd better make a move!" Debs said. "I'll see myself out, chic, but get yourself to bed, you look exhausted!"

"Yes, come on chubby, I'll tuck you in!" Lyndon hauled me to my feet.

I didn't know what I'd do without Lyndon. He'd been a lifesaver, sleeping over regularly when he wasn't working and rallying around after me – almost like a boyfriend. Sometimes I forget he wasn't my partner. In fact, he'd offered to be my birthing partner. To be fair, all the girls had, but somehow, I leant more towards Lyndon. He was just great. Not only was he funny and handsome and would probably pant more than any of the others, I just liked having a male around, regardless of how feminine he might be.

As for James, I wasn't sure if he would be panting with me or not. It was his bloody panting that got me into this mess in the first place! I hadn't seen or heard from him since Friday, so I presumed he was still in shock. Or died of shock! Lyndon saw me drifting.

"Do you think you'll hear from him again?" He asked. "He is the father, for god's sake!" He had made himself another hot chocolate (with a kick) and was stirring it like crazy as I got myself into bed.

"Yes, he is the father, Lyndon, and for god's sake, I'm sure you're making that poor mug dizzy, stop stirring!" I smiled at him with affection. I took him for granted sometimes. What would I do when he was gone?

"Soz, just want to make sure the alcohol reaches every mouthful. Do you want a sip?" He offered, but I shook my head as I seriously needed some shut-eye.

"Lyndon?" I asked, making his name linger childishly as I snuggled under my duvet.

"Yes?" He replied in the same childish tone. "What's up, babe and baby?" He gently patted my stomach.

"Will you always be around, do you think? You

know, here, staying at mine like normal?" I could be direct with Lyndon as it wasn't a romantic relationship, so I wasn't afraid of scaring him off. It was like having your brother as your best friend. It's funny, really, how we got so close. We could sleep in the same bed, cuddle each other, walk around practically naked and it just didn't feel weird. It felt ok, really comfortable, but would a baby change all that? Maybe it would become weird.

"I will be around for as long as you need me, babe." He kissed my forehead. *God, why did he have to be gay?* "Or, of course, unless George Clooney decides to be gay and chooses me to be his happy ever after!" He grabbed his bollocks as he said this and ground his hips! Gross!

"I meant what I said earlier though, Lillian, about work?" He turned it into a question.

"Yes, yes, I will get a plan, I promise!" I mumbled as I nodded off into never-never land, knowing that I wasn't going to think about work until I really had to.

NINETEEN

I had no job, no man and no baby... as yet... with a due date looming and feeling every single minute of it. I had never been so huge and swear I was the largest pregnant woman on record! Apparently, the average weight gain for pregnancy is one and a half to two stone. This depressed me somewhat as I had gained over five stone, so if you took away ten pounds for the baby (and whatever else comes out with it!), then I was carrying over four stone of pure lard! What the fuck had I been eating? I was heavy, large and very uncomfortable. Nothing fitted me and I looked a bugger in anything that did! The only footwear I could get my huge fat feet into was a pair of flip flops, but as my feet were so swollen, I couldn't keep them on my feet. I didn't look pregnant, more obese, and was seriously concerned as to where the four stone of extra lard would place itself once the baby had appeared. My boobs were excruciatingly sore and leaked constantly with the slightest touch, and my nipples were at least five inches long. I couldn't get comfy, no matter what position I tried; sitting, lounging, standing, lying down or standing on my head, I couldn't find a comfortable position, not even for five minutes. My body was so distorted it was never going to recover.

Using all the energy I could muster, I waddled slowly to the bottom of the garden to get some fresh air. As I peered over the fence across the fields, I noticed a couple jogging, their bodies synchronised with each step, happy and free. I couldn't help but feel envious of these strangers. She was tall, slim and very attractive – everything I wasn't – he was lean and athletic looking, and there was something about his hair that... *Is that...?* Oh god, it was him! I flashed back to our first meeting with his surfboard, then again at the chemist, and watched them float into their happy life. His Australian accent played over and over in my mind. Although I was not in a position to move forward with anyone new, I did wonder why our paths were out of sync. Was James on a different path too? My heart sank yet again.

This baby was truly ready to drop as he/she/it was wriggling around so much I swear he/she/it was trying to find a way out! Sleep was impossible with all the fidgeting, so I could add exhaustion to the list of problems pregnancy created. I was head-butted, kicked and thumped throughout the night, so it would appear that I'd 'baked' one of god's nocturnal beings who would probably become a 'hip DJ', hanging out until the early hours, so I was never going to sleep again and would probably lie awake worrying as to where they were for the rest of my life – parenting is a lose/lose situation! The pain in my back was debilitating and the only relief was to sleep on my side with pillows between my knees, stomach and boobs! Maybe the lack of sleep was nature's way of preparing you for what was to come. I wished this bloody baby would arrive. Not long to go now – not long to go!

Standing naked in front of the mirror (not recommended) it took a while to overcome the reflection. My breasts were humongous and veiny, my legs were swollen and dimply and my thighs chafed. There were also weird sensitive pigmentation patches decorating my body – would I ever get my pre-baby figure back? I thought of Jenny Ward and what she would see in her reflection – a stunning figure, lard-free, perky boobs, slender legs and a neat bump. I was curious to know if she'd had her baby and tortured myself frequently, visioning her with James, running off into the sunset. I was no further forward in that area, as I hadn't heard from him, but respected his need for space. I wasn't sure how much longer I could hang on to his words that *things* would be ok; I could barely hold on to my waters!

Trying to have a moan-free day, I ventured out of the house to go shopping. It was an exceptionally hot day, but at least I could escape the rising temperatures in the cool air-conditioned precinct. Maybe I'd treat myself to a new outfit for after the baby appeared, whether James *appeared* or not. The sun was bright and glorious, lifting the mood slightly, offering a more positive outlook on life. *I may be alone now, but once my little bundle arrives, I'll never be alone again.*

Just as I was leaving, I caught sight of my packed maternity bag sitting by the front door, waiting, ready.

I pondered aloud whether it would be needed. With no reply, after asking my bump if it planned on making an appearance that day, I left the bag and headed for the shops.

People adorned the streets and recreational areas, baking in the sunshine, absorbing the summer mood. I was too excited to rest after a successful few hours with my smoking hot credit card. Even the string of adoring couples dripping off each other couldn't spoil my mood.

Baby clothes, blankets and booties filled my bags, with some new tincy wincy knickers for me, clearly not designed for a pregnant woman, but I wouldn't be pregnant for ever. The thought of my arse in a G-string wasn't good, but I was determined it would be once this sprog was out, even if it might take some time. One thing I had noticed was all the new summer fashion – I was totally out of touch. I'd tried to keep up during the early stages, even having my midriff on show at one point, but this was not the look for me in my current state, although I did feel slightly frumpy in my oversized smock. Flicking through the rails, admiring each garment, imagining them decorating my post-baby figure, I suddenly noticed a familiar face that I wrestled to place. Then it dawned on me exactly who it was... Jenny Ward.

I tried to hide in my oversized smock, too ashamed of my attire as she gradually moved towards me, her beautiful midriff on show. Her bump was still intact. *Hadn't she had her baby?* Oh god, I couldn't possibly let her see me, I looked hideous! *Shit, she is looking over!*

Hide! I took cover behind some skinny jeans, unaware I was in the petite section. Then I came face to face with the female goddess.

"Lillian? Lillian, is that you!" Jenny had spotted me just as I was picking up some jeans, busying myself with the label. "Are they for you or the baby?" *Bitch, Bitch, Bitch...*

"Jenny!"

She must have seen the look of outrage on my face. "Sorry, I'm only kidding. I can't wait to shop for some kind of normal clothes again. They're gorgeous, but I don't think petite will be long enough for you!" She smiled at me then suddenly, as if in unison, we both spoke together.

"How are you?" We both sniggered.

"I... fine thanks, how you are feeling? I thought you would have had the baby by now – are you with James?" Oh god, he was on the brain, now I sounded desperate! I was so nervous – god knows why – not realising I'd asked the question until I had asked it. I felt a little sick at the thought of seeing him again, especially as I hadn't heard from him, only imagining he'd run off to Gretna Green with the underwear model standing right before me!

"I was going to ask you the same question!" She replied, quite directly.

"I haven't seen him or heard from him since the evening I told him I was pregnant. Look, Jenny, I'm so sorry about that night..." As the words came out, it suddenly dawned on me that she wasn't a bad person. It wasn't her fault she was in this mess.

"Lillian, I know this is a surreal situation, but do you fancy a coffee?"

She seemed a little lost so I agreed immediately. Well, my feet were killing me, and I could kill for a latte and some chocolate cake! I tried not to stare at her middle region; she must have been near full term but looked amazing: stunning, glowing. My eyes ducked to my covered midriff. I'd better make my latte skinny!

We left the store together, heading for the nearest bistro.

"You look great, by the way, great boobs!" Jenny was paying *me* a compliment.

"Thanks, although I have to say that pregnancy really suits you, you only look about six months pregnant!" I replied, giving her a shy smile.

We headed towards the counter and I caught sight of all the beautiful sugary delights. Jenny must have seen me dribbling.

"Look, this is my treat and almost a time for celebration, so let's have lots of cake. What do you fancy? I'm having a very large piece of that and a large cappuccino!" She said, pointing at a particularly large and moist-looking carrot cake.

Was she trying to make me fatter? Why was she being so nice?

"Make that two!" I slobbered, unable to resist the luxurious frosting. I could feel myself warming to the enemy; she ate carrot cake and drank cappuccino and was still THAT skinny – but she seemed nice!

We found two available sofas, taking one each

and sinking our bodies gently into the leather. It felt amazing and, once settled, I realised how tired I felt.

"This tastes so great!" Jenny splurted as she shoved the cake into her mouth. "It's sooooo delicious!" She closed her eyes, losing herself in the taste. After a few swigs of coffee she told me about life as a model and how it wasn't as glamorous as it sounded. The reason she'd not gained much weight was that she was on a special diet provided by the agency. They were monitoring her closely as she was booked for a catalogue shoot only six weeks after the birth! She confessed all about her diet over the past nine months and it sounded rather bland. She'd practically survived on cabbage soup and lentils, with some special drinks to ensure the baby received the right nutrients! Maybe that's a little exaggeration, but following a strict exercise and diet plan throughout your pregnancy didn't sound like a barrel of laughs. She also confessed that she'd always had to watch her weight and was unable to eat what she wanted as, pregnancy aside, just looking at sugary delights would attract unwanted pounds. It was a total sin that she was eating the carrot cake and if the agency found out they would probably drop her. On hearing that, and receiving her genuinely lovely comments, I started warming to her. How wrong can you be about someone? Or was it the Stockholm syndrome?

As the remaining forkful of cake fell into my big drooling mouth, Jenny slipped out a few tiny words.

"James left me."

My eyes widened in shock and some relief, and I replaced my fork, thankful I'd managed to finish it before the drama.

"Oh my god, Jenny, what? I can't believe it! When did it happen?" My mouth was still open.

"You mean you haven't seen him? You didn't know? I thought maybe he was with you!" She looked shocked.

"No, like I said, I haven't seen him since you gave him a bloody nose in my house!"

"I haven't either!" She gasped. "It felt great though!"

"You mean he's run out on both of us?"

As I looked at Jenny's stomach and then at mine, I felt the urge to giggle, as did Jenny. Two pregnant women, same father, about to drop at any moment, stuffing their faces with cake and coffee, in uncontrollable laughter. We were shoulder shaking and teary-eyed with euphoria – that was until Jenny no longer found it funny. Clutching her stomach, she looked across at me and very calmly announced, "The baby's coming!"

Still smiling, I asked, "What? Sorry, WHAT?" No more laughter.

"Don't panic, Lillian, but I think the baby is coming... now! It's ok, it's ok, stay calm!" I was calm(ish), but why the hell was she so calm? "Stay calm, stay calm, deep breaths, deep breaths!" She mumbled. Was she talking to me?

"Jenny, it's ok... are you sure?" Stupid question.

"Yes, I'm BLOODY SURE! Worst pain EVERRRRR... contractions... they're coming in THICK AND FAST... OH DEAR GOD!" She screamed loudly. The whole café glanced our way. "I'm a little overdue, it all fits into place really... oh, I've just wet myself!" Her forehead crumpled and she feigned a smile.

"Eh?"

"My waters have broken!"

Jenny screamed again. By this time there were a few spectators, including the barista.

"Is everything ok?" He offered.

"Please call us an ambulance…" I asked, but Jenny interrupted.

"No, No, please not an ambulance, Lillian. Can you take me?" *WTF?*

"You'll never make it to the car, Jenny, it's miles away!" I replied, getting agitated.

But she wasn't giving up. "I will, I will. Just grab my stuff and I'll hang on to you!"

Hang on to me? I'd fall over, we'd both bloody fall over! I was going to kill James. Where was he when you needed him? Jenny must have seen the stress shadow my face.

"Lillian, I'm so sorry to do this to you, you don't deserve it (*No, I don't!*), but please, I don't want any fuss, let's just get to your caaAARRRRR! (more screams) Pleeeaease, Lillian?"

Within minutes, it would seem that one order for an ambulance had been cancelled. Instead, two fat ladies were waddling towards the car park, one taking the weight of the other whilst laden down with a zillion shopping bags! Offers of help came flooding in as we'd clearly attracted an audience, but much to my dismay, Jenny refused, focused on getting to the car. As we shuffled along, a sharp pain shot through my body like a bolt of lightning, stopping me in my tracks.

"Lillian?" Jenny asked concerned, thinking exactly

what I was thinking.

"I'm fine, I'm fine, come on, keep going," I replied, hoping it was just the strain of carrying that extra load. If I just ignored it, it might go away. It didn't.

"Argh...HELP ME, HELP ME..." *Help me!* "...here comes another one! Arghhhh!"

Shit, shit, shit, shit, shit, shit, shit, shit! I also felt another pang.

"Ok, ok, we're nearly there, just hold on, hold on..."

"IT'S COMING! FUCKING FUCK, SHIT, THE BABY IS COMING!!!" I wanted to shout 'so is mine' but thought better of it!

"Hold on, we're almost at the car, let me call an ambulance, for god's sake, Jenny..."

"NO... shove me in and put your foot dooWWW-WNNNNNNNNN!"

I did just that, not even bothering with seatbelts – far too stressful! As the suspension dropped with the elephantine weight, I just prayed my little Mini would see us through.

Jenny's contractions were seconds apart, her screams louder and longer. Something was also happening to me as the twinges in my stomach became far more powerful. I kept my legs together and stamped on the peddle! *Oh god, was I going into labour too?* Fucking James! I was going to skin him alive! The pain was unbearable, so I too screamed, alarming Jenny, who continued to pant and shout. The giggles returned intermittently. Oh, the irony! Was this really happening? We felt every bump in the road, as did my poor Mini, the suspension scraping on the surface of the tarmac with each and every jolt.

"Oh, fuck, Lillian, faster, FASTER... put your foot down. PUT YOUR BLOODY FOOT DOWN!"

I did as I was told.

"OWEEEEEEE!" I yelled. OMG, another twinge. *Please tell me this isn't happening!* I felt all funny.

"What, Lillian? WHAT?" She asked frantically. "Keep driving! Breathe with me, breathe with me," she panted

I began the breathing exercises that most people do around pregnant women, and in unison we breathed in and out, in and out all the way to the hospital. We were laughing and crying, breathing and panting, until finally we could see the lights of the Emergency Department.

"Do you need to call someone? Your mum? A friend?" I asked.

"My mother!" She shouted, clearly in discomfort as I tried to manoeuvre her from my car. "She's away, back tomorrow."

"Tomorrow? But Jenny, who is your birthing partner TODAY?"

She looked at me questioningly. "You are?" Her eyes pleaded before her head dropped towards her lower region upon realising that she'd completely wet herself... and my seat!

I felt another twinge. Never mind *her* birthing partner, I was wondering if I was going to need mine! I pictured my bag sat waiting by the front door, missing all the action.

I dumped my urine-sodden car outside A&E and

called for assistance, my pleas falling on deaf ears as the audience in the waiting room looked on horrified and soon returned to their own personal traumas. We waddled through noisily as two ambulance men came to our assistance. Before we knew it, Jenny was in a wheelchair on her way to the maternity ward, slowly followed by me dragging behind. *Where's my bloody wheelchair?*

"Don't leave me, Lillian, please don't leave me!" Jenny shouted, clearly in pain, afraid, alone. Delivery was imminent.

"Take deep breaths, just keep breathing!" I shouted after her. "You'll be fine!" Holding my stomach as the contractions attacked, I questioned if I'd just dreamt the previous forty minutes. I wouldn't have imagined this scenario in my wildest dreams, we were practically enemies but now possibly could we be friends?

"Get this bloody thing OUT OF ME! IT'S COMING... NOW!"

As more staff attended to her needs, I looked for an opportunity to escape, but it was too late.

"Lillian!" Jenny howled in between screams. "Lillian, I need you!"

I rushed over, taking one of her hands as gas and air occupied the other.

"Take this whenever you feel the urge to push," a midwife advised.

Jenny held it tight to her mouth and was soon as high as a kite! By this time, my contractions were every ten minutes. I couldn't disguise the possibility that my baby might also be on its way. Oh god, where was my support team when I needed them? There were signs everywhere not to use mobile phones so I couldn't ring anyone, but at least I'd managed to sneak a quick text to Lyndon in all the commotion:

HELP!!! HSPTL NOW!!!

"Ok... Jenny?... I need you to push as hard as you can. Push, Jenny, push... PUSH!" The midwife looked concerned. "You've got to push harder, Jenny. Come on, just one more push and we are nearly there!"

Jenny didn't seem to care. She was practically pissed on gas and air! It was hilarious.

"Lillian, my darling Lillian, I can't tell you what it means to me that you are here with me. I mean, what a doll you are! I run off with the father of your baby and then he becomes the father of my baby and here we are in hospital together!" She rambled euphorically as I smiled awkwardly. How embarrassing! Jenny took another gulp of gas and air and continued with her babble, so I took it away. She'd clearly had enough.

I watched her pushing and wriggling and screaming and swearing – you name it, Jenny was doing it. I discretely brought the mask to my face and inhaled. Then again and again... bloody hell, it was good stuff! I could feel myself floating, listening to faint words from Jenny.

"Lillian!" Her words came drooling out unclear. "There is something I have to tell you, it's really important!" More slurring and dribbling...

"Jenny, just concentrate on your baby, breathe with me, breathe with me," insisted the midwife.

"No, Lillian, you don't understand, it's the baby's

father, James, he isn't..." Before she had a chance to finish her sentence, she disappeared... probably with the fairies.

"Jenny, love, Jenny! Can you hear me?" Shouted the midwife, her tone firm. "Hold on, just hold on!" She banged down hard on the emergency button, concern written all over her face. "Jenny, Jenny!" She shouted, tapping Jenny's face. Panic filled the room as a team of doctors raced in, poking and prodding Jenny, then whisking her away.

"Oh my god, what's happening? What's up with her?" I demanded, concerned for her welfare, the baby's welfare, James' baby's welfare! Holding on to my stomach, I inhaled the gas and air one last time with all the energy I could muster.

"She'll be fine, don't worry!" A nurse took over as available midwives scuttled off with the drama. "How about you? Let me take a look at you." She led me to a side room where I climbed up on the bed. It felt wonderful,

"What about Jenny? Is she ok....?" I mumbled as she focused on my pillows, fluffing and fussing as I drifted in and out of my own unbearable pain.

Moments later, a gush of hot fluid travelled down my thighs.

"Your waters have broken!" She exclaimed.

This baby was on its way. *Is this really happening?* I needed some back-up and, as Lyndon was my birthing partner, he'd make a good start. Although a little wobbly from the gas and air, I secretly managed another quick text:

In labour, where the fuck are you?

Should I call James? Would Jenny have called James? Was Jenny even able to call him? After the day's events, was that my responsibility? I had to call him, it was only fair, but it might not be the right time. I texted Lyndon again.

Please come now, both in labour, I need you!

Scrolling through my recipient list, I pressed send. I don't know how, but the text delivered to all my contacts – including James. For all I knew, he could have changed his number, met someone else and got them pregnant… whatever… bovverrd! If I was honest with myself, I was, very much so.

I waited and waited for a change to occur, but nothing happened apart from the increased frequency of my contractions. But at least Lyndon decided to put in an appearance.

"Lillian, I'm here, I'm here. Are you ok?" It took him a moment to catch his breath. "What did you mean, 'We're *both* in labour'? Who's the other poor bugger?"

Overwhelmed by the reassurance of his familiar face, I burst into tears, turning into a quivering mess. The shock of the day finally caught up with me and, if I was honest, I was frightened to death.

Lyndon was great, although far more interested in

the gossip than fussing over me.

"Lil, I know you're in labour, but what the fuck's been going on?"

Having missed his subtle turn of phrase, I burst out laughing as I unravelled the day's events piece by piece. Laughter truly is the best medicine, but there was no remedy for the battle that lay ahead.

"I feel something, it's different. OUCH!" I screeched as Lyndon stood to attention. "It's unbearable... OW! OW! OW! The contractions, they're torture, faster!" Right on cue, the midwife returned.

"Is this your husband, Lillian? Lovely to meet you. I hope he's been looking after you!" She obviously had a dysfunctional gaydar! "Right, this baby's ready, are you?"

I wasn't sure.

TWENTY

My beautiful baby boy slept peacefully in the glass cot next to me. It had been a horrendous twelve hours, an experience I hoped I'd never have to repeat. Lyndon was still recovering; it had been a bit of an ordeal for him. Bless. Unfortunately, I'd vomited all over Lyndon – who then threw up at the sight of my vomit. There were a few slippy moments as the midwives skated around the bed before the sick was removed and the floor disinfected, but of course the smell of bleach made me sick again. I didn't care, I was in agony.

The contractions had been coming every few minutes, but my baby hadn't been quite ready to leave his warm, cosy home. To relieve some discomfort, I was offered a bath, which would also aid the process along. I lay there naked for over an hour, waiting, something I was getting very good at. Lyndon wasn't comfortable with this arrangement and, although he tried to be supportive whilst standing as far away as he could from his naked, nipple-leaking, freaky friend, he wasn't feeling the vibe. However, as I'd managed to text most of the contacts in my phone, I wasn't short of company.

Of course, the girls appeared, but so had Mum, Dad, Lou, Sadie, Jim from Wytes, a distant aunt and a few other long lost relatives that I hadn't seen in years. There was no sign of James. It was all very embarrassing as I had to send most of them home.

As I was in the bath, the baby moved: turning, rolling, jabbing, poking, clearly ready to come out, but I couldn't even heave myself into a sitting position. Then the bolt came.

"I can't move, I can't get out of the bath!" I screamed. "OH MY GOD... PLEASE HELP ME!" This I directed at Lyndon as I grabbed his shirt. "Please help, help me, take me home. I don't want it, it's torture! Oweeeeee!"

After a horrendous journey from the bathroom, I found myself back in the delivery room, regretting my choice of partner as Lyndon was as much use as a chocolate fire guard. I pushed, pulled and panted, on my knees, on my back and standing, anything to release the pain as Lyndon looked on in horror. Then, of course, the baby's head slid down the canal, causing more raw, screeching pain.

"I HATE you, James! I'm going to KILL YOU for putting me through this! OUCH... I HATE YOU, I HATE YOU!"

Lyndon was very relieved he wasn't James.

"I feel the need to push. I can't stop it. I can't, I can't. IT'S COMING! IT'S COMING!"

My baby finally arrived.

"Is everything ok? Are all fingers and toes intact?" I managed to ask, exhausted.

Thank god it was over. I'd done it. I'd bloody done it. Relieved, I turned to face Lyndon, but he was on the floor, unconscious. Hopeless! But as he came to slowly, rising to his feet, the first thing he saw were my legs in stirrups, followed by the delivery of the afterbirth, and he fainted again. Within minutes, Lyndon was taken away and placed on a bed. Would you believe it? Anything for attention! As I said, as much use as a chocolate fire guard!

TWENTY-ONE

Sitting in my hospital bed, staring at the gorgeous bundle sleeping peacefully, I drifted off into thoughts of what would happen if James were ever to show. I had messaged him to share the news of his beautiful son, welcoming him to come and visit, but disappointingly he hadn't replied. I wondered if he was already at the hospital with Jenny, only a stone's throw away, playing happy families with his new little baby. Although there was still no news on Jenny. I mean, for all I knew, something terrible could have happened.

My thoughts were interrupted by a gentle tap on the door and a tall god entered my room. This handsome, charming and sophisticated man took one look at me and said, "Oh, so sorry, I do apologise, wrong room!"

Gone in a flash, just like that, off to some lucky girl's room to see his beautiful child, every bit as handsome as he was. Sighing at the thought that everyone was playing happy families except me, I lay reminiscing on my last days with James at The Wyte Shed and why our relationship had broken down. It didn't help my already melancholy state of mind to acknowledge that maybe I was to blame. Was I too pushy? Should I have stayed and ridden the storm? Was I a little too hasty in leaving?

"Takes two to tango! It's NOT your fault... what will be will be!" I said out loud, disturbing my little baby boy, who wriggled slightly as he made that awful noise, that horrendous racket – yes that was it, crying!

Presumably he was hungry, so I took care in lifting him and settled him onto my right breast. Yuk, this was not nice. What the hell was all the fuss about? But looking down at his adorable little face, his deep red heart-shaped lips sucking away at what I had previously considered sex objects, I could see he was peaceful and content. Although I hated every minute of it, I allowed him to carry on. Let's face it, they do say that if you breast feed you'll lose your weight in no time!

Another tiny knock (it was definitely a gay knock) and Lyndon walked in, taking one look at the scene before him and turning on his heels to exit.

"Sorry, sorry, will wait outside!" He whispered.

"Lyndon, come back here, you mouse. It's only a breast, and anyway, I could do with the company."

"Fine! What does it feel like? Do you like it? Does it hurt?" He asked, obviously over his initial fright.

"Weird, No and Yes in that order!" I replied.

Lyndon was fascinated. "God, you women really are hard as bloody nails. You do go through the paces, I'll give you that..."

"Yes, thanks for your support, you were wonderful!" I interrupted sarcastically, smiling.

"Oh god, Lil, I'm so sorry. My stomach couldn't take it. I tried, I really did, then when I saw the head thingy..."

"Crown!" I stated.

"Yes, crown, I mean it just threw me. There was so much hair, I didn't know if it was an extension of your bits or the baby, then the blood came and the squidgyness of it all, then the next thing I remember is waking up on a hospital bed!" He looked at me with puppy eyes. "Lil, I am soooo sorry I left you alone, I really am, but at least it's over now... and... I will be at your beck and call for as long as you need me. Tell you what, though, there are a few dishy dads on this ward. There was a gorgeous man in the waiting area earlier. God, I bet he's hung like a horny donkey – phew, you should have seen his hands!"

"Yeah," I laughed, "he popped his head round before, got the wrong room... unfortunately!"

Drifting off again, I wondered if all the daddies were here except my little boy's.

"Have you thought of any names yet? More to the point, what about the surname? Will he take James' or your own? Cheeky bastard doesn't deserve the right! I mean, where is he? I can't believe he hasn't been in touch!"

"I can't either. You know, I kind of coped with it while I was pregnant because I really thought he would show when I needed him, but now it's all over I'm starting to panic. What am I going to do?"

"You're going to brush yourself down, my girl, and carry on, that's what you're going to do. You're a strong woman, Lillian White, and don't you forget it. You don't need a man to make you feel complete and god knows most of the population only has one parent these days, plus just look at that cute little face."

I peered down at the tiny china doll as a well of tears gushed.

"Lillian, don't cry. It will all work out. It's just the hormones. You'll get stronger, you'll be fine," he encouraged. "As for James, I really don't know the answer to that one, having never met the guy, so try and put him out of your head for now. Enjoy the moment; this may be the only time this creation happens for you, Lillian, don't let him take these precious moments away!"

He was right. Of course he was right. I wiped my eyes and squeezed his hand. "Thank you."

Hearing a commotion outside, we both looked up as the door flew open and an invasion of beauty appeared, my support team – animated, eager and intoxicating, bearing balloons, nappies, clothes, food and, most importantly, a hip flask. (Although I soon realised that I couldn't drink any of it due to a last minute decision to breast feed – argh!)

Acknowledging the no alcohol disappointment etched on my face, Lyndon rolled his eyes. "I'll go and get some coffees."

It was so wonderful to see the girls, which brought more tears – joy and relief.

"Lillian, darling, oh come here," coaxed Sam, squashing both baby and I in a bear hug, stroking my hair. She was soon joined by Jess and Sal. "It will all work out, I promise. Things will get better. God, you've just had a baby, don't be so hard on yourself."

At that moment, Lyndon walked back in. "Bloody

hell, what have you said? I've only been gone five minutes! Anyway, I'm glad you've put that breast away, it was enough to make anyone cry!" He winked, watching as they cooed over my son – my son!

Having decided that my little boy was quite happy with his new found friends, I tried to slip out of bed as I needed the bathroom, but it was just too painful. It took a little help from my friends to heave me into a sitting position and a kind of push for me to stand. I was conscious that my undercarriage would fall out at any moment, it certainly felt that way.

"Why are you walking as if you've just shit yourself?" Asked Sam, with no decorum whatsoever,

"You've shit yourself?" Asked Lyndon, only tuning into the latter part of Sam's sentence.

I clearly hadn't but had experienced a second-degree tear so, as I literally had no feeling *down there*, I was a little concerned. I mean, was this normal? Women had babies every day, it's supposed to come so naturally to us, but what's natural about having pads in my knickers and ice packs on my arse? It just wasn't right. I was wearing a bigger nappy than the baby! The pain killers were losing their intensity, so every step was excruciating, any movement involving the gluteal muscles was a task in itself.

"Can someone help me to the toilet?" I asked, scrunching my face.

"Er, I think I've done enough," said Lyndon, "so that's a no from me!"

Luckily, Sal has a big heart, so she offered to escort me.

"We might be gone a while, so who's up for some babysitting duties?"

Sam and Jess looked petrified.

"Lillian, unless you hadn't noticed, none of us are lactating right now and this little darling looks like he's hungry. He keeps going for my right nipple!" Cried Lyndon.

"Well, you should keep them covered up. You're confusing the poor little thing!" *I wonder if he'd notice?* "There's a bottle on the side that I expressed earlier. Try him with that!"

They exchanged looks whilst mouthing to each other 'expressed?' Rolling my eyes, I took hold of Sal and we shuffled to the ladies.

It was an ordeal just lowering myself on to the toilet, only manageable with Sal's help, who was relieved to wait outside after performing her duty. Closing my eyes just for a second and embracing the harmonious peace and quiet, I took some deep breaths at the enormity that I had now become a mother. Fuck! I must have fallen asleep as an eager knocking broke my rest.

"Lillian! Open the door!" It sounded like Sally.

"Are you ok in there, hello?" I didn't recognise the second firm voice lacking any gentle tone in its delivery, but before I could reply, the door was forced open and a stern looking nurse barged in.

"What happened?" She asked. "You raised the alarm!"

"Oh, I thought it was the toilet flush, sorry!" I hadn't realised that I had accidentally pulled the emergency cord!

"Where's your baby?" She continued. "You're supposed to take it with you everywhere!!"

I was a little taken aback and Sally looked petrified as I explained that my son was with friends. The nurse wasn't impressed, pointing out that visiting time was over, this wasn't The Ritz, and maybe I should return to my room! Hearing her own sombre words and seeing the surprise on our faces, her tone softened and she escorted us to my room.

"You'll have to make it quick, I'm afraid, as your friends really should have gone by now."

I'm walking as fast as I can!

"We only allow husbands and partners to stay on to help.

Knock me while I'm down, why don't you?

"Well," I pleaded, "as I don't have either of those, can at least one of my friends stay for a while?"

Apparently not. They didn't cater for single mothers. Oh joy, I was a single mother.

"We have to go," said Lyndon apologetically, "we've outstayed our welcome!" He had hold of the baby, and had fed, watered and changed his nappy. "We've had a telling off!"

"Yes, I know, so from now on you are my husband or partner so you can stay a little longer, but unfortunately, the rest of you have to go. I'm sorry, I don't want you to, but Matron says, rules are rules!"

Threatened with another run-in with Matron, they soon made a sharp exit, which was just as well, as she appeared moments later to check!

"See, they've all gone except my partner," I stated.

"I thought you didn't have one?" She questioned.

"I do now!"

And that was that. Lyndon stayed for a further hour: he sipped the flask, I drank coffee, we both laughed, cried, laughed and cried a bit more, and changed babe's nappy for the night. He fed and tucked me in, then the baby!"

"Good night, Lillian White!"

"Good night, you big skinny gay lover!" I smiled, then promptly fell asleep.

The waves were crashing against the rocks, splashing onto my bare tanned feet as I lay baking in the glorious sunshine, but I couldn't settle as the faint cry of a baby approached in the wind. I altered my bikini, admired my slender bronze figure, and lay back down awkwardly on the rocks, but the sound of crying grew louder, fierce, wailing, piercing. What was that noise? Woken from my dream, I came back down to earth with a bang. It was my baby making that horrendous din! Unfortunately, his little lungs had also disturbed the nurse, the Matron.

"My goodness, he must be starving. He's going to wake the other babies. Hush, darling, hush, hush, hush." She fussed over the little bundle and asked if I was going to feed him.

I thought she meant this as 'did I want to feed him?', or 'do you mind if I feed him?' Maybe I could get back to my dream.

"I don't mind, do you want to feed him?" I asked in all innocence.

"I don't think he will get much nourishment from me, my dear. I stopped lactating a very long time ago!"

Oh, she meant were my tits going to feed him, but as there were some difficulties, I'd changed to formula, which also worked a treat. God, he really was gorgeous – huge big blue eyes, tiny cute little nose and the biggest lips you've ever seen. A big mop of hair, looked like he'd been here for weeks. I took a deep breath of his wonderful aroma, just gorgeous.

Once he was fed, clean and ready to return to his nap, I felt quite proud of myself. Maybe I was taking to this mother thing quite naturally. I swaddled him in his blanket, placing him on his back in the glass crib. I checked my phone to see the time. You had to be kidding me! 2.45am! What the fuck! I also caught a glimpse of my stomach, unslender and unbronzed, the reality check of motherhood was being cashed quicker than I thought.

Too restless to sleep, I sat up in bed, catching a glimpse of the time again. 3.26am. This wasn't fun so I headed down the corridor, baby in tow, to the day room and kitchen area, which was laden with biscuits, crackers and fairy cakes. Although tempting, I managed to refrain, pouring a bland glass of water instead.

Walking past the day room, just popping my head round for a quick nosy, I was surprised and relieved that I wasn't the only person awake. I mean, of course I wasn't, this is what babies do, they wake up in the middle of the night. This was normal! New mothers and babies fought with bottles, boobs and nappies, troubled and tired at this god-awful hour. A baby with beautiful mocha skin caught my attention, resting peacefully, the mother at ease, calm... OH MY GOD, it was Jenny! FUCK, had she seen me? Relieved that both mum and baby were alive and kicking, I wasn't sure what my next move should be, so stepped back quickly in case she'd seen me. Wait a minute, how come her baby has beautiful olive skin when mine is all chubby and pink? Can they really be fathered by the same person? James must have some exotic blood in his heritage. Trust Jenny's child to inherit this enchanting gene.

"Lillian, is that you?" She whispered. "Lillian?" She said a little louder."

Oh fuck, she'd seen me! She looked bloody gorgeous too. She looked like the girl in my dream, with the bronze body. She was a doctor; she was a model. I'd got jelly belly and marmalade down my nightie! I fastened my dressing gown and took a deep breath... "Jenny!"

****

James

I'd been set up, I was certain of that. The unmarked police car came to a grinding halt, almost running me over, four heavies jumped out, wrestling me to the ground. I'd retraced every step, covered my tracks, so how did they know I was here? This is bad. I thought my life was over before, it might as well end now!

TWENTY-TWO

Jenny was a real beauty, natural, unaware and her brains were exploding with IQ cells. I don't have many of those. I felt sick forming, my heart sinking as I waddled over with my pink baby, trying to disguise my humongous extra weight.

"Oh, he's gorgeous, Jenny, what have you called him?" I had so many other questions that were far more pressing, like 'Why is your baby black and mine isn't?'.

"*She's* called Lucy-Lee, and Lillian, don't tell me you haven't noticed that this baby can't possibly belong to James?"

It took a moment for the news to sink in. *What?* Well, of course I had, but I was still bewildered. *Why is she being so nice and smiling at me like that? Oh god, she's waiting for me to speak!*

"Oh, really, oh, er… of course I noticed, but I'm really confused," I forced myself to answer.

"I know, listen Lillian, what happened at the coffee shop, thanks for being there for me. You were an absolute star and I hadn't realised that you had gone into labour too until much later. I was moved to the private ward. I work at this hospital, I'm a doctor here. I came back up here because my daughter's father, Lee,

191

works on the ward. You may have seen him? He actually delivered our baby!"

Jenny continued to chat, but she looked tired, as was I, so she asked if we could meet for an hour the following day, which I was keen to do as I needed some clarity. We said our goodbyes and planned to meet the following morning. She wouldn't have long because she was being discharged that afternoon – no such luck for me as I had a numb undercarriage to fix!

When I met with Jenny, she told me the truth, the whole truth and nothing but the truth. I don't think I could have been so honest. She clearly wanted a clean slate. Yes, she had met James just as I had moved out of Wytes, so was well aware of the situation. She too had come out of a long-term relationship with Lee, which had only just ended as he was going to take a job in the Far East and she hadn't wanted to go. James was in the right place at the right time, helping her come to terms with things. One thing led to another and they fumbled around. She had an idea she might be pregnant before she got together with James, so knew full well it was Lee's baby, but when she told James, he just presumed it was his. Bewildered with it all, she went along with it, not really sure of the outcome, but still making James believe it was his.

She hated herself and was truly disappointed in her behaviour at the time, but got carried away with the roller-coaster. She and Lee hadn't fallen out of love, it was just circumstance. She'd not mentioned this to James, appallingly, and had never got the chance to tell him the truth. She knew full well that he wasn't quite over me. (Wow, a triumph at last!)

"What have you called him?" She asked. "There is no mistaking that he belongs to James, he's a mini version!" I hadn't really noticed that much but now that she said it, I was glad.

"I haven't thought of a name yet, to be honest. I really thought that James would show up and we would decide together," I confessed. "I was getting into a state thinking that he was with you and you were playing happy families. Anyway, he's not been in touch or replied to any of my messages. Bizarre, really, it's just not like him." I looked at Jenny for some reassurance.

She regarded me straight on and put a friendly hand on my arm. "Lillian, I promise you, I haven't heard a dicky bird since we came to your house, I promise you." She squeezed my arm and returned her hand to its place around her daughter's body. "I thought maybe he was with you and you were playing happy families. It does seem out of character, it just isn't like him!" Her voice raised a decibel, so I believed her.

"How come you came to my house with him?" I was quite direct, having gained some confidence from her honesty.

She took a deep breath and sighed. "He told me he had to take a detour. We were on our way to my parent's house. He said he had to pick something up and that he hadn't seen this friend in a while, so he might be a few minutes!" She seemed to be telling the truth. "He was gone ages, I mean bloody ages, and I was getting really uncomfortable in the car. You know what it's like, Lillian, when you get bigger." She was in full flow. "So I decided to knock at the door and just ask if he was going to be long. I think I may have called him and he didn't answer, I can't remember, to be honest, but when you opened the door I..." She was reliving our nightmare. "I just couldn't believe what I saw. Hitting him was a reflex action. I think I was in shock!" Jenny continued to say that deep down she knew that he would always choose me over her and really, she couldn't expect anything else as she would have chosen Lee over James.

"Well, Jenny, I had no idea you were pregnant, and I had this fairy tale ending I was living out in my head!" I told her my story. "It was a shock to me that I was pregnant. In fact, I was in the middle of an emergency landing when I realised it!" I let out a nervous giggle. "No woman really wants to do this alone, so I contacted James to tell him I needed to see him but didn't tell him what about. When he came to my house that day, it was the first time he knew I was pregnant. He was just as shocked as you were. Oh god, what a mess!" I held my head in my hand and held my baby tighter in the other.

Jenny gave me another squeeze. "Ironically though, Lillian, it's turned out for the best, don't you think?" She looked at the bundle in her arms. "I have Lee's baby and you have James'. You can still have your fairy tale, I think I may have mine!"

"Are you back with Lee now, then?" I asked.

"Well, he delivered her and, although there's a few hills to climb, the road ahead looks straight." Jenny told me that Lee didn't actually take the job but was too pig-headed to contact her as he was still cross with her for not wanting to go with him and support him in the first place. "If things work out, the job will always be there for him, so we all might end up going anyway. What about you? What are you going to do about James? Do you still want to be with him?"

I admired her directness.

"I think I want him; it's too early to tell, and with all the hormones flying around, maybe it's good that he isn't here, but part of me longs for him and desperately wants to make it right again."

She asked if I'd spoken to his parents, his friends and colleagues, but I hadn't really looked into that at all. I didn't get on that well with his mum. Being an only child, no one was good enough for her James, including me, but maybe it was time to go down that route.

We said our goodbyes, wishing each other all the best, even exchanging telephone numbers.

"Look after yourself, Lillian White, and thanks again for everything. Enjoy your new gorgeous little bundle."

"You too, Jenny Ward."

TWENTY-THREE

Freddie knew from an early age how to get Mummy's attention and, like any other baby, soon discovered the art of *Dummy-gate*. I'd regretted not going cold turkey, as he knew that no matter what time of night, I'd rush to return it to its rightful owner. He was three months old and our routine worked. It had been a huge learning curve for both of us, but one thing was certain, I'd fallen in love all over again and hadn't realised that he'd been missing from my world before he'd even entered it. I'd not heard anything from James, not a peep, and not a day went by when I didn't long for him and for Freddie to have a father figure, of which he was innocently unaware and one day would clearly miss.

Things were settling a little, but when I first came home from the hospital I was not in a fit state. After a few days of being home and the elation of guests diminishing, I felt an overwhelming disappointment that James had become a no-show. The first few nights were a nightmare: wake, feed, burp, sleep, repeat. Was he breathing? Was he too hot? Was he cold? Would he suffocate? I didn't sleep, the exhaustion was unbearable, and of course I had it all going on *down below*.

One particular night, Freddie was crying, reaching the highest of all decibels. Whilst his bottle was warming, a fart slipped out and I was so numb from the waist down it took a while to realise that I'd literally passed a *number two*. Freddie was hysterical by that point. The microwave alerted me that the milk was done, and I didn't know what to see to first, my arse or the baby's!

Your body tries to adapt to the lack of sleep but you're barely functioning, existing as a zombie, and you just about manage to operate. You can't hold a conversation, you're grumpy all the time and unliberated. I missed my freedom the most and hadn't taken into account that when you have *another* to take care of, even nipping out for milk is a mammoth task; you practically take the kitchen sink with you.

One afternoon I needed chocolate. NEEDED. The shop wasn't too far away, and I could have run there and back twice in the time it took me to prepare Freddie for the short journey. The thought, *Can I leave him?* did cross my mind, I must admit. It started raining, so the canopy was required for the pram. Another twenty minutes passed. By the time I had finally got it on, the rain had stopped and the sun had come out. Freddie was now in a makeshift greenhouse. I didn't give up as I NEEDED the chocolate So arriving at the shop with one sweaty baby, I picked up some other groceries too, placing them in the hood of the pram. Freddie was fast asleep but would be due feeding shortly. In fact, I had been very brave coming out before his feed, knowing how much noise he could make, but I wasn't far from home and was sure I would make it back in time. I was more concerned about my chocolate fix.

The queue was long, so I joined the back, collecting more groceries as I moved nearer to the checkout. Literally a minute before it was my turn to be served, Freddie woke up with his usual screaming. I didn't have a bottle with me, so I put the dummy in his mouth and hoped this would suffice. *Nearly there*, I thought. I could picture us back at home, all fed and watered, and me enjoying my chocolate fix. Freddie's cries got louder and louder... and louder. I could smell a soiled nappy too and prayed it wasn't me! People were beginning to stare at my crying, smelly baby and I could feel myself getting hot. Then, oh no, it was that man again, that Aussie hunk. Why did he keep popping up when I was not at my best? Oh lord, he was so drop dead gorgeous. Although he'd clocked that I was responsible for the horrendous noise, he offered a polite smile. Other shoppers just gave me the daggers! Thank god, it was my turn to be served. Smiling apologetically at the assistant, I searched for my purse, which turned into a frantic hunt to no avail as it dawned on me that I'd left my purse at home! Feeling all eyes on me, including hunky Aussie's, I started to cry. I had to blink away the tears and couldn't help but think that the whole world was against me and why did everything go wrong for me? Why was I on my own? Why me, why bloody me? So, I made my excuses, apologised again and headed home, gutted that I wouldn't be getting my chocolate fix.

I had never craved chocolate more or cried more! Of course, I blamed James. Where was he and why had he not made contact? I thought of Jenny Ward, imagining her hunky dory-tastic life. Smugsville, would I ever make it?

I did everything Jenny recommended. I'd been in touch with old colleagues and friends, but they hadn't seen him. No-one was aware of any work in London, so I had no choice but to contact his folks.

Over the years, they were used to him hopping from country to country at the drop of a hat, so didn't seem overly concerned. However, when I told them that he'd become a father, that caused a raised eyebrow, as they clearly had no idea. I even took Freddie to see them. Thinking they'd immediately report him as a missing person, I was a little unnerved at their lack of panic and thought maybe I was the fool. Maybe the father of my child had taken off across the other side of the world? Who wouldn't if they thought they'd got two girls up the duff? What a predicament to be in! Was he struggling to choose? The gorgeous ex-model and doctor *or* the dragon with her wagon selling tea in a posh coffee shop thirty thousand feet above sea level – it was a no-brainer! Maybe Lyndon was right, how would you get your head around two women with two babies. If only James knew the truth.

My visit with Freddie had been short and unwelcoming. James' father appeared to fidget, pacing the room. He was either bursting to share something or he just wanted rid of me. I prepared to leave, saying my goodbyes to his mother, promising to visit again with Freddie, even though I didn't quite think she believed he was her grandson. His dad offered to see me out.

"He's got mixed up with the wrong type of people again!" He blurted in a hushed tone.

"What do you mean, 'the wrong type of people'?" I whispered.

"The sort that don't play by the rules..." He began muttering about how James used to take weird calls at all hours. "Once we had a bang at the door at two in the morning. His mum nearly had a heart attack."

I listened intently as he raised his concerns over the previous life that James used to lead. My cogs began to turn.

"Do you mean when he set fire to cars?" He was clearly surprised that I knew these details. "I thought that was all behind him?"

His dad explained that it was in the past, but he'd been asked to help out in France or Spain or somewhere. He looked down at the floor, avoiding eye contact. He knew more and I could sense it.

"Look at Freddie, don't you think I... we..." I pointed at Freddie, "...have a right to know?" He was hesitant. "I don't shock easily, just say it as it is!" I demanded.

"He got caught setting fire to cars again... abroad... somewhere!"

"WHAT?"

He looked anxious, perplexed, as if he didn't quite know what to say next, but something told me there was more to come. "Oh god, Lillian, I don't know how to tell you this!" He shook his head slowly and checked that his wife was still inside.

"I'm confused. Tell me, do you know where he is?"

"His mum doesn't know. I can't find the right moment to tell her, but…"

Oh my god, the father of my son is dead! I know it, I just bloody know it! "For god's sake, just tell me. I have a right to know, just for peace of mind, if anything." I couldn't help it, but my voice was beginning to rise, causing James' father to look over his shoulder.

"Lillian, he's in jail," he said abruptly.

What the fuck! "Jail?" I couldn't believe it. I looked at Freddie then back at his very distressed grandfather. "Where? When?… er… How?"

"In Spain… he was arrested for fraud!"

TWENTY-FOUR

"JAIL!" Sam's voice echoed down the receiver and out across the fields. Who needed British Telecom with a voice like that? "What the fuck is he doing in jail? What's he done now? You always like the bloody dangerous ones, don't you? Well, does this turn you on?"

I didn't dare tell her that well, yes it did a little! I was bursting to tell someone and was still in shock at the news of James' arrest, and had described my disappointment that he'd not called me himself.

"I thought they had payphones for the criminals' use?" Sam said tersely. I cringed as the word 'criminal' left her lips. "You need to forget about him, Lillian, you don't want to get mixed up in all of that."

"But he is the father of my child!" I demanded. "I can't just ignore it!"

"You've acknowledged that he's in jail, now move on. He's not your problem anymore!"

"But we made plans... sort of," I offered.

"Plans?" She asked. "Did he not say he was going to London? Did he not say he was going to call you? Lillian, I'm sorry, honey, but I think we all know that *his* plans are slightly different to yours!" She was right, but what was I supposed to do? "You hadn't seen him for the whole of the pregnancy; you called him, he didn't call you back!"

"He did... eventually!" Was I defending him?

"Well that's ok then!" She responded sarcastically, then softening her tone, "Lillian, if it was you he wanted, surely he'd make contact. He's had ample opportunity!"

She was right. He wasn't in my life when I realised I was pregnant and he wasn't in it now. Was that a sign to let sleeping dogs lie?

"What about Freddie?" I asked. "He deserves to know his father."

"Yes, he does, and when the time is right, he will!" She said. "You don't even know how long he's in jail for. You can't just hang around! Nope, no way. Life moves on and so will yours!"

I knew she was right, of course. I couldn't wait around for him, not that I knew what I was waiting for.

Sam hung up and was soon at mine to join the rest of the gang.

Noise filled the air as did the smell of wine and tortilla chips. Things had obviously changed since I had Freddie. Being the first of the girls to branch off and have children, excluding Lou of course, was kind of a shock to the system for both parties and, although I still saw my friends, it wasn't as often as I'd have liked. I felt the pull at my heart strings at first. I was the sociable one, the events planner arranging outings, gatherings and gossip and, although I missed that part of me, I was adapting to my new role as a mum and the fact that someone needed me. My love for Freddie was all-encompassing. Things were changing, but at that moment, they were all here together at my house. I was child free and enjoying every minute.

Lyndon was over with his new boyfriend, Ben. I hadn't seen much of him since they'd been together. Ben was drop dead gorgeous and by all accounts performed the best blow job in the country, and knowing Lyndon, he's had the experience to judge!

So here we all were and it was fantastic, although Sally wasn't quite herself.

"Sally, are you ok, chic, you look like you've seen a ghost?" I ruffled her hair and poured her a huge glass of wine! She picked it up and swigged half of the glass before wiping her mouth on her sleeve. This was not like Sally at all so something was definitely up!

"We've set the date for the wedding!" She blurted out, then went to take another swig but hesitated, returning the glass to the table with a frown. We all started to cheer and congratulate her. "Wait, wait, there's more." She took hold of the glass once again but didn't lift it to her lips this time, although something in her eyes indicated a desperate need to devour the contents. She stared at the glass. "I think I'm pregnant!" We all cheered and congratulated her once more, but then she spoke again, after another tiny sip of wine. This time, her voice was breaking. "Wait, wait, there's more," she bellowed over our chinking glasses. "It's not Lloyd's baby!" And at that she burst into tears.

We all surrounded her with reassuring hugs and squeezes as she sobbed uncontrollably, exchanging quizzical looks with each other, wondering what the fuck was going on. Every time she went to speak, she would break down again.

"Let it out, darling, it's ok. You're not on your own. Let it out. It will be alright, we'll sort it." We all chipped in our words of wisdom, but it was obvious it was going to be a while before she could be consoled enough for her to speak a clear sentence without tears. Usually I would pour a brandy, but she'd had wine, so I thought she had already had too much in her condition. I felt helpless. Oh, my Rescue Remedy – quick thinking, Batman. I grabbed my bag and demanded she open her mouth as I sprayed the expensive medicine on her tongue. At this, her tears turned into light giggles, then into fits of laughter, which gave us no choice but to join in with her, although none of us knew why!

"You and your bloody Rescue Remedy! Give me some more!" She grabbed it from me and sprayed half the bottle on her tongue, under her tongue and jokingly went to spray under her arms as well!

"Sally?" Sam's gaze was direct.

We all listened as Sally told us what had been going on.

"You know Lloyd took me away to London about three weeks ago? Well, we decided on some arrangements for the wedding and he gave me a ring."

"But you've got a ring!" Piped up Sam.

"Shush!" We all squealed.

Sally continued, "An eternity ring! It was such a fabulous weekend; he'd sorted the hotel, the room, the flowers…" The tears came again. "There were so many flowers in the room, and attached to a bouquet was this long trail of pink ribbon which I had to follow, leading me to a bottle of chilled champagne. As he filled my glass, there it was, glistening in the bubbles!" She was crying uncontrollably again.

"But that's wonderful, Sally, you couldn't want anything more, so what happened?" Lou was sincere, but we were all eager to hear about the baby and who the mystery man was.

She carried on. "We had so much sex that weekend, he was telling me that he wouldn't want anyone else to carry his children and that if we never got pregnant together, he would still be happy, just me and him! I just went with the flow, knowing that I had been really awful. God, how could I be so stupid?"

Sally was grappling with her words, but a little more Rescue Remedy did the trick. She continued to explain that Lloyd had been working away for weeks and, with deadlines to meet, only returned for the odd weekend. He felt awful about it, hence why he thought he would treat her to a weekend away with another fabulous diamond ring. Bloody hell, how many did she need? I hadn't even got one! Lloyd was a great guy and adored the ground that Sally walked on and he was only working so hard so he could provide for her in the future. Sally had moaned many times in the past about Lloyd's workload and how lonely she was, but I suppose we had just taken it for granted that they were happy despite it all and things were ok. Obviously not. Sally worked for a huge organisation with mostly male employees. She was a high-flying PA to Sean, who was married. She had met his wife and family on many occasions, even bought gifts for them on his behalf. Lloyd had met them too and they'd been to several work engagements together over the years. Literally, the week before her weekend away, she had been at a charity auction with Sean which, as these auctions do, went on until the early hours. Lloyd was working as usual and, instead of going home to an empty house, she was quite happy to be entertained by her boss. The bubbly was a flying, so was Sally, and at the end of the evening her boss asked her if she wanted a nightcap. She innocently said yes but woke up in his bed, starkers! Although drunk, she knew exactly what she was doing. "I just felt so lonely and it was so good to be wanted. He was like an animal possessed." She cracked a little smile. "We had sex all night, several times. Lloyd can only manage the once, then he's fast asleep within ten minutes!"

We all laughed at this, familiar with such men!

I couldn't help but ask, even though I didn't really have the right, "Didn't you use anything? Protection?" I bit my lip nervously, instantly regretting the words as they escaped my mouth! I knew what was coming.

"Did you?" Sam asked me cheekily.

"Ok, ok, stupid question, please continue!"

"No, I didn't use anything and yes, he fired those hungry babies straight into my fertile womb and I haven't seen or heard of a period since. I've done a test and I'm definitely pregnant. Oh my god, what a tart! I have a ring on my finger with a bun in the oven, but no idea who I'm supposed to be cooking it for!"

Shit! We all consoled the poor girl, with the help of a few bottles of wine... which Sally declined!

Lyndon looked at me, I looked at Lyndon, then we both pulled that face of 'Oh shit, now what? How do we make this better?' I felt a bit sorry for poor Ben. This was his first time meeting the girls. What must he think? I'd better not mention where James was! My thoughts were broken by Sally's frantic questions.

"So, what am I going to do? Do I tell Lloyd that I'm pregnant?" She pleaded with us for some advice.

"You mean he doesn't know?" Blurted Sam incredulously.

"How the hell can I tell him I'm pregnant when I don't even know if it's his?"

"Good point, good point!" Sam bit her lip.

Sally dropped her head into her hands and screamed, "Arghhhhhh!"

Ben stood, moving over to Sal, embracing her, followed by a kiss to her forehead. "Sal, it's a beautiful thing to be carrying a baby, to bring a child into the world. Don't worry about the politics of it all, just worry about you, ok?"

What a wonderful speech! He is definitely gay!

"Right, listen, it's really quite hard to get pregnant, ok." I found some words but was interrupted by Sam.

"But you didn't have any problems, did you?" God, she has a big mouth!

"Let me finish," I insisted, "you have to work out exactly where you were in your cycle, Sal. You have to sit down and work out to the absolute day where you were and work out what day you had sex with your boss and count the days to see if they fall into when you would normally be ovulating."

Sally said she had done all that and that she had not had sex with Lloyd over that time but had the sex with her boss on the fourteenth day! That did not sound good.

"Well then, you're fucked, Sal!" Sam was so matter of fact. "You're absolutely fucked! Did you do more than one test to be sure?"

"Is ten enough?"

"I've been there myself. Oh god, I know exactly where you're coming from!" I really felt for the poor girl. I had been there but at least I knew who the father was – well, I was pretty sure – even if it wasn't him, it wouldn't have mattered as I wasn't engaged to him. My heart jumped a bit as part of me wished that I was.

"Are you going to tell Lloyd?" Lou asked.

"Do you think I should? It will destroy him."

"But you didn't set out to do this intentionally. You were lonely, Lloyd was working long hours and, if I remember rightly, you did challenge him about this several times and said that you were lonely and sick of him working all the time!" Said Lou.

"I have said this to him many times, but it's still not justified!" Replied Sally. "The other thing is, do I keep it or not? I don't want to lose Lloyd and I will if I tell him it's not his baby."

"You don't know that for sure, Sal. It might still be Lloyd's baby. I mean, would he know straight away? What ethnicity is your boss?"

"Lillian!" Jessica pinched me in the ribs.

"Ow! What? Well it's true. Unless there are *obvious* cultural differences, Lloyd wouldn't instantly know, would he?"

Sally grimaced as she explained there was no confusing her boss's dark brown eyes and olive skin with Lloyds' baby blues and milk bottle tone!

"Oh dear!" We sighed in unison.

"You're right, Sam, I'm fucked!"

"Let's have some more wine. Come on, Sal, you're pregnant and you're engaged, or have an eternity thing going on, so we have to drink to that, no matter what the occasion. Does anybody else have any news which can top that?" Sam looked at me with encouraging eyes, which meant I had to let them know about James.

"James is in jail!" I announced.

The screams were coming from all directions, the firing of questions, the disgust, the excitement, disappointment, everything in one ball of noise. Then the question of where he was in jail.

"In Spain!" I responded, then for some reason, I burst into tears, as did Sally, and before we knew it, we were laughing and crying, hugging each other and cracking open more wine. You can't beat a night in with the girls!

TWENTY-FIVE

The park was fairly busy for a Sunday morning. Freddie was happily throwing bread for the ducks as I attempted a few stretches. We were meeting Jess for one of our power walks. Fingers crossed she'd left the Lycra number at home. Debs had called a few weeks previously to confirm my date for returning to work and to ask if I was ready. I wasn't ready. I had a fat face, skinny shoulders, jelly belly, and a lardy arse and legs! I was definitely not ready! Before I could fly again, I had to go through a refresher course and resit some exams. All I could think was, not those bloody exams again – 10% of this and who the fuck does this and that. I ask you, why do you need to know this bullshit, and who the hell cares? However, I had to care as they were bringing the course forward, so I was returning to work in just over three weeks. I wasn't so much bothered about the exams; I was more worried about my figure and my street credibility. I wanted to look like everyone in Heat magazine, you know, hot!

"Have you heard from James?" Jess was cringing as she asked as she knew it was the six-million-dollar question. Even though we occasionally made a joke about the whereabouts of Freddie's dad, the reality of it had hit home.

"Nothing, not a bean. I can't believe he hasn't called or written, and I half expect him to just knock on my door." This was true. I would often jump out of my skin at the appearance of an unexpected visitor, hoping it might be James. "To be honest, I've lost all sense of how I feel or felt about him. It's like he is at the surface of my mind on a daily basis, but at the same time he is a distant memory." I often wondered that if I hadn't got pregnant, would our paths have ever crossed again. Did I only want him in my life because of Freddie, or was it that I still had feelings for him? I really wasn't sure. So much had happened since we had seen each other, *and* he still thought he was the father of two babies. I would have loved to have seen his face on the labour ward – hilarious!

Anyway, I was returning to work imminently, so I had more important things to worry about. Weight, revision, childcare! At least I was addressing the weight issue.

Since Jess had been diagnosed with diabetes, her diet had changed completely. She followed a low sugar and carb-free diet, exercised regularly and was looking pretty damn fabulous, I must say. You wouldn't believe it was the same person who'd passed out on me! Thomas had called her a beached whale and it had kind of kicked her into action. See, there's always something to be thankful for.

Pushing harder on the pram, we picked up speed, turning into a sprint. God, where did she get all her energy from?

"Last one to the lamp post stinks!" Were her words as she gained speed.

"I can't go any further, can't breathe, can't breathe!" I panted.

"For god's sake, Lillian, think of your saggy arse in your uniform. We'll have to spray you into it if you don't keep running!"

Good job I knew her well or I could take offence.

"Come on, just to the second lamp post!"

"Biatch!"

After an exhausting morning, we went our separate ways as I was meeting Mum and Lou for lunch. A quaint French café had become our regular haunt and, although it had been there for years, I'd never ventured inside until recently. It was tucked away beneath a narrow path, just behind an exquisite art gallery and sweet shop, not visible from the road, but they did a mean coffee and the crêpes were to die for.

"Come on, quick, tell us before Mum gets back. What's the latest?" Lou asked.

I hadn't told my mum about James being in jail. She would be mortified. Things like that don't happen to our family so, no, this information was best left from her little world for now, so I'd just told her he'd gone travelling. Obviously, that was enough for him to go down in her estimations, but if she thought he was in jail, there'd be no return and none of our lives would be worth living!

"There's still not much to tell, I've already told

you." This was true. Although I had seen his parents about childcare a few weeks previously; his mother now knew where he was and was clearly devastated at the news.

"At least there's some reassurance knowing that they haven't heard from him either. They're his parents, for god's sake, they must be worried sick!" I paused for a moment as I'd just realised that I *wasn't* worried sick. In fact, it had only just occurred to me that I was cross with James rather than concerned for his safety. He wasn't at the forefront of my mind. Well, he was, but only because I was angry and disappointed that the fairy tale in my head hadn't come to light, but I wasn't going to lose sleep over him anymore. I was annoyed that he hadn't been in contact and that was all I could manage for now.

"What's up? You've gone quiet and all serious looking. It doesn't suit you!" Lou woke me from my reverie.

"I was just thinking, I wonder what's really happened to him, I mean *really happened* to him. Do you think he is getting hurt, picked on, or even...?" Oh god, I couldn't even say it.

Lou could, though. "You mean shagged up the arse by hard, vicious, evil inmates – lucky James!"

"LOUISE! Yes, that's exactly what I meant!" I could hear Freddie's adorable giggles approaching. "Shh, Mum's back... no wise cracks, ok?"

Mum appeared with a very sleepy Freddie covered in chocolate.

"You can't hide it from us, what's he been eating?"

Lou pinched her nephew's cheek. "God, Mum, you could have wiped his face!"

"Well, I did try, but he was tired and agitated. He's been fighting sleep for ages, so I decided to leave well alone! Anyway, kids should be covered in tasty chocolate." Mum parked the pram, taking care to secure the brake just in case her precious grandson rolled down an invisible hill.

"Any more coffees, girls?" She asked. "Any cake?"

We'd been drooling over a calorific thick sponge for ages, a bouncy Victoria Sandwich with a layer of jam and a blanket of coconut with each delicious bite. You could almost hear it whispering, 'eat me, eat me'. We each tried to coax the other to make the purchase, so we could still sample, guilt free. With a promise to run it off later, we eagerly cried, "YES PLEASE!"

"I might get a filter coffee to go around. Any takers and any preference?" Asked Mum.

"Oh Mum, see if they have any Spanish coffee!" Suggested Lou.

I almost spit my lukewarm tea over everyone.

"Lillian!" Cried Mum in disgust.

"Sorry, sorry, went down the wrong way!" I kicked Lou under the table.

"Now then, Lillian," said Mum, unsure of what she had just witnessed. "When do you start? Is it six or eight weeks? Well, listen love, your dad and I wondered if you and the little one wanted to come away with us for a few days, well a week actually, you know, before you start? It might be a good way to get some studying in, by the pool or the beach. Your dad and I will watch over Freddie."

"Sounds great, Mum."

Argh! She never listens! I told her I returned in three weeks not six!

"Wonderful!" Lou agreed.

"You coming then, Lou?" I asked.

"No, I can't. I have work commitments, *your* work commitments, I might add." She was having a jibe at how much extra work she'd taken on since I left. "But it'll be great for you. Any thoughts of where, Mum? Have you found anywhere yet?"

"Well your dad was looking at Greece but I rather fancy Spain for a change!"

Lou and I both spit our drinks out, unable to hide our gasps of hysteria.

"What on earth is the matter with you two?" Asked my poor innocent mum.

"Sorry, private joke!" Said Lou.

"Your father's found a lovely little village off the coast of Barcelona. It looks absolutely gorgeous, although I did read somewhere that it's a bit smelly and not very clean!" Mum continued. "Anyway, Lillian, think about it. It would do you the world of good to get some rest, some colour and, who knows, you may even have a little holiday romance!"

Yes, because that was all I needed – not!

After consuming the humongous tasty cake, it was time to leave and, as Mum made a quick trip to the Ladies, both Lou and I burst into serious giggles.

"You might be able to visit him!" She said. "Maybe James could be your holiday romance!"

"Oh yeah, right, 'Where are you off to, Lil?' 'Oh, nowhere too exciting, just off to *the nick* to see Freddie's dad!" I couldn't help but see the funny side.

"She wouldn't even know what the nick was!"

More hysteria. We shouldn't laugh, really; only five minutes ago I said I should take the situation more seriously. A holiday sounded great, but I didn't have a week to spare! In theory though, if I knew what jail he was in, maybe I could visit, but we had no idea where he was, not an iota.

TWENTY-SIX

Replacing the receiver and staring into space, I questioned if that had just happened. Debbie had rung and dropped an almighty bombshell. I almost didn't take the call, letting it ring a few times as I was watching my favourite romcom, *Maid in Manhattan*. Don't you just love Jennifer Lopez? But just as she was about to steal a Chanel suit from the penthouse suite, I picked up. Debbie was bouncing with excitement. It must have been my lucky week for holiday offers as Debbie had an interesting proposal of her own.

She had been promoted to Manager, a position which overlooked the crew. She had been asked to put together a mixed scale team for a contract in Orlando, and to my astonishment she was struggling to fill the last few spaces! She wondered if I could wangle six or twelve weeks away. How wonderful! *Wonderful* but not really *do-able*. It sounded AMAZING, just what the doctor ordered to get on with my life, but how could I do it with Freddie? Again, I blamed James. Debs knew it would be difficult, but it would look great on my C.V., making promotion more achievable. Also, the fact that I was a parent now, it would look as if I'd clearly put the company first!

"Difficult! You're not kidding, Debs. You're teasing me. This is like dangling the carrot, knowing I'll never reach it." I was excited but disheartened, knowing it was a great opportunity but Freddie had to come first. "How the hell am I going to wangle six weeks away?"

She interrupted and said that actually it was twelve weeks, but after six I could go home, maybe!

"What about Freddie? I don't know if I want to leave Freddie for that length of time; it kills me just going out for one night without him!" This was true.

Debbie continued, "That's the good part, Lil. Maybe if your parents had him, they could come out and visit as often as they liked, and you could go home on your days off!" She went on to convince me that I should give it great thought. I had a week to decide or they would have to offer to someone else! "Just one more thing," she added, "the places left are really only available to pursers and bar. If you decide to go, they will place you on a bar course immediately, so you'd become a temporary bar and even possibly a temporary purser, which eventually will become permanent!"

"Now you're dangling the Cadbury chocolate… keep talking!"

"You'd get more money, the chance to be a lazy bitch and boss people around!" She was laughing as not all of this was true.

"Oh, you bitch!" I was laughing with her. "Oh bugger, why do opportunities come at the wrong time?"

I was lost in thought for a moment. It would be more money, which always comes in handy, or at least I would be making my own money rather than having to rely on handouts. She made it sound so simple. But it did sound fantastic. How could I make it possible? Was it bad parenting to leave your young one for a career, even if it was only temporarily? Was I the sort of person that wanted to leave him behind? I would pine terribly. I wasn't even sure if my parents could have him for that length of time. I knew my mum would say what a terrible mother I was for leaving him, but if it was work related and I had no choice, or I would lose my job…

"Ooops, I forgot…" Her voice cut through my thoughts. "The contract starts in four weeks, so we will have to bring your refresher course forward, maybe a week on Monday!"

I almost choked on my own saliva. "Monday?" I squealed. "There's no way I can arrange…"

Debs interrupted me, "Hold your bloody horses, girl. The crew rotate so you wouldn't actually be needed in Florida until after Christmas, possibly even January/February? But you need to get back into flying as soon as."

"Oh, right, ok, that gives me a little more time to completely freak out!" How things can change. What an opportunity to earn lots of cash! Paid hourly for flight duty the whole time we were there, basic and commission… was I dreaming?

"We get our own apartment, two crew sharing, possibly three, but I'll get the best one, of course, so you can share with me. Honey, we're quids in, get it sorted… Ciao!"

Could I manage this? Could I really bugger off to Florida, leaving my baby son to fend for himself (with help from my parents), especially when his father, who he hadn't even met, was banged up abroad! Decisions, decisions. I had to give an answer by Thursday, so I had some time to stew on my response.

I put the film back on and poured myself some more wine, but I had to keep rewinding it, because even though my eyes were fixed on the screen, my mind was fixed on Florida. Florida! Wow, it would be great! I wondered if I could do it. Maybe I could. I could do it, I could wangle it. Could I be going to Florida. I smiled to myself and thought, *things are looking up, Lillian White, things are looking up*. Maybe it wasn't right for me to leave Freddie, maybe it wasn't right for me to leave James in some jail, maybe it wasn't right for me to leave while Sal worked out who the father of her baby was, but it also wasn't right for me to put everyone else's needs first and miss an opportunity, so I was going for it. I could hear the girls now: "Go girlfriend, go, go, go!"

"No, Lillian, you shouldn't go. It's not fair on your mum and dad. I take it you are going to leave Freddie with them?" This came from Jess.

"But Lillian, what about me? I need you now too. Please don't leave me. Oh god, you're leaving me. Lloyd will leave me eventually. Oh god, this is terrible!" This came from Sally.

"Well, if you really think you can leave Freddie for all that time. I mean, he'll know, and it will all be different when you return. You will come back, won't you?" Asked Lou.

Maybe it was a different set of girlfriends I could hear saying "go, go, go", but I was sure they'd come around, especially when they realised they could visit! If I could sort the logistics out, then I was going. Six weeks, it would go in a flash! I just had to butter up my mum and dad and sweet talk the girls!

TWENTY-SEVEN

I was returning to work the following week and, although it was extremely difficult to make the final decision, I was overwhelmed by the support from my family, who encouraged the opportunity. However, as the contract in Florida drew closer, the enormity of my decision and the future upheaval played on my brain. What about Freddie? He was my life. Was I rushing into it? Would I be homesick? I started to doubt if, when it actually came down to it, I would mentally be able to go. I debated ringing Debbie to cancel the whole thing, but that would just leave her in the shit and make me look bad.

Instead, I phoned Sam, who I have to say had been far more supportive and soon brought me around, reminding me that the whole thing was 'temporary, Lillian' so 'get a grip'. She also reminded me that, more importantly, I should be focusing on getting my body Florida-Bikini-Beach-Ready. The cheek of it! She did have a point. Looking down at my body, it really wasn't good.

The disappointment just made me hungry, so I headed for the kitchen, making a bee line for the goody cupboard. Every house should have one: chocolate twirls, Turkish delight, crisps, Twix, Jaffa cakes. I closed the goody cupboard and opened the fridge: Sauvignon Blanc, Pinot Grigio, full-fat milk. I looked down at my stomach again and acknowledged things needed to change.

The morning was filled with *Tweenies*, *Fireman Sam* and some weird looking *Tombliboos*, which initially encourage suicide, but once you've seen Iggle Piggle and Upsey Daisy get groovy in the Night Garden and push Makka Pakka off his bicycle, it wasn't so bad! I dragged myself away easily as I had some serious work to do, leaving Freddie securely in the world of the Pontipines, happy they would zombify him into a very deep coma.

It was time to face my body and bikini saga. I rooted out my uniform and slid on the size 12 skirt – a little ambitious but I was feeling ambitious, even though I couldn't get it past my thighs – it had *obviously* shrunk! This was a major problem. I had a size 14 skirt which I used to call my *comfy skirt;* however, this also was a snug fit. I make a decision *not* to have any more babies. Actually, once I got my jacket, beret and gloves on, I didn't look half bad. In fact, not that different to when I first got pregnant. I slipped into the miracle high heels. Amazing! They make the thickest of calves instantly slim, turning any cankle back into an ankle – every girl should own a pair! Feeling pleased with myself, I returned the uniform to its rightful place in my overcrowded wardrobe.

Taking a deep breath, I prepared myself for the

beach wear, visualising an image of a whale in a yellow polka dot bikini. I stripped to my undies to see what I was working with, chanting to myself *don't look down, don't look down.* I did look down. I also tried not to look in the mirror, but I had to be brave and face the music. *Come on, girl, you can do it.* The first bikini went on. A whale in a yellow polka dot bikini would look far better than me. Disgusting! What had happened to me? What had happened to my boobs? My stomach? *This is all your fault, Freddie, I hope you appreciate it!* Tucking my stomach into my knickers and my boobs into my bra, and standing in a Victoria Beckham style pose whilst breathing in gave an instant lift to my body and my mood!

I couldn't face a full bikini session, so thought I'd do a little studying instead. Rummaging under my bed, I came across some of the previous year's exam papers, written in jest by Lyndon, and sat howling.

```
If a passenger smells smoke in the
toilet do you:
    A) Jump out of the aircraft door and
hope for a soft landing?
    B) Ask her if she has farted? or
    C) Grab a fire extinguisher (BCF) and
call for assistance?

If a passenger asks you for a flight
deck visit, do you say:
    A) No, fuck off?
    B) The captain's asleep? or
```

```
C) Pretend you didn't hear them?
(this is a trick question as 'all the
above' would suffice.)

When a passenger asks you where we are
at the moment, do you say:
A) In the fucking sky?
B) Do I look like Einstein? or
C) I don't care?
(Again, all the above!)
```

Still in my bikini and heels, I flopped onto the bed, reading over some safety drills: Oven Fire, Toilet Fire, Seat Fire, Overhead Locker Fire, Engine Fire, Decompression, Emergency Landing (pre-planned, unplanned), Ditching (pre-planned, unplanned). I wondered why anyone would want to fly with the possibilities of all these catastrophes!

I couldn't go through with it. What was I thinking? I hadn't thought it through. I couldn't go, I couldn't leave him, not for a minute. My palms started to sweat, my heart was pounding, and I felt a flurry in my throat and a full-blown panic spread through my veins. Where was my Rescue Remedy? As I was frantically looking in my bedside drawers, I heard my phone beep downstairs. I kicked off my heels and ran downstairs in my bikini.

```
Are you in? Just had scan. 10 weeks
pregnant. Baby not Lloyd's!
```

Oh dear! Sally's text was definitely a Jeremy Kyle

moment. Twenty minutes later she appeared at the door loaded with Rescue Remedy (thank god!) and a bag full of goodies. Oh no, more rubbish for my cupboards!

It was clear she'd been crying, but I didn't ask questions as her face told the story. In her hands was the scan of her baby boy. She'd seen a private doctor and held a 3D scan of her future. She dropped on the sofa and forced a smile as I handed her a cup of tea and a packet of Jaffa cakes from the bag. Unfortunately, it was a twin pack, so we ended up with a sleeve each! *I think size 16 will be my comfy size!* She'd broken down in front of the doctor, who offered comfort and reassurance, covering all avenues to consider, and had left with the same leaflet of choices that I was given, which she too tore into pieces. Both Lloyd and Sally were desperate for a family, having been trying for years. Surely the most important issue here was that Sally was actually pregnant? Anyone can provide sperm, but it takes a great man to be a father! Understandably, Sal would prefer Lloyd to father her children.

"The dates don't fit, they just don't." She was going over in her head again just how long it had been since she shagged her boss senselessly! "Lloyd was away for almost two weeks solid, so if it was his baby, I would be at least eleven weeks! It was 'that time' the week before he went away and I was full of cold the week before. I remember he wouldn't come near me as he didn't want to be ill for his trip. No, it's definitely not his. We hadn't had sex for almost a month. This is such a mess." She shoved another Jaffa in her mouth, then another!

"Sometimes doctors do get the dates wrong, Sal,

it happens all the time. Come on, let's do the maths again." I got the tiniest calendar off the fridge, which was attached to a painted footprint of Freddie's feet, dead cute! "When was your last period?"

"I can't remember. I'm getting all confused, but I'm positive, Lillian, it's not Lloyd's baby!"

She was pretty adamant, so I put the calendar back. I sat next to Sally and took a Jaffa cake. I bit half off. "Half moon!" I said. "Full moon!" I mumbled as I shoved the second half in. I took another Jaffa cake and did the same again, then again.

Sally cracked a smile at my struggle to speak or even breathe with a mouthful of Jaffas. Her smile grew wider, then she burst into a fit of giggles. There was no alternative but to join in. Of all the people this could happen to, it happened to Sal with all her values. I knew exactly why she was laughing. It was kind of funny! We howled for ages, then had to stop as Freddie was a little freaked out! It didn't take long. The laughter turned to tears, but only sniffles. She was calming down and in control.

"It's just so unbelievable!" She put her head in her hands. "What am I going to do? My life's over! This is my punishment for sleeping with Sean. I didn't plan it. No-one could have known this was going to happen, it was literally spur of the moment. I'm never drinking vodka Martinis again!"

"Vodka Martinis?" Even I knew they were deadly. It was exactly how I got pregnant! "You know how lethal they are. Didn't you learn from me?" I was making light humour of this difficult situation. "Well at least you can call your baby Martin!" I offered flippantly.

"Er… no! But I suppose it's better than what they'll call the mother!"

"Why, what will they call the mother?"

"Martini! Any time, any place, anywhere!"

You had to see the funny side!

"Is this your homework then, Miss Trolly Dolly?" Sally picked up my safety manual. "Shall I test you?"

"Yeah, go on then, but I've not had much chance to look!"

"What's this?" She took out some notes. "If a passenger asks you for a flight desk visit, do you say A) No, fuck off…" She burst out laughing. "Lillian, this is hilarious. Can I work for this airline?" She carried on reading and started sniggering again. "Wouldn't you love to say this to someone? Fancy a brew?"

We stood in my kitchen, drinking tea and dunking biscuits – all the Jaffa cakes had gone! We were silent for a moment or two, which was fine: we were comfortable, respecting each other's thoughts.

"Does Sean know?" I asked, intrigued.

"No, god no. He would think I was trying to trap him or something, or maybe blackmail him into promotion!" She looked mortified.

"Sal, why the hell would he think any of the above? You're fantastic at your job and Sean knows it. He respects you as an employee."

"Oh yeah, he really respects me!" Replied Sal.

"Well, put it this way, he respects how 'by-the-book' you are and how professional you are in every aspect.

He knows you're committed to Lloyd, why on earth would he think anything else?"

"Maybe, but I didn't show that much commitment to Lloyd when I slept with Sean!" She retorted. "He has a wife and family; there's no way they can find out!"

"Er… I think it's a bit late for that, don't you, Sally. You owe it to him and to give him a choice whether or not to be involved." Sally began biting her fingernails. "Stop it!" I shouted. "So what about Lloyd? What are you going to do?"

"I'm not sure I can face telling him, but I know it's the right thing to do."

"Would you consider…?"

She knew what I was talking about and stopped me from saying the alternative out loud by admitting, "The thought came into my head for a microsecond, get rid of the evidence and no-one need know. We've been trying for a baby for so long, how could I possibly get rid of it? No way – this baby is a keeper!"

"Excellent, good choice!" Still holding on to Freddie, I gave Sally a hug. "Another brew?"

"One more then I must get back to work. I'll be peeing all day at this rate. Pass me a biscuit!"

She was heading back into the lounge with Freddie when my phone rang, but as Sally needed my time, I decided to ignore it.

"It's ok, Lillian, I'm fine," she shouted from the living room. "Answer the bloody phone!" She knows me too well!

When I answered, there was a long beeping sound like an old fashioned payphone (or maybe a current one

– I hadn't used one in ages). It sounded long distance.

"Hello? Helloooooo?" I said as I walked back into the living room giving Sally a questioning look. The line went dead. I threw the phone down onto the sofa. When Freddie picked it up and began to dribble on it, it suddenly dawned on me that I might know the caller.

"Lillian? Who was it?" Asked Sal.

I could feel the blood draining. "…I think it was James!"

****

James

Shit, this is just hopeless. What the fuck's up with these phones? I slammed down the receiver in temper, kicking the console until my foot throbbed. The prison guards looked over but I'm not stupid, I got the message and headed back to my cell, knowing full well that any eye contact or engagement of any kind would attract unnecessary attention. I didn't want to cause any more trouble, couldn't afford to, didn't want them to throw in another few weeks or months for bad behaviour just because they could.

I can't begin to describe my life over the past four months, probably similar to how an animal might get treated living in a cage. Human Rights? I've forgotten what those mean. Yes, I've been a naughty boy, yes, I've done a silly thing, but do I really deserve this? I'd done this type of thing many times before, crossing the channel by ferry, sometimes by tunnel and sometimes in one day! Straightforward run there, straightforward trip back. A bit of a jolly, pick up a few beers on the way back, earn a decent crust and head home to Mamma. Only this time, this job had gone wrong, turned completely sour, which left a bitter taste in my mouth. This Dougy chap has set me up. A wealthy chap, ex-criminal who needed some cars taking care of. His nephew used to do the dirty work for him but he's lying low as the police are on his tail. I wasn't on the radar so by all accounts the coast was clear. I wasn't interested, not at first, but the money was too good to be true. Literally! Little did I know that this Dougy had managed to throw all charges against his nephew in my direction, leaving him scot-free, which is why I'm in here. I'd only scorched one car, one! Dougy must have been following me and called the police, it's the only explanation.

I exist in a cramped 6 x 8 cell which I share with intolerable men, a constant stench of human faeces, blood and sweat drowning my senses. I'm hungry, desperate and lonely and honestly don't think I have ever been so low. I have no mobile phone, which is my lifeline, so I'm out of touch and miles away from everyone. In this jail, you have access to the telephone once a month! Once a fucking month and that's only if it's working, so you wait for weeks to use it only to find it's out of use. But it's not like anyone complains; head down and get on with it until something changes. It's really difficult not having your phone at hand though. At least my phone bill will be at an all-time low, always a silver lining!

I'd managed a very brief conversation with my father when I got arrested and I could sense, understandably, he was devastated. The connection had gone before I could tell him what part of Spain I was in. That was my one call, the guards prevented me trying to redial.

I think about Lillian a lot. She's going to think I've forgotten her and that was my last privilege for three weeks. I had been trying to contact her for ages. She would have had the baby by now. And Jenny, I wonder if she's had hers, ours? What a fucking mess to be in! How on earth did I get here? I'm a decent chap. I must have taken a wrong turn somewhere, but I'm genuinely excited at the prospect of offering my father skills to both of my children. How the hell did this happen to me? Talk about being fertile. Maybe I should sell my sperm!

Lying on my filthy bed, just about big enough for a 12-year-old, I go over again, piece by piece, what happened:

On leaving the port of Calais in a hire car, I was to head towards Rennes, then through Nantes, then Bordeaux, buying a few wines on the way, then Toulouse, the home of the Airbus. My target was just on the border of Barcelona, so once I was done, I'd stay a day or so in Spain then fly home. The equipment was there waiting for me. It was all prepared, I just had to light the match. Simple. I changed my clothes and headed for the border, but as I handed my passport to the Guardia, he frowned as if something wasn't quite right. It most certainly wasn't. "Wait here!" Within seconds I was wrestled to the ground then dragged off, surrounded by guns as if I was some kind of drug dealer. Forced into the car, they took me to the local police station in Barcelona. I was stripped of my passport, wallet, phone, loose change and jewellery and thrown into a cell. I called Dad from the cell, but within 24 hours I was bundled into the back of a van and brought here to Hellsville. And I fear this is where I'm going to spend the rest of my days.

TWENTY-EIGHT

The Christmas holidays were gone in a flash and the New Year began. I'd not received any further silent phone calls, only seasonal well-wishers and family good tidings. The house was filled with toys and leftover pine needles, which the vacuum still rejected. The cupboards continued to store the long, slim toffee sweets and the round ones that break your teeth. I thought about James on Christmas day and what he might be doing. Did he get turkey or a Spanish omelette? Did they even celebrate Christmas at all? I had no answers and yet my mind wandered when I was alone. We had fun things going on, so the time passed quite nicely but, believe it or not, I was lying by our private pool in Florida.

Yes, I made it to Florida! After all the uncertainty, I'd decided that life was too short and went for it. I had also decided that I couldn't wait for James to call or show up or get an out of jail free card, I just had to deal with this situation as best I could. I needed to get on with it and do the best for my son, my gorgeous little Freddie! It wasn't an easy decision to make, but after endless discussions with the girls and with my parents, we all came to a decision together – put that part of my life behind me and go to Florida, start new.

My wonderful parents, my fantastic parents, decided to rent a property in Florida near to Debbie and me for the whole time I was there. How fantastic was that! Lou wasn't happy as Dad had left her in charge of Wytes, but he was supposed to be retired anyway. I had my boy with me, as well as my parents (and instant babysitters). What more could I ask for? I was in Florida – did I mention that already?

My folks and Freddie flew out a week before me. My mum was eager to get out there to get as much sorted as they could before I arrived, which gave me a chance to sort things out with the house in the UK. I wanted to make sure there was enough money in my account to cover the bills while I was gone, and I didn't want the house to be empty, so at the last minute I tried to find someone to house-sit but failed miserably. My elderly neighbours said they would pop in from time to time and water the plants (I didn't have any), which was the best offer I had had, so couldn't look a gift horse in the mouth!

The night before I was due to fly out, I nearly didn't make it. I was all packed and ready for an early night before my 8.00am flight to Sanford when Sally rang, distraught and asking if she could come over. Well, of course she could.

As she sat in the same spot on the sofa as she had some weeks earlier, I handed her a brandy. I knew she was in a delicate situation, but she could sip it slowly.

"I decided to take your advice," she sobbed. "I told Lloyd everything!"

"Oh Sally, shit, what did he say?" I was gob

smacked.

"Well," she sobbed, "he'd noticed something wasn't right, but he's worked away so much that he thought that was it. I thought long and hard about how to tell him because I had to try and put it in some order. If I had told him I was pregnant first, he would have been thrilled for a minute then distraught the next, which would have been just awful." How very thoughtful, even thinking of the order she had to give bad news. "So, I told him about Sean and the vodka Martinis and how one thing led to another and you should have seen his face, Lillian, he didn't have a clue what I was talking about..." Sally started to cry again. "He trusts me that much that he just wouldn't think I could do a thing like that!" The poor guy would be heartbroken. Lloyd really was a nice guy, the best, but Sally was great too, and this couldn't have happened to a nicer person. She continued with her story. "I had to spell it out for him. Lillian, you should have seen him, he was broken... and at this point I hadn't even told him about the baby!" I told her to sip her brandy, take a big gulp and no, it would not harm the baby at this stage! "Then I told him I was pregnant, and he asked if it was his baby and I had to answer that I didn't know. I felt like such a tart, such a prostitute. Who the hell wouldn't know who the father of their baby was?" I didn't comment on this; it had passed my mind for a second many months ago...

"Sal, I know it sounds bad, but bad things can happen to good people, and anyway this isn't all bad. You have a gorgeous little baby growing inside you and that's a good thing, right?" I held Sally's hand. "Sally, darling, you have been waiting for this moment for so long."

"But so has Lloyd," she added.

"Yes, I know Lloyd has too, but it's done now. You can't turn back the clock. You have to move forward!"

"He told me to get rid of it," bawled Sal, "but he has no idea how far gone I am!"

"How far gone are you now?"

"Fourteen weeks, I think. He said that if the baby isn't his and if we have any future at all, then I must get rid of it because it would be a reminder of what I did. Otherwise, he said it was over and he took his ring off, he took his engagement ring off!"

I felt sick for Sally and sick for Lloyd, neither of them deserved this, although I did think it was odd that a man wore an engagement ring!

"He said to go and that I had some thinking to do, but I couldn't get rid of this baby, Lillian, not now. But I love Lloyd and I don't want to lose him either!" Sally was crying uncontrollably. "He asked me to give him some space while he gets his head around it so I'm going to move out, but I can't think straight, and I don't know where to go!"

A big smile crept upon my face. "You can stay here!" I was delighted for me, but still sad for Sal. "I'm off to Florida in the morning and the house will be empty for months, so why don't you move in here. It's perfect!"

She hugged me so tight I thought I was going to pop. She was so grateful and relieved. "I have a few things in the car, which I grabbed as I knew he wanted me out, so is there any chance I can stay here tonight?"

"Yes, of course, you silly thing, you can wave me off in the morning." I snuggled into Sally and gave her a reassuring squeeze. "It will be fine, Sally, I promise. These things have a way of sorting themselves out. You'll know what to do, you both will. You're like salt and pepper, fish and chips and cheese and biscuits, you're meant to be together!"

She leant her head into my shoulder and we both had a little sob. Sally for her baby and Lloyd and temporarily losing her home, me for leaving my home and venturing into something new. It was a scary place for us both to be in but exciting all the same.

"I'll really miss you, Lillian."

"I'll really miss you too, Sally, the girl who shags her boss just to get a promotion!" We both fell into fits of giggles at the absurdity of it all.

It was January, but the weather was fantastic in Florida. I reckoned it was about 28 degrees every day, with the occasional shower thrown in for good measure, which was duly appreciated. Both apartments were near to Orlando's International Airport, which was a bit noisy, but you got used to it. In fact, both apartments were within walking distance of each other, which was pretty cool as I could just flip from one to the other in no time. The local beach was great, and the night life wasn't too far in a taxi. Ruby Tuesdays was my favourite place as they served Mississippi Mudslides – Baileys, cream and chocolate ice cream – the best orgasm ever. So, if I'm ever lost, you know where to find me!

Our flights were all scheduled short hall within the

sunshine state, with the earliest check-in being 4.30am and the latest finish being 1.00pm, which wasn't bad. I was liking this set-up. We were flying on the Airbus A320, with four crew instead of five, and I was in charge at the back, but it wouldn't be long before my promotion and I could kick ass at the front, with more money and respect – groovy!

My first flight was on Tuesday. It was Sunday, so I had a few relaxing days to chill. My parents were dying to take Freddie to the theme parks, even though I kept telling them that there was no rush and we didn't have to do it all in one day! But then my mother reminded me that even if I was here to work, it was still a holiday for them, so let it bloody begin! She had a point, so theme parks here we come. But you are so spoilt for choice, and it's quite a decision as to which one to go to first! There was Aquatica, Busch Gardens, SeaWorld, Universal Studios, Epcot, to name just a few – Phew! My mother was so excited and, even though I said we could get some family vouchers to make entry cheaper, she didn't care and said, "It's only money. We'll pay at the gate – get your coat!"

So, within a few hours we were outside the gates of Walt Disney World's Magic Kingdom. We chose this one first as it appeared to be more 'Freddie Friendly' and, if I was really honest, I'd always wanted to go to Cinderella's castle. I was dead excited. I just loved the film *Pretty Woman*, when Julia Roberts' character, Vivian is falling for Edward, played by Richard Gere, and she asks her friend, Kat, "Who gets it all? Kat, just name one person?" To which Kat replies, "Cinder-Fucking-

Rella!" Well, I wanted to be Cinder-Fucking-Rella just for one day! We asked Deb to come as she had kind of become part of the family, but she declined, but did say that she had a surprise for me when we checked in on Tuesday! Oh goody!

The queue seemed to go on for hours, but at least it was a structured queue with entertainment along the way, so we wouldn't get too bored. This didn't help Freddie, though; he wasn't interested in the entertainment, he just wanted to cry, which in turn didn't help my stress levels. No matter how much milk or juice or rusks I put his way, he still wanted to cry. And cry he did. Already I had changed my mind about it being a good idea, but hey ho, only about another forty minutes in the queue! We were handed lots of leaflets, which normally you would shove in your bag and bin on the way in/out, but as we had half an hour to kill and there wasn't much to do but listen to Freddie crying, we actually read them. They were mostly advertising accommodation within the many Walt Disney Resorts, which did look absolutely fantastic, from Disney Deluxe Resort Hotels to Disney Deluxe Resort Villas. If we booked immediately, yes, whilst queuing, we could get two nights complimentary, so like a bloody sucker, my dad had booked us in before we hit the end of the queue! I tell you, the Americans know what they're doing!

At least by the time we had entered the park, Freddie was asleep! Thank god! But wow, it was breathtaking. I was Cinder-Fucking-Rella entering her magical castle with everyone gathered to greet her. There was Micky and Minnie Mouse, Pluto, Tom and Jerry, all surrounded by little people dying to have their picture taken. This was the bit that Freddie would actually like but no, he decided to take some zzz's instead.

We decided that because Freddie was in such a deep sleep, we would grab a coffee and a sandwich and plan our route for the day.

There were attractions for all ages, so we thought we would get some of our fun out of the way first while the baby was sleeping. It turned out that he slept for most of the afternoon, so the three of us had the chance to be children again. We had such a good time. Freddie was probably a little young to appreciate it. Dad wanted to go in the Hall of Presidents, which I couldn't help but yawn at, but as Mum insisted on staying with Freddie, I went along with Dad. God, it was so freaky! They all moved their arms and legs and actually spoke. Mum and I went in the Haunted Mansion, which Mum screamed through. God, she could be so embarrassing at times.

We walked past Dumbo the flying elephant and the many adventures of Winnie the Pooh. As we approached the Country Bear Jamboree, Freddie began to stir! I think he had been awake for a few minutes because he looked bright-eyed and bushy-tailed, just like the characters, and was giggling as the bears sang along. Oh, I could just eat him sometimes, he's so cutey-cute! Happy that Freddie was up for some fun, we headed over to Tomorrowland to see Buzz Lightyear – Space Ranger Spin – and looking at the map, we were in Frontierland, so we had a slow walk to 'infinity and beyond!'

I carried Freddie for some of the way before deciding to sit and watch the world go by. Mum and Dad had taken a stroll and left us to it for a bit and it was really lovely, just me and Freddie. We sat on the bench for quite a while. Freddie was happy to just sit on my lap with no fuss. He didn't cry, he didn't wriggle, he just sat, like me, watching. The noise surrounding us was deafening but we'd zoned out. It was peaceful, it was lovely.

After an amazing but exhausting day, Freddie was finally asleep, so I joined my folks on the veranda for a late-night tipple to discuss our adventure, but I was distracted by voices, one in particular. I knew that voice.

"Lyndon! OMG, it's Lyndon and Debbie, come up, come up!"

My lovely Lyndon! I'd not seen him since forever! Mum and Dad politely retired for the evening so the three off us polished off the Pinot!

"Oh, by the way, this was your surprise for Tuesday!" Said Deb. "Only the rosters have been changed. We're not flying on Tuesday now."

"Not flying, why not?" I asked.

"Because we have a four-day trip to Miami, girlfriend, that's why not!" Deb replied.

"Miami!" Blurted Lyndon, "and I'm your bar person all the way!"

"You mean you're not here on holiday, you got the contract? Yes!" I jumped up to hug him.

"It's going to be brilliant, just brilliant!" Said

Lyndon. "And well done you on your promotion, you big fat purser you!"

I had a temporary promotion to purser, which would become permanent when we got back to the UK as long as there were no hiccups in Florida and I stayed until the contract was complete.

"So, darling," Lyndon continued, "we form part of a permanent crew that will be rostered together. We are going to have soooo much fun, starting on Friday!"

"Friday?" I looked at him questioningly.

"Yep, we fly out Friday, back Tuesday, so we have a weekend in Miami!" Sang Debbie as we put our glasses together.

"Here's to Miami!" We chorused.

I was woken by my throbbing head vibrating through my skull, accompanied by Mother making as much noise as she could in the kitchen and Freddie banging his toys as loud as he could on the kitchen floor.

"Morning, how's your head?" My father's eyes didn't leave the newspaper as he sipped his tea.

"Morning!" I managed, whilst dissolving some pills into a glass of water. "It hurts!"

"You're not the only one with a bad head, it would seem, you left something on the sofa!" Replied Dad.

I did vaguely remember saying to Lyndon that he could sleep in the spare room just before I dragged myself to bed, but he'd clearly not made it that far and was sprawled out half naked on the couch!

"Lyndon, Lyndon, cover yourself up!" I whispered.

"Oh, my head!" He groaned.

I handed him my dissolved paracetamol as my mother shouted us for breakfast. Just in time. Feed a hangover, that's what we needed to do!

"Oh Mum, you are a star! This is just what we need!"

"Yeah, thanks Mrs W, this is just great!" Added Lyndon.

"Well, not only did I hear you all scrambling in and out of the bathroom at a ridiculous hour, but Lyndon, you get rather windy in your sleep!" Mum laughed, setting us off.

Lyndon was crimson. "Sorry! I'm really sorry!" He replied as he mumbled "how embarrassing" into his breakfast.

I scooped Freddie onto my lap and he stole my toast, or rather sucked the butter off the toast, leaving me with the soggy bread. I felt his warmth as he fumbled around on my knee. It was so great to have him here. He could cure any hangover, including Debbie's, who wandered in, still in her PJs, stealing Freddie from my lap, along with my other piece of toast. She could smell the bacon from her bedroom.

"One advantage of having the apartments close together!" She said.

We had a wonderful breakfast discussing our trip to Miami and the days ahead. This was the life!

****

James

Well, my life is truly over, completely fucked in more ways than one as my roommate fancies the pants off me! Great! I've told him I'm getting out of here soon and promised him a lot of money, anything to stop him staring at my arse!

It's all just shit and I can't get hold of Lillian. I'm desperate to sort things out. She's the mother of my child, one of my children. I don't even want to ring Jenny. It was never Jenny I wanted to be with, it was always Lillian, and being locked up in here is making it worse. I can't stop thinking about her and wondering about my son – or daughter – I don't even know what she had. She must think I have completely abandoned her, run a mile, emigrated! God, if only she knew why I was here in the first place and why I took this last job. I was offered it weeks prior to meeting with Lillian, but of course turned it down. They offered ridiculous money, in the thousands, but still I turned it down as that part of my life was truly over. Then when I saw that Lillian was pregnant, as well as Jenny, I'd decided before I'd even left her house that maybe one more job wouldn't hurt. But now the pain is excruciating. I only did it to make some money for us, our family. It's the only thing that keeps me going.

Lillian White... she's beautiful... weird, strange or maybe just unique, but certainly different. When I went to her house, it was the funniest thing really, I had no idea she was pregnant, especially as I was hiding a very pregnant Jenny in my car! What a mess! What the fuck am I going to do? I just want to get out of here, make it right. You think of everyone and everything when you're in a place like this. There isn't much else to do! But what I keep thinking is that I just might ask Lillian White to marry me. Let's hope no-one gets there first!

TWENTY-NINE

After our first night in Miami I swore to myself that I would never drink again. Lyndon just wouldn't take no for an answer, practically forcing a mix of cocktails upon us. I spent most of the evening speaking into thin air, presuming I was in discussions with Lyndon, until it was pointed out that I was just seeing double! Debbie had fallen asleep whilst standing and Lyndon remained quite composed until our short walk home to the hotel turned into an amusing detour.

"Can you smell that?"

"Smell what?" Asked Debbie, her eyes fighting closure.

"You can't mistake those fumes, someone's smoking weed! Isn't it illegal here?" Lyndon began marching on ahead of us.

"Lyndon, where are you going?" I asked as his pace increased, leading us further into the darkness. "Lyndon, wait, where are you going?"

But he wouldn't halt. We reluctantly followed with only a phone light for torches, aware that we were leaving our familiar path and comfort zone behind us, entering somewhere we clearly shouldn't be.

"Come on!" Lyndon shouted. "I've found

something."

"What do you mean, you've found something...?" But the stench was overwhelming as we found ourselves surrounded by rows and rows of identical plants, millions of them, which rather resembled marijuana.

"My favourite kind of sweetie factory, girls. We've won the lottery!" Lyndon was overwhelmed with excitement.

"Yes, but they're not your sweets, are they?" I retorted.

"Who's going to miss a few little leaves?"

"I'm sure someone will, Lyndon, otherwise why would they be protected by high security fencing. Look at those spikes... LYNDON, STOP!" Ignoring anything I shouted, he began climbing. "Lyndon, stop, you'll get arrested!" I screamed. "You'll get us ALL arrested!"

"By who? There's no one around!"

"How do you know? We don't even know where we are!" I started to panic as Lyndon climbed to the top of the wired fence and began straddling the top. "Lyndon!" I screamed, but it was too late, he was already hanging from the spikes.

"Shit!" He screamed.

"What? What's up, Lyndon. You're scaring me." I could barely make him out in the darkness.

"My shorts, they're stuck. I can't unhook them." I could hear him struggling. "OUCH!" He screamed. "Bloody hell!" Lyndon cried as he caught his leg and ripped his pants!

"Are you ok? Serves you right!" But just as I spoke, I heard a big crash to the ground! "LYNDON!"

"I'm fine, I'm fine!" He reassured me. "Wow, this is amazing! Bloody hell!" He brushed himself down, examined his cuts and bruises, then began walking up and down the lanes of weed, leaving his silhouette for us to follow.

"Debbie!" I shouted, waking her from a drunken heap on the floor. "Get up. Lyndon's gone rogue!" Dragging her to her feet, I directed her to the fence.

She rubbed her eyes and put one foot up to climb. "Oh wait, look we can squeeze through there!" She'd noticed a tiny hole in the fence, just large enough for the smallest of rabbits.

"You'll never get through there!" I exclaimed, even though she was already almost through.

"Lyndon!" Debbie shouted. "Wait!" But he didn't return so she began scratting around in the darkness, the distant whoops of Lyndon's excitement spurring her on.

"Debbie! Bloody hell, not you as well. Wait, let's head back."

"We can't leave him!" She replied as she got down on her hands and knees, scrambling under a barbed wire fence. "Come on, you can get through here!"

Riddled with fear but too afraid to be left on my own, I got down on all fours and heaved myself through the tiny hole. What the fuck was I doing?

"Shit, Lillian, get down, there's a car!" Shouted Debbie, forcing our heads down in the grass.

"Oh god, shit!" I whispered. "What are you doing to me?" My heart was thumping faster and faster as a station wagon slowly rode past. Thank god it wasn't the police; we could have been arrested!

"BOO!" Screamed Lyndon as he jumped out of a bush. I could have killed him.

"I got us some smokes, girlfriend!" He dropped a bundle of leaves, soil and flowers on the ground.

"Hang on a minute, since when did cannabis have bright coloured flowers growing out the end of it?" Asked Debbie.

"Smell it, it's weed, gange, whatever you want to call it, but I'm going to smoke it!" Replied Lyndon, shining his mobile onto the brightly coloured pile. He looked a little perplexed as he examined the flower, feeling it, crushing it and practically shoving it up his nose!

"Oh, I know what it is… It's that… erm… Phlow… flix… erm… omg, what is it?" Demanded Debbie.

"I have no idea! What the hell is Phlow? Oh, do you mean Phlox?" I asked.

"Moss Phlox?" Asked Lyndon. "Moss Phlox!" He sighed, throwing a handful of his stash on the floor.

"Oh, yeah!" Debbie explained how a couple in America received complaints and were raided by police as neighbours reported they'd been growing marijuana, when it was in fact Moss Phlox, which has the same aroma as weed.

"Can you smoke it? Shit, there's a car!"

We all ducked down again, completely shitting ourselves.

"Great! Now what? How do we get out of here?" I asked.

"Get down, more lights!" Whispered Debbie.

I could have bloody killed them. We hadn't been there five minutes and we were stuck in the middle of nowhere, surrounded by insects and spider-ridden plants!

"I'll never climb up there!" I screamed, realising that the hole we climbed through wasn't as easy to return through, so we would have to get over the fence.

"You'll bloody have to," said Lyndon.

So, the three of us began climbing, with me complaining, shouting and moaning. I was so angry and a little sore from the fencing, but when we got over the other side, I supposed I could see the funny side.

"Quick! Car!" Lyndon shouted. "Shit, it's the cops!" He began legging it.

We ran as quick as we could to catch him, but he hadn't got very far. He was rolling around in fits of giggles as there were no cops or cars in sight! Twat.

The weeks were flying by and, although riddled with guilt at my new found freedom as Freddie was with my parents most of the time, I was secretly loving it! The flights were quick and easy, the crew was great, mad but great, and with regular trips to Miami, one couldn't complain. We were always excited to be on South Beach, the place to see and be seen, otherwise known as *the* Miami hot spot! Well, that was if you had a 'body beautiful' which, thinking about it, I didn't, but was content just watching the slinky bodies zooming by on their blades or boards, no helmets, just the whiff of sun lotion they'd leave behind them. On South Beach you're showing off all that hard work in the gym, which

I have to say is pretty spectacular. Bodies to die for, boobs to die for, everywhere, no-one seemed to care. 'Get them out' was the motto and get them out they did!

"I'd like to go to Coral Castle tomorrow, does anyone fancy it?" Piped up Lyndon as he waded through his boring tourist leaflets.

"Lyndon, all I want to do is chill out, relax and sunbathe, so it's a NO from me!" I replied.

"How about you, Debs, are you up for it?" He pleaded. "Go on, pleassseeee!"

"Yeah, go on then, I'll come with you. May as well make the most of it!" Easily swayed, Debbie didn't quite get the lying on the beach all day thing, but that was fine. I was quite happy to be Billy-no-mates for the rest of the day. There was lots to see and do, lovely bodies to drool over and a constant drip of sunshine.

James seemed to be fading from my mind as I did have rather a lot to occupy it. Freddie, Mum and Dad, work, Florida, my house back in the UK and a pregnant friend to look after, so there wasn't much time to dwell on James and his jail sentence. Harsh as it may sound, but he got himself into this mess, so he'd just have to get himself out of it. What I couldn't understand is why he hadn't made any contact with me. I was sure they had phones in Europe! I'd lost count of how many months it had been and I hadn't heard a dicky bird, so I couldn't sit around moping. It all had to come out in the wash one day!

The guys had gone off to Coral Castle, leaving me

to enjoy my own company in our luxury hotel. I was rather looking forward to it. Most of the crew had gone shopping, so it was great just being by the pool relaxing, drinking and eating… whatever I liked. Something you couldn't usually do on South Beach as it would just confirm that 'you are what you eat'. But just for one day, I was quite content to tuck my tummy in my knickers!

I had magazines, my phone and my purse, which was all the company I needed. I also decided to pick up a handful of touristy leaflets and educate myself on the places I would not be visiting, so if anyone asked me on a flight at least I could offer some guidance. I read each leaflet cover to cover: The Everglades, The Seaquarium and the Metro Zoo. This brought me back to my gorgeous Freddie and how he would love the zoo. Taking out his picture from my purse, I studied his little face staring back at me, such a sweetheart. I was still smiling as I answered my phone.

"Sally!" I think I may have shouted a little too loud. "I was going to ring you. How you doing?"

"Well it's all kicking off here big style," she said calmly. "You know I finally told Sean about the baby?"

"What? You never told me that! So he knows it's his?"

"Yes, I did, Lillian, a few weeks back, I told you!"

"You didn't!" I lied, suddenly recollecting a hazy conversation.

"I did! Anyway, do you want to hear this story or not?" She was getting angry, which always made me giggle. She told me that Sean had told his wife all about the baby and she'd insisted that he fire Sally.

"But they can't just fire you, it's against the law," I said.

"I know!" Sally explained that Sean's wife had told him either Sally got fired or she'd leave him, taking the children with her. So, he had been to Lillian's house to plead with Sally to see if she would take redundancy.

"Redundancy?" I think I shouted that quite loud too. "The cheeky sod!"

"I know," was Sally's reply. "Can you believe it?"

"So… what have you decided?" I was really interested in what Sally had to say, but I was suddenly distracted by the cutest smile from a handsome stranger sitting on the lounger just opposite. Gosh, was I flirting?

"Lillian? Lillian? Can you hear me…?" After I grunted a response, Sally offered in-depth details, but I was totally oblivious. What a shit friend!

"Sorry, my phone went out of range for a second, Sal, say again, what are you going to do?" I shifted my focus as she explained how she needed her job as she might be a single mum and, not only that, she needed the maternity pay and leave so couldn't possibly find herself unemployed. She wouldn't get a reference, never mind a job, once the baby was here, so she was going to fight her corner all the way. "Well good for you, I just wish I could be there for you. I hope you've gained some weight when I see you next and get as fat as I was!"

"I'll try!" She giggled. "There's more. I told you it was all happening." She sounded a bit more excited at this and told me that Lloyd had been in touch and asked if she was still 'with baby'. He asked if there was any hope that it could be his and were there any tests that could be done while she was pregnant to confirm this, but Sally didn't know and was looking into it.

"Bloody hell! Does he forgive you, then? Does he want you back?" I couldn't help but think of poor old Lloyd, who had done nothing but treat his fiancée with complete and utter respect and was only guilty of loving her.

"He's been trying to come to terms with what has happened and says he still loves me and can't believe the mess we're in. One minute he is sad and calls me crying, saying that he can't live without me, but the next minute he is really angry and says he doesn't think he can raise another man's baby, especially if Sean wants to be involved with the upbringing. It's all such a mess!" She got a little tearful, but with good reason. I wished I could be there for her. "Oh Lillian, there is just one more thing, Jess and Tom are definitely back together and she's wearing her ring again!"

"No way!" Again, my pitch was a tad high. "I knew he was back on the scene, but wearing his ring? Oh, I feel so out of the loop!"

Sally brought me up to date with all the goss: the girls had been round to my house for a catch-up; Jess looked fantastic as she'd trimmed down considerably, and the diabetes was under control; Tom was back on the scene, claiming his undying love and begging for her forgiveness.

"So basically, he has seen Jess back to her old self and decided he wants a piece of it. Why the bloody hell has she gone back to him? Where was he when she needed him most when she struggled at the beginning? What a shit!" I soon lowered my tone as the guy opposite caught my attention again. Either he found my conversation riveting or maybe he liked what he saw! I sucked everything in, checking that all was still tucked in!

"Well, I'm not really sure, but she did say to give you all her love and she would be in touch soon. You know she has a busy life and she's still running around after her family, so don't be too hard on her. I'm sure she has her reasons, but she does look pretty fantastic!"

With that, Sally and I said our goodbyes and I lay back down on the lounger, soaking up some sun. I couldn't help but think of Jess and Tom and how she must love the guy to take him back after all he had done to her. I couldn't help myself and dialled her number, which went straight onto answer phone. I left her a lovely message followed by "PS – what's the news with Tom?" Then she would know I know!

Sinking elegantly back into my lounger, just in case the guy was still looking, I picked up one of the leaflets which was about the historical 50-acre Vizcaya Estate – bored already!

"Are you planning on getting married?" Said a very manly voice attached to the shadow which was blocking the sun's rays.

"Married?" What was he talking about? Omg, he'd actually come over! He was gorgeous!

"'Vizcaya Estate – popular venue for Galas and Weddings', it says right there on the back!"

He sat on the lounger next to me. I checked my stomach yet again. Phew, still tucked in.

"Oh, right, no, well not yet anyway, I haven't been asked!"

"Well maybe it's a bit too soon to ask, but how about a drink? You must be pretty dehydrated after all that talking?" He extended his lovely muscular tanned arm and offered me his hand. All I could think of was what would he do if I just licked it all the way to the top? "Robert, pleased to meet you. My friends call me Rob."

'Rob with a big knob' was all I had running around my head. "Lillian, Lillian White, and yes, a drink would be great!" *Cute, cute!* I put the leaflet down and sat up on the lounger, taking care not to disturb my belly as he caught the waiter's attention.

"What would you like to drink?" He asked.

"A coffee would be great?" I answered with a question, already feeling that a coffee was rejecting his offer of a drink.

"A coffee sounds good." He asked the waiter for two coffees with brandy! Well, I could cope with that, even though I seemed to be nursing a permanent hangover! I couldn't tell if he was looking at me or not as he wore shades. I wondered what colour his eyes were. "Cheers, Lillian White!"

"Cheers, Rob..." I waited for him to offer his surname.

"Lomax!" He smirked.

"Cheers, Robert Lomax!" I smiled back and we raised our cups.

Rob and I spent all afternoon drinking and chatting, and I found out that he worked for the same airline as a Senior First Officer and was staying at the same hotel! He was based in Miami and had been for a few months, while I had been based in Orlando, but we were pretty much working from the same contract. We both recognised names within the company that we had mentioned, and thanks to the nature of our work, we became immediately familiar. In fact, I swear that as the night drew closer, our loungers did too! I was really enjoying the attention and, as selfish as it may sound, I was enjoying the fact that someone was interested in me again and not just the mum side of things. Even though I missed the little man terribly, it was great to be the centre of attention. It had been quite some time since I had been intimate with someone. Not that Rob and I were getting intimate, but the fact that it could get a little 'fresher' (and that if it did, at least I wouldn't have to dash home to relieve the sitter or ruin the evening by thinking of how many hours I had left before Freddie would drag me out of bed), was most liberating.

The pool lights were on and the staff had begun preparations for the evening's entertainment when Lyndon appeared.

"Lillian, there you are!" He shouted across the pool.

As I waved Lyndon over, I could feel Rob backing off a little, offering the same distance we'd initially had some hours ago. Lyndon sat on my lounger and gave me a big gay snog, which he always does. I was hoping Rob would catch on that he was gay. If he didn't, then there was something seriously wrong with him. Lyndon was going on and on about his trip to Coral Castle, failing to acknowledge that Rob and I were kind of in the middle of something until it was too late. Rob jumped to his feet.

"Right, well I'd better be going, I guess. Nice to meet you, Lillian, enjoy the rest of your evening." And with that, Robert Lomax was gone, out of sight and out of reach.

I was secretly cross at Lyndon and disappointed that he'd interrupted. Was Rob interested? Would I see him again? It was draining. I didn't miss this one little bit, the dating game. I hated it but couldn't stop my mind rehearsing exactly that.

"Lyndon!" I whispered.

"What? Oh no, I didn't realise! Sorry Lillian, were you two…?" he broke off in the middle of his sentence, then his face split into a big grin and he started singing, "Lillian and Robert in a tree – k i s s i n g…"

How childish!

"Where's Debbie anyway? Has she come back? Are we eating out?" I asked.

Debbie had gone to her room to transform herself with evening attire, so Lyndon suggested I followed suit as we were meeting back downstairs in one hour for the hotel BBQ dance!

"BBQ dance? Sounds groovy!"

"It's a Miami thing, now get your skates on!"

Heaving me up from the lounger, he listened to me telling him all about Sally and Jess, and of course my afternoon with Rob. Just as Lyndon innocently put his arm around me, kissing my cheek farewell, Rob walked by, offering a look of 'you win some, you lose some.' Nooooo! I felt sick. 'No, no, no, this is not my boyfriend,' I wanted to shout, but he obviously thought that he was! Had he not clocked Lyndon's bright pink, tight budgie smugglers?

Back at the poolside, I was a little disappointed that I wasn't meeting Rob Lomax. My heart sank at how the afternoon had unfolded, but there was no sign of the handsome officer. On the bright side, I was slightly lifted by the stunning display of glittering lights around the pool and the romantic aroma of flickering candles. The food looked magnificent, not that I had much of an appetite, although I could easily be persuaded. This wasn't a typical British BBQ of burgers and bangers, this was a seafood delight of dressed lobster, grilled salmon, seafood skewers, and tuna steaks sitting amongst a colourful display of healthy salads and garden vegetables. It really was a sight for sore eyes. I scoured the area yet again for a shimmer of hope, but if he thought Lyndon was my fella, what would he think of me flirting with him? I had to put the record straight. I was a single parent, for god's sake, and although not particularly looking for a new man, I quite liked the way he made me feel.

"Shall we get some food, guys? I'm starving!" Thank goodness for Debbie's interruption. "Just look at this tucker. I can't wait to get stuck in!"

"I'm not hungry!" I replied.

"What? Lillian White turning down food? There must be something wrong with you!" Piped up Lyndon, feeling my forehead with the palm of his hand.

When I looked up, guess who I saw in the distance, once again witnessing the closeness between myself and Lyndon. Damn! I couldn't believe it. Rob didn't make it obvious that he had seen me, but I knew that he had, so I made my way over to him. Just as I got within touching distance, he embraced a pretty girl and headed towards the bar. Argh, I'd lost him. He'd slipped between my fingers even before I'd had chance to take hold! I needed a drink! Lyndon had disappeared in the same direction, probably to get some food, but then I saw that he too went to embrace the same girl. She must have been cabin crew and work for the company. Trying not to stare, I watched him giggle away with the young, slender beauty. Lyndon then turned and began talking to Rob. I could feel my cheeks warming, thinking of what he could be saying. Rob looked over towards me, making me blush even more with those eyes. As I looked towards Lyndon, he winked at me, enticing me to join them. Feeling completely stupid, I found myself slowly walking over towards them. I didn't hold eye contact as I was far too embarrassed, but as I approached, Rob had disappeared. Lyndon was engrossed with the buffet, stacking his plate high, so I ended up standing awkwardly by the dressed lobster.

A tanned, manly hand offered a vodka Martini.

"I don't believe we've been properly introduced!" A voice said. "Robert Lomax: single, available and child-less at present!" Rob held out his hand.

"Lillian White: single, with child and have gay friend!"

We shook hands, exchanging nervous giggles. Rob kept hold and kissed my cheek. "Let's start again!"

I woke in a bit of a haze, not quite sure where I was until I took in the sexy dude odour still lingering. I felt a cheeky smile appear as I rolled over to fall neatly under the arm of sexy, single Robert Lomax, but as I edged closer, I realised he wasn't there. Creeping out of bed, wearing one of his T-shirts and still wearing kickers – bonus – I tip-toed towards the bathroom, anticipating a wet, soapy body in the shower for me to join. No Rob. Feeling a little silly, I quickly pulled back the plastic curtain, just in case he was hiding! No Rob. Checking the rest of his suite, which wasn't huge, I opened the wardrobe doors. Maybe he was playing hide and seek. At one point I even shouted "coming, ready or not!" No Rob. Was I that shit in bed? I feared that he had shagged and left. Then, I found the note: "Lillian, been called out. Left at six. Didn't want to wake you. See you soon, Rob." And that was it. No kiss, no telephone number, no 'I had a great night, can't wait to see you again. Miss you, miss you, miss you!' None of that. I felt so sick I could have cried. I really liked him. But at least we had slept together and had amazing fun. We didn't actually *sleep* together. Don't get me wrong, there was touching, feeling and erupting of volcanoes, but I'd drunk too many vodka Martinis and had learnt from previous experiences. So, I was more than relieved that nothing (everything but) had happened! He had a good size penis, not quite up to James' standards, but hey, you can't have everything.

I had been hoping I would get to spend more time with Rob today, or at least have sex and scrambled eggs, but as this was clearly not on the menu, I thought I would scour his room. Before I knew it, I was quite at home in his paisley decorated lounge, placing my freshly ground coffee cup on his marble coffee table, stretching out across his silky cotton sofa listening to the morning unfolding from the slightly ajar window with a pool view. Bliss. Why wasn't my room as fabulous as this?

I daydreamed about the previous evening. We were probably the last to leave apart from a few waiters fussing around us as we snuggled down on one of the loungers. It was just perfect, and it was well into the early hours before we headed up to the suite, so Rob must have been absolutely knackered! Shit, his hotel phone was ringing. Should I answer it? I hoped it wasn't a wife he forgot to mention! Oh god, I hoped he wasn't lying. No kiss, no number... oh no, it was his wife, wasn't it! *Calm down, he's single. Just answer it*, I told myself. I pondered over it until it stopped ringing, but seconds later it rang again. Oh, sod it!

"Hello?" I tried to sound cool.

"Lillian, it's Rob!" I felt all warm and fuzzy inside and wondered if he could hear the tension draining from my shoulders? "Did you get my note?"

"Morning, Robert Lomax, how's your head? I can't believe you got called out!" I put on my sexy voice to match his tired and sexy tones.

"Well, I do feel pretty rough, but the flight's been delayed. There's a thunderstorm heading our way. I'm going to grab forty winks in the crew room. Anyway, I just wanted to say a quick 'good morning' and to tell you what a great night it was last night. I wondered if we should do it again. I'll be in Orlando next week for three days?"

He'd called me, he'd called me in his room, while I was eating his room service food and lying over his manly paisley furniture. My heart skipped a hundred beats.

"Yes, that would be great. Do you have my number?" Oh god, how keen was I?

"Err, no I don't, only your bra number!" I could tell he was smiling. I blushed a little. "Can you leave it for me?"

Feeling smug and gaining back my appetite, I devoured my English breakfast in style, washed down with the finest coffee beans whilst nibbling on a shiny powdered pastry. I may as well make the most of it!

I decided to leave my number written in lipstick on his bathroom mirror, and to prevent it being cleaned, I placed the 'do not disturb' sign on the door handle! Feeling pleased with myself, I called Debbie to spill the beans on my dirty night, but the poor girl was full of flu so I headed for her room with as many flu relievers as I could get hold of and we spent the day watching old movies and drinking Lucozade, which is also pretty good for curing hangovers!

THIRTY

I had been back in Orlando for two days and had even had a trip to Miami and back again, yet still had not heard from Rob. It was just ridiculous that I found myself waiting for two guys to call me. Why did this keep happening to me? I thought he liked me. I thought both of them liked me! I felt like screaming, 'GO AND FUCK YOURSELF, ALL MEN!' No, I didn't really mean that. 'Please call me, please call me, PLEASSSEEEEE!' Yes! The phone began ringing, making me jump out of my skin. He must have heard me! But it was Lyndon. I couldn't hide my disappointment.

"Oh, it's you!" I sighed.

"Well thanks a lot! What's up with you, you miserable devil?"

I told him that I hadn't heard from Rob, and as I started to tell how I was giving up on all men, I could hear him chuckling.

"Lyndon, what is it? Does my depression amuse you?"

"Lillian, just shut up and let me get a word in!"

I shut up.

Lyndon told me that he had just seen Rob on a bullet flight to Miami. Rob had been asking what I had been up to as he hadn't heard from me and he didn't have my number!

"But I did leave him my number, on his bathroom mirror. I feel a complete idiot now!"

"Well, he didn't get it. Maybe the maid cleaned it off!" Said Lyndon.

"But I put the 'do not disturb' sign on the door so the maid wouldn't go in!" I screamed.

Lyndon demanded I lower the octave a little and explained how Rob had to check out over the phone because of the thunderstorm and mega delay. He was being transferred to Orlando. He did ask, apparently, if there were any loose papers or numbers for him, but nothing came to light, so he obviously didn't get to see my little lipstick number in the bathroom! Anyway, Lyndon gave him my number, he was on his way to Orlando and would be calling me at 8PM!

Throwing myself on my bed, I allowed myself a little smile. I was beside myself thinking I wasn't worthy of his phone call when all along he just didn't have my number. Now he'd rung me, part of the chase had been crushed. I wondered if the same would happen if James were to call. My thoughts then went to James, then back to Rob. Why is life so complicated?

We had a good chat though. He was keen and was rather sweet with it. He'd said that he felt sick when he got the call from crewing giving him his changes and had no choice but to agree for hotel staff to collect his belongings as the room was required. He was laughing at the thought of getting back and seeing my lipstick scrawled all over his bathroom mirror. In fact, it quite turned him on. I felt the chase return! He was sexy.

"I know where I'd like to see your lipstick!" He teased.

"Robert Lomax, what are you suggesting?"

"I have to see you!" He urged.

I arranged to see him the following night. And as it turned out, we had a few flights together in the near future too, which could be fun!

He was a perfect gentleman, hiring a two-seater sports car to take me to a quiet tapas restaurant downtown. The hustle and bustle of local bars faded around us as we each poured our lives on the table. He was open and honest, updating me on a previous engagement, his recent promotion and why he ended up in the US. I wasn't as honest and was far more comfortable omitting the jailbird story, but he knew about Freddie and that he currently didn't see his father. I managed to change the subject rather swiftly to avoid further questions – you can't reveal all on the first date! Rob was fun and easy to be around, and I felt as if I'd known him for ages. Gorgeous food, great wine and brilliant company was just what the doctor ordered. I could get used to it.

We ended the evening back at his hotel for the perfect night cap. Call me a tart, I don't care, it had been a long time and, although I was a little out of practice, he didn't complain that part of his anatomy ended up wearing my lipstick.

Our relationship grew rapidly, and we became very

close, almost inseparable. We spoke each day, flights permitting, and during that first week we saw each other several times, even meeting my folks back at the apartment. However, I had this nagging feeling at the pit of my stomach – what about James? But I soon silenced them. Was I supposed to put my life on hold? Was I supposed to travel around Spain trying to find which jail he was locked up in? Was I meant to rescue him and be his happy ending? Was he ever really in jail or had he just scarpered to avoid all responsibility? I just didn't know the answers any more, but I did know that I deserved some fun and why couldn't I be the one getting rescued for once, just for once?

I'd had long conversations with the girls about Rob and long conversations with the girls about James and they all agreed that I couldn't put my life on hold and would just have to bloody well get on with it.

Rob and I headed for Sanibel and Captiva Island in a hired 4-wheel drive. It was a fair drive from the apartment, but we had a 36-hour window in which to have some fun. We drove down Alligator Alley, shopped at some malls, ending up in one of the island's spectacular hotels. We played tennis, went swimming and had hours of saunas. It was truly amazing. He took me to the Clam Shack, where we shared seafood and lobster and watched the sunset over the bay. We'd become as one, united, a couple. I was no long an *I* but had become part of a *we*. I loved it.

He met Freddie a few times and Mum was getting used to having him around. I couldn't fully close the compartment in my head labelled 'James' but accepted that it could be reopened when the time came. I still hadn't heard from him, but I guessed Freddie still needed a father figure. Not that Rob was trying to replace James, he just got on with whatever role he fell into when he was around Freddie: friend, plaything, semi-father figure. It worked.

It didn't seem possible, but in such a short space of time Rob and I became even closer. We seemed to fit somehow, and I was very happy. Were we becoming a family? Was this what it felt like in Smugsville?

Our time was coming to an end in Florida and we were due to leave in a few days. Mum and Dad had already flown back to the UK with Freddie, leaving Lyndon, Deb and me to finish our contract. I was really looking forward to going home and getting back to normality, hoping that Rob would slot in somewhere without too much disruption. Anxiety kicked in at the thought of losing him and I wondered if maybe this had all been a holiday romance. He still had a few more days on his contract so wasn't returning immediately, but he didn't live local to me so would have a fair commute on his hands.

It would feel quite strange being just the two of us again, Freddie and I, after being surrounded by family and colleagues. I wondered if maybe it wouldn't just be the two of us, maybe there'd be the three of us? Would Rob be in the picture? I really did like him. There was just a slim barrier stopping me from going full steam ahead, but I wasn't going there, I still wasn't opening that compartment.

To be honest, we hadn't really discussed life after

Florida in too much detail, even though I was desperate to bring it up. I was very fond of him, couldn't stop thinking about him and wanted him in my life. I wasn't passionately in love with him, but I wanted to be with him, loved being with him and loved the feeling of being with someone. I worried in case he didn't want a parental role just yet. Would this be a stumbling block for him?

It had been a fabulous ten weeks, but I had missed the girls. I hadn't seen them since forever. We'd survived on texts, calls and Skype. I couldn't wait to see them, especially Sally, who was keeping my house warm while I was away. She would be over five months now. I tried to picture her round and chubby, ankles inflamed, boobs inflated, but I betted there'd be no difference to her tiny, petite frame. I still didn't know if she would be there when I got home.

With just one flight remaining on our rosters, Debbie manoeuvred the crew so we could all work together on the grand finale of flights. Our route was Miami – Barbados – Miami – 3 hours 25 minutes each way. Due to there being several seniors on-board, I offered to be the galley slave, so I was looking forward to having some fun, especially as Rob was our captain.

Midway through the drinks service, the first officer entered the cabin, probably to scan the cabin for innocent women he could charm. Deb wanted to escape him as she'd been there before, so she disappeared to the back galley as I slipped into the flight deck unseen.

Rob looked very pleased to see me, immediately

locking the flight deck door and raising his sexy eyebrows. I felt an air of excitement below my waistline. What was he thinking? As he mumbled into his radio, feeling naughty, I put on his jacket, folding my skirt up to my waist so all that was seen were bare legs and stocking tops, and grabbing his hat for effect! Hovering suggestively, I soon discovered it was a mistake as the horrified expression on his face said it all. Holding one hand up to stop whatever I was going to do, it was clear his conversation was serious. I hadn't clicked that of course it was weather related and, within a split second, Rob had switched on the seatbelt sign. Suddenly, the aircraft had fallen several feet, lifting me hard into the air, hitting the roof of the cockpit, knocking me to the floor.

With my bleeding head blocking the entry to the flight deck, Rob had no choice but to carry out an emergency call.

"Will the senior crew member please report to the flight deck immediately!"

This was not the first time I had heard this type of call. Although, to be fair, I hadn't actually heard it this time either as I was flat out on the floor. The first officer, along with Debbie, rushed to the front of the aircraft, having to force the flight deck door open because my bottom was against it. You can imagine what they were presented with! The poor crew, having no idea what going on, continued preparing for an emergency, as for all they knew this could be an emergency landing, ditching or decompression.

The aircraft was being thrown all over the place,

as were the crew, who were soon updated with *some* of the details and ordered to sit down and fasten their seatbelts until the storm had passed. They also had to deal with fretful passengers who clearly thought their plane was going to fall out of the sky. As I opened my eyes, head pounding, I was somewhat confused as to why I was lying on the floor in the tight hold of Debbie, who had me held in her grasp whilst her feet were clamped into the back of the flight deck chairs, trying to secure the pair of us. The vessel was tossing frantically as the flight crew dealt with the chaos. I clocked the first officer, who hadn't been there before, and Rob was still on the radio. Something had happened here. What had I done? As my brain sobered from the cracking pain, realisation overwhelmed me. Debbie held her finger to her lips to keep me quiet and so that I wouldn't distract the flight crew in their moment of heroism. I wouldn't dream of it.

Eventually, I managed to sit up and secure myself, naturally feeling for the area of pain, which was bleeding through my hair, ears and the top of Rob's jacket. It was a superficial cut, but a little blood goes a long way. Debbie held a cloth to my head whilst shaking her head and smiling, trying her best not to laugh.

"What the fuck were you doing? Where is your skirt?" She mouthed. She looked away, knowing that if she continued eye contact, she would be overcome with ridiculous giggles.

After an eternity, which only turned out to be about eight minutes, the flight crew secured the aircraft into autopilot. Rob took off his seatbelt, turned his chair towards me and stared at me lying on the floor. The first officer, smiling, didn't move or turn, he just kept on staring out of the window into the clouds, which were now clearing.

"So?" Rob paused. "How are you feeling, Lillian?"

At that point, Debbie and Rob began tittering at the sight of me.

"I'm not saying anything!" Piped up the first officer.

"I think that's best!" Replied Rob, winking at me. "Are you ok to stand?"

Debbie helped me to my feet and perched my bottom on the jump seat just behind Rob.

"You took quite a fall!" Rob examined my head. "But I think you'll live!"

Without speaking, Debbie helped me out of his jacket and I slowly pulled my skirt from around my waist, covering my stocking tops and legs.

"I'll go and see to the crew," offered Debbie, who tried to contain her sniggering as she left the cockpit.

"I'll come with you," I offered, embarrassed and desperate to escape.

I followed Debbie into the cabin, slipping quickly into the toilet to examine the damage. I looked shocking. There was blood on my face, neck, ears and shirt and it was clogging nicely in my knotted ponytail. There was a knock on the door and Debbie offered me her cosmetic bag, so I rebuilt my hair.

Luckily, all was well in the cabin, but of course the crew needed to know 'what happened to Lillian?' Thank god for Deb, who omitted the finer details, although Lyndon knew some of the puzzle was missing.

After sweet tea and chocolate, a new hairdo and shirt, although a little battered and bruised, I was fine. However, Debbie couldn't allow me to operate, due to health and safety reasons, and she had to carry out a full flight report. I spent the rest of the flight sat in the flight deck – but at least this time I was fully dressed! Rob saw the funny side and was pretty gutted that he'd missed out on whatever it was I'd had planned, although I made a mental note to myself never to strip in the flight deck again during severe turbulence.

THIRTY-ONE

After a tearful farewell to Rob, it wasn't long before we'd arrived in Manchester to be greeted by Mum, Freddie and Sally. More tears of relief at the realisation of how much I'd missed them, all of them. It was so great to be home and Rob and I had vowed to keep in touch. Freddie stared at me, listening excitedly at the sound of my voice and smiling sweetly every time our eyes met. He was truly scrumptious. I was never leaving the little man again. I burst into tears at the enormity of what it must have been like for him, not only being away from home and being left with grandparents most of the time, but returning home without Mummy. He probably thought I was going to leave him again. Never. I squeezed him tight and he wiped away my tears, which made them flood even more. Sally squeezed my hand. I knew she had lots to tell. I couldn't wait to hear it, but I needed to rest first.

Back at the house, I felt complete. Sally had made a little 'high tea', although I was way too tired to appreciate it.

"Your bed's all made and ready. I'll put the kettle

on while you get sorted."

"Thanks, Sal. Sorry, it all looks lovely, really, although it feels bizarre being here again after so long."

"No need to explain, we've a lot to catch up on and maybe some news that you might need a fresh head for?"

"What do you mean?" I asked eagerly, presuming she meant the saga between herself and Lloyd. Although keen to catch up, I hoped it could wait.

"First things first, dump your bags, sort Freddie and I'll get the coffee on!" She demanded.

It was late and I was absolutely knackered. My head was still bruised from my little incident, as was my pride, but with the emotion and upheaval again, I was drained and couldn't wait to get my head down on my own pillow and start the next day fresh, so when Sally came to check on us, Freddie and I were snoring away on my bed.

Freddie and I slept the whole night through in the same position, both relieved to be back together again. It was a lovely welcome home.

"You're awake!" Sally appeared with the perfect British cuppa. "Reheated from last night!" She joked.

"Sal, I'm so sorry, and the lovely sandwiches with the crusts cut off. We'll have them for breakfast!" I replied, making room for Sal. The three of us cosied up under the duvet. "Oh my, look at your lovely bump now. It's growing! Or should I say he? He is growing?" I looked at her questioningly as I'm sure she had said she was having a boy, but she wasn't giving anything away, not yet anyway.

We caught up on a few events whilst sipping our tea and nibbling on slightly stale triangular butties, not quite the norm but yummy all the same. Sally told me all about Lloyd and her ex-boss, his wife, her scans, her midwife – who was a male, shock horror. I was surprised at how she'd turned things around in such a short space of time. Sally looked amazing and was truly glowing.

"So? You and Lloyd? I've missed so much, so before I left it was over, dead and buried-ish?"

Sally knew she could not miss out any details. Lloyd didn't know she was staying at mine, he'd heard this news from Tom (yes, Jess was still wearing her ring) and had turned up at my house to see Sally, bringing chocolate and flowers and some items for the baby.

"Oh my god, I can't believe he did that, really?" I was shocked.

"I know, it's really sweet considering he must be desperately hurting inside, knowing it might not be his baby. No, no, I'm not going to cry any more. I'm trying to move on from the guilt!"

"Might?" I asked. "There's still a good chance then that's it's his?"

"Wait a moment, wait, wait... right!" She contained herself and stopped the tears dead in their tracks. She continued to fill in the details about the first few weeks that she hadn't got around to telling me about in her phone calls. She'd had a terrible time, pretty much keeping herself to herself, trying to process what she'd done and the outcome she was left with and how truly gutted she was. Her parents had disowned her for a while, not to mention Lloyd's parents, and she'd found it hard to function, to put one foot in front of the other, let alone see or speak with anyone, so she just kept a low profile for a while. Lloyd had also been through hell because, let's face it, those two were the perfect couple; they were in love, happy, and making plans for the future, then after one drunken evening it was gone in a flash. Surely, they were strong enough to get through this, which was why Lloyd came to see her.

"Although he's truly broken, he asked me to rethink the dates and asked if I'd forgotten about the sofa saga!"

I looked at her questioningly.

"Lloyd was due to be away for a few weeks but hadn't realised there would be a 36-hour window when he returned to Manchester for a connecting flight. Rather than stay in the hotel provided, he came home to surprise me. I'd totally forgotten about it. Our lounge sofa was for sale and I was at home waiting for a prospective buyer to collect. I was trying to move it when Lloyd arrived home, so he sneaked up on me from behind and shoved me down on it and *things* happened. He returned to the airport and it was the next evening that I had the works party, but I had totally forgotten about the cheeky moment on the sofa, so there's a 50/50 chance it could be Lloyd's baby."

"OMG!" I was very confused. "Did you not always think there was a glimmer of hope there anyway?"

"Although I joked about not knowing who the father was, deep down I thought that we hadn't had sex in ages as Lloyd's always away, which is why I panicked, but now I'm not so sure." Sally told me that she may have been able to avoid all the upset with her boss and his wife, but then admitted that she couldn't live with herself if she hadn't. "Lloyd knew there was no way that I could ever abort this baby as, either way, it's still my baby. He knows how desperate I've been and realises he shouldn't have asked this of me and he wants to be with me, regardless."

"So, will you do a paternity test?" I asked.

"Yes, of course, but not until after the baby is born."

"But you could have a test done now while you're still pregnant," I suggested.

Sally paused for a moment, staring at me. "I know," she whispered.

"So… why wait?" I asked gently.

Sally put her head in her hands. "I'm too scared! Say it's not his and it changes things again. I'm not sure my emotions could go through us falling out again and I'm worried that the stress of waiting will harm the baby." Sally clearly wasn't sure what to do. "Plus, I haven't told Lloyd that such a test exists. I've led him to believe that you have to wait and take bloods from the baby!"

"Sally! You little liar!" I joked. We both sat in silence for a bit. "Maybe there's a way you can do the test without him knowing, then you have the power of the answers and can prepare yourself and plan forward."

"How am I going to do that?" Sally asked.

I confessed that when I was first pregnant and doubted who the father was I did quite a bit of research on how I would find out. The mother has a simple blood test as the baby's DNA is found in her blood and all she would need from Lloyd is a mouth swab.

"Oh yeah, simple? What's simple about getting a mouth swab from someone without their knowledge?" She asked.

"Do it with your tongue!" I replied.

We both giggled.

"Coffee cup, beer glass, beer can? Or, tell him he has something in his teeth but accidentally on purpose scratch his gum then the skin will be under your fingernails!" I suggested.

We both flinched at the thought. Sally said she would think about it and keep me posted.

"I'd better jump in the shower!" I said, leaping from the bed.

"I would, can smell you from here!" Offered Sally.

Wrapped in towels and turban, I almost tripped on the landing where Sally's bags were packed.

"Sal?" I demanded, "What's this?"

"I'm just getting my things ready for later as Lloyd is picking me up and I wanted to be out of your way so you can relax."

She was smiling, so it must have been good news if Lloyd was collecting her. All the same, I was shocked she was leaving so early. Freddie endearingly closed my surprised mouth with his chubby little fingers.

"You don't have to leave now though, surely there's no rush?" I panicked in case she felt she had to leave because I'd returned. "Please stay a little longer, pleassee!" I begged.

"I'm not going just yet and anyway, it's all good.

Seriously, I'd planned it this way so had already packed."

"And… this little thing?" I asked, rubbing her extended stomach area. "Promise me you'll think about what we've just discussed?"

Sally held my hand over hers whilst enveloping her bump. "Yes, I will think about it. Come on, I've time for another cuppa before Lloyd turns up."

She updated me on the recent events with the girls and what had been happening with Jessica and Tom, before moving on to Sam. She'd met this gorgeous doctor only to find out that after weeks of dating and *getting close* he was only one of the porters! Poor Sam! I could imagine how mad she was.

"To be fair, he is studying to be a doctor and works as a porter for extra cash, so he's not completely fibbing!"

I brought her up to date on what had been happening with me.

"We've all missed you and are so glad you're back. And what about Rob? Seems like things are moving quickly, he sounds pretty amazing." *Is there a but coming?* "I don't want to be the one to burst your bubble, but there's just one more thing I need to bring up," Sally said hesitantly.

"What are you going on about?" I asked, but she didn't have to say anything as she presented a handful of letters from behind her back.

"These came for you!" She said. "Only a few days ago so I thought I may as well leave it until you got home." Noticing the blood drain from my cheeks, she kept hold of the envelopes as I tried to take them, knowing full well who they could be from. "Lillian!" Her voice was reassuring. "This doesn't change anything. You're with Rob now. Just take a breath, you don't have to read them!"

I was shaking as she released the letters from her warm, hands. I examined every letter, date and stamp and felt sick to the bone, fearing my life would be turned upside down once again.

"They're from James," I whispered.

****

James

I've been sat in the same spot, on the same damp bench, same dreary park for the last five hours. My tears have dried, there's no fluid left in the system. I want to continue but nothing seems to be happening, trapped in my own phenomenon. The clothes on my back now hang loose. I have my passport, a ticket home and £25 cash. That's it, this is all I'm worth. I didn't even know where I was until I asked a passer-by who appeared threatened by this tramp of a man who may beg for money. I'm that tramp. I slept on this bench. I'm out of jail. I'm free.

This has to have been the worst point in my life. Lost time, time I needed. Months of not sleeping, not speaking, away from familiarity, filthy clothes, disgusting leftover food. Just not being your normal human self. I'm a survivor of jail, a foreign jail, a not-so-nice foreign jail. I've established I'm on the border of Gerona and Barcelona!

But, where am I? I still don't know.

I have the things that I had when I was first arrested: bag, wallet, credit cards, key to my folks' house, but this doesn't register for a while in this zombie state. My release was a stressful blunder of events. The guards told me I was to be released, then they said they'd made a mistake, then another guard said a similar thing, then he too changed his mind. The next thing I knew I was being bundled into a van, driven at slow speed to another 'place' – god knows where. I was taken from the van and led into a darkish room with two further guards. One spoke broken English, which I just about understood. They threw a white bag at me which contained my items, and demanded I got changed there and then. Which I did. Nothing else was said. Back in the van again, I was dropped here, this park. I don't even know what it's called but it's been my home since I was dumped here. I can feel the hunger pains attack my stomach and I desperately need a drink. I can feel the heat from the morning sun increase. Without thinking, I get up and start walking, I don't know where, I just walk. I stop at the first sign of accommodation I can find and check myself in using my credit card. Luckily, I don't need to pay until departure as my mind is clear of all pin numbers and necessary information. Hopefully they will return. There is a hotel shop selling souvenirs, so I buy a T-shirt, sweatshirt and shorts, again putting these on the tab as I search my brain for the pin number to my card. I have 48 hours to leave the country otherwise my ticket will expire and they'll re-arrest me. I don't really know who 'they' are. I need to *shower, I need to eat, I need to sleep.*

I wake with a thin towel still around my waist, hair damp, but the strong aroma of soap indicates I'm clean. Just to be sure, I jump into the shower once again, scrubbing any remaining smells reminiscent of my cell. I call for room service: burger, chips, salad, ice cream, English breakfast tea. Feeling full, I turn on the TV and update myself on recent events and try and adapt to normal living again. How do people do this when they have spent a lifetime in jail?

Twelve hours later, I'm on a plane to Gatwick. It was the first UK flight, so I just took it. Anything to get away from this country. I won't return.

On UK soil, I reversed charges to my dad. Mum answered and broke down on hearing my voice. I didn't have the heart to tell her where I'd been. She passed the phone to Dad.
"Where are you?" He demanded.
"Arrivals, Gatwick Airport!" I replied. "Terminal 2."
"I'm on my way!"

THIRTY-TWO

Sitting stunned on the sofa, I stared at the crumpled envelopes for quite some time before opening them. I was far too afraid of what I may be presented with, afraid of the truth unfolding. Could I have been wrong about James, would he really abandon me? How selfish had I been burying any ordeal he may have faced, brushing aside a possible agonising experience under the carpet. I dug deep into the buried compartment at the back of my brain that had put this chapter on ice and now it was melting all over my frontal lobe. I had no idea what would be in those letters.

On the flip side of the coin, I felt my strength surround me and reminded myself that James and I weren't together, we had been split for ages, he had moved on with the luscious Jenny Ward. I wasn't even in the equation when he disappeared to Spain or wherever it was. Nope, I should not feel guilty. I didn't need permission to move on with my life.

Freddie weaved in and out of my space, the perfect reminder that this was his father after all. I poured myself a small sherry, sat down and began peeling away at the seals.

Twenty minutes later I was holding a picture of a love heart bearing the names James and Lillian. Inside a small heart were the words 'I love you'. I then read the text on a not-so-clean lined piece of paper and, as my brain absorbed the words, it dawned on me that he still thought he was the father to two babies! He still thought Jenny had his baby. He was going on about supporting the both of us in the correct way, but of course it was me he loved and somehow, he would get home to prove it. It was me he loved all along, he wanted to be with me but hadn't realised just how much until he saw me on that fateful night, and Jenny punched him in the face. I smiled as I recalled the moment.

The third letter I opened was another love heart with the words:

'WILL YOU MARRY ME?'

As the words sank in, I couldn't believe what I was seeing. He was asking me to marry him? Why would he do that? Is this what he really wanted? Freddie was pulling on my top, but I hadn't noticed, too distracted by the compartment I wished I'd kept closed in my brain.

"Mama... Mama..!"

There was a banging on the door.

"OK, honey, let's go and see who it is, shall we?" I opened the door to the biggest bunch of flowers I had ever seen. Red roses, pink roses, white roses and some other colour I hadn't known existed, all in the most luxurious glass vase. I took them, exchanging smiles with the driver as I signed my name, Lillian White. For a split second, I heard my inner voice call 'Lillian

Dickenson' in my head, just to feel how it sounded. Searching for evidence of the sender, my blood froze. Was this a dream or could this be a nightmare?

'Miss you so much, Lillian White. MARRY ME! I love you,
Rob xx.'

My legs turned to jelly and I collapsed in the chair, swiftly followed by a giggling Freddie, who for some reason thought that my turmoiled life was funny. It wasn't funny. It seriously wasn't funny. I wished that the compartment in my brain labelled 'James Dickenson' had been opened sooner and that I wasn't so god damn good in bed to make Rob Lomax want to marry me. Did I really just get two marriage proposals in one day, one morning, one hour? That's got to be a world record, surely? I poured another sherry. It's fine to drink Harveys Bristol Cream from a wine glass in the afternoon, don't sweat it. But I was sweating it. It was exciting getting two proposals from two great guys (ok, so one might have been in prison, but hey, you can't have everything, it's still a bloody good bona fide proposal). I pictured myself with them walking down the aisle – not together, naturally – but then that thought was in my head too. Which one would I choose? Would I end things with Rob and make a go of it with James? After all, he was Freddie's father (*I think, gulp!*). Or would I continue my beautiful relationship with Rob? I really did like him. He was amazing, only I wasn't expecting things to move so fast. But what was stopping me from moving so fast?

A fuzziness clouded my brain and the anxiety escalated. I'd been back five minutes, but that's all it took for me to completely fuck up my life. Sally wasn't long gone; I couldn't break down on her as she had her own shit to mop up. Jess would be busy planning her life with two-timing loser, Thomas. I called Sam, who answered instantly. This was the first time we'd spoken since my return from Florida, and her animated response was a welcoming sound.

"LILIIAN, LILLIAN, is that you? Oh darling, I've missed you. Are you really back?" She squealed, totally out of character for my strong, dry Sam.

"Yeah, I'm home and I've missed you too. Can I see you when you're free?" I asked.

"Well, now I know you're home, I'll cancel all my plans. Shall I come over later, pick up a takeaway? I've loads to tell you!"

Although I wasn't sure it would be the same load I was carrying.

Whilst waiting for Sam's arrival, I'd had several missed calls from Rob, eagerly awaiting my answer, and my heart-shaped proposal from James was stuck on the fridge. I couldn't ignore Rob much longer, so I asked myself if it wasn't for the letters from James, would I jump for joy and scream YES at the top of my voice? I thought I probably would, so I began thinking it could be a yes for Rob and a no for James. But then I thought if it wasn't for Rob, would I say yes to James, and I thought probably that could be a yes too. Back to square one. Oh shit, what a dilemma! How dare they put me in this situation! How selfish! I wondered how they'd feel if each one knew of the other's proposal. Should I tell them? Oh no, more secrets! My heart was pounding and a panic rose from within as the fear of indecisiveness took over. Downing the sherry, I refilled the glass.

By the time Sam arrived, I was half-cut and a bottle of sherry down. My mood had lifted slightly and I was halfway through a second family bar of milk chocolate and fumbling for some cups.

"Lillian, LILLIAN!" Sam shouted, heading for the kitchen, wondering where I'd got to. "I'll bloody make it. How much have you had to drink?" She laughed. "I think a strong coffee is in need, don't you?" Shoving me from her path as she worked my kitchen, she stopped upon noticing the fridge display. "Well, that needs to be taken down for a start! You've not heard from him in forever and now he's made prime position on your fridge?"

I brought her up to date on my recent news over the last couple of hours.

"Lillian, of course you should marry Rob. You've not stopped talking about him since you met him. All your messages involved Rob. Yes, it's moved quick, but so what? He sounds wonderful and wants to get to know Freddie more. You were never right with James, not at the end anyway, so you must ask yourself if you never got pregnant, would you still marry him?" She summed up.

This was a good point, as probably not.

"I appreciate you've only known Rob a short time… a very short time!" She didn't have to remind me! "But there isn't a rule book on this type of thing, so just go for it, full steam ahead. You deserve some happiness, don't you think?"

"I know, it's just thrown me seeing that!" I waved towards the display on the fridge.

"And, how do you think Rob would feel if he thought you were comparing the two of them before making a decision? Does he even know about James?"

Oh dear, she was giving me the lecture. She'd clearly matured whilst I'd been away.

"Fine, fine, you're right!" I replied, sipping my incredibly hot, strong coffee.

We sat staring at the flowers, which were just beautiful.

"Lovely flowers!" Sam said.

"Yes, stunning!" I replied.

"Worth a yes in my book." She smiled at me.

"Yes, mine too!"

"Sooooo, does that mean you are going to say yes? Mrs Lillian Lomax? Lillian White-Lomax? I bet you've sounded out Mrs Lillian Dickenson, haven't you? You have!" She laughed. "It's ok, I would too, but to be honest, none of them sound great, do they?"

"Oh, cheers!" I giggled. She had a point. Maybe I would just stay as Lillian White.

After copious amounts of coffee and as Freddie was settled for the night, Sam decided it was time for wine! Still squiffy from the sherry, debating if this was a good mix, I tipped the remnants from my wine glass, holding it high to be filled. What the hell! Sam and I sipped our way through the chilled crispy white, catching up on months of gossip. Bringing me up to date on her dating saga, I could tell she was smitten as her face glowed with the sheer mention of the new man in her life. Porter or doctor, it clearly didn't matter, she was hooked. I'd missed this!

Hearing my phone for the umpteenth time, I didn't answer. It was Rob, again. I would ring him back later, when Sam had gone, and give him my answer.

"You can't keep ignoring him forever. Put the poor bugger out of his misery!"

"Which one?" We broke into a tiddly fit of giggles again.

Eventually, Sam hauled herself up and said, "Right my friend, I have to go, my cab is here. I'll get my car in the morning, and I want to hear that you've said YES to the pilot." Her voice raised, "and NO to the jailbird, ok?"

I pursed my lips, "OK!"

This predicament had dampened my homecoming euphoria bubble. I was really cross at James for that, but I was also cross at Rob for not giving me chance to get my breath. Was he that needy? Give me strength! But then again, our time together had been fabulous and what was so wrong with a man showing his hand early?

It wasn't too late when Sam left and as her enthusiasm had snowballed, I took a deep breath and dialled

Rob's number, taking in the long slender ringing tone as the international lines connected.

"Hello Lillian, is that you?" Caller ID, international call, cell call or whatever it was displayed on his handset so he knew it was me. Upon hearing his voice, I felt a sudden urge to shout my answer from the rooftops, giving him the answer he deserved. Was it the wine?

"YES, YES, YES, I will marry you! Oh Rob, yes of course I will!" A rush of excitement emerged from within and both our voices raised in pitch as an explosion of delirium roamed the link. For those few seconds it felt absolutely right, and for once maybe my life was moving in the right direction. But just as we started to calm a bit, with adrenalin still pumping my veins, there was a knock at the door. Believing it was Sam, who'd probably forgotten her keys (or marbles) I slowly opened the door, my hand still clutching the receiver.

"Forgotten something...?" I asked breezily, thinking I was talking to Sam.

"Where have you gone? Hey sexy, are you still there?" Rob's voice echoed through the receiver, but it wasn't Sam at the door. It was James.

THIRTY-THREE

Frozen like a statue, shocked to the core, I stared at the man in front of me. Time stood still.

"Helloooo? Where have you gone? Are you still there?" Rob asked innocently into the open line as James mouthed 'Hi' at the door with a nervous wave of his hand. He entered slowly, walking straight past me as I stumbled over my words to Rob.

"Sorry Rob, it's Sam messing around. She's forgotten something," I lied. "I'll call you straight back," I said, then hung up.

James looked at me, shaking his head. "Sam?" He asked. "Why lie?"

"It's a long story!" I replied, "But JAMES you're HERE!" I practically shouted in a mix of emotions.

"Yes, I'm here!" He replied, tense, uneasy, not sure what he'd just walked into.

We stood staring, each trying to read the other, fumbling for the right words.

"Where have you been, what...?"

He interrupted gently, "I know we have a lot to talk about, Lillian, maybe a drink first?"

I couldn't face any more alcohol, although I'd sobered rather rapidly.

"Do you mind?" James continued easing past me into the kitchen as my brain failed to register what this would entail. Shaking, I pulled myself together then followed him. He was leaning against the work surface, already holding the card from the flowers in one hand and his note from the fridge in the other. I died right there on the spot! Mortified, embarrassed, ashamed. However, *JAMES* was standing in my kitchen! After all that had happened – jail, weird missed calls, months of silence – he was stood in front of me looking DROP DEAD GORGEOUS and all I wanted to do was lick his face!

"My, my, Lillian, you have been busy! Two proposals?" His eyebrows raised. "Who's the other lucky boy then? Sam? Rob?" He asked, attempting to add humour, but I could see he was hurting. "You have two proposals and feel it necessary to flaunt them for all to see? Well that's just fantastic, Lillian, thank you. You sure know how to make a man feel great and also very stupid."

"James, OMG James, I didn't know you were coming, I've only just read your letters!"

"What do you mean? They were sent ages ago!"

"I've not been here, James, I've been out of the country. I've only just seen them!" My voice broke, full of emotion.

"Been in jail too, have we? What for? Bigamy?" He was angry, I could tell, disheartened, disappointed... as was I – neither of us expected our first meeting to be like this.

I softened. "James! Can we start over? I've literally only just come back from Florida on business, so yes,

I've just read your letters and yes, it does look bad having two proposals on display for all to see, but it's not supposed to look like that!"

"Oh well, that's ok then. So you've been swanning around Florida, have you, found yourself a new daddy for my child, have you? Where is he or she that some other bugger is raising?"

I no longer wanted to lick him, but I could rather smack him right now. This was not the James I knew.

"James, it's not like that. I haven't heard from you since forever. I had no idea where you were, which prison. What did you expect me to do?" I asked.

"I don't know, Lillian, but I didn't expect you to run off with the first man you meet, leaving me to rot in jail!" He shouted.

"We weren't even together, James, so you getting arrested was none of my business!" It was all coming out wrong. "Last time I saw you I do believe you were with someone else yourself!"

He fell quiet, couldn't really argue that card.

I dropped down an octave, "You got arrested! I thought you'd given all that up!"

James backed down, manoeuvring himself around the kitchen for cups, coffee and milk, knowing quite well that he couldn't challenge the prison card – or the Jenny Ward one for that matter!

"Yes! I'm quite aware of the situation and feel bloody awful. I disappear, land myself in jail, leaving two women up the duff! Doesn't sound good, does it?" He continued, "Lillian, I had no idea that Jenny was expecting a baby. It's all fucked up!" James slammed the spoon down on the side.

It dawned on me that James still thought he'd fathered two children. "James, there's something I need to tell..." I attempted to tell him the truth, but he wouldn't let me speak.

"No, Lillian, it's fine," he sighed, running his hand through his dishevelled hair. "I've had time to think and come to terms with it, a lot of time actually, to try and plan my way forward so I can be a good father to both of my children..."

"But James, I..." He interrupted again, so I raised my voice. "James! Listen! You are not father to two children!" I screamed.

Silence.

"What?" He whispered. "Oh, so you're telling me that your child is not my child. God, I still don't know what sex it is!"

"His name is Freddie. It's a boy, James, you have a son!" I blurted, seeing the tears in his eyes. He covered his face with his hands. I peeled away those hands – rough, manly, hard-working hands. "Look at me. Look at me, James. It's fine. You have a beautiful son. He's gorgeous, look!" I placed a photo of Freddie in his hands. "He's asleep, but you can see him. He's yours, James, a son."

His fingers outlined the image in the frame, his eyes fixed. "He's perfect Lillian, just perfect."

"Come on, come and see him!" I offered, but he hesitated, smiling at his son grinning back at him.

"Not yet, it wouldn't be fair to wake the little fellow and..." He paused. "I'm a little nervous. What's it like...

being a parent? Even saying it out loud seems… surreal!"

As he absorbed the image of our grinning child, I thought it right to apprise him about Freddie: the way he held his bottle, how he slept, his hair, smell, how he communicated, everything, cramming it all in, careful not to omit something vital. James fell silent. It must be hard to take in, knowing he'd missed out on those all-important first months.

"Sorry, Lillian, I have to ask, what about Jenny?"

I explained that Jenny's child had a different father and that she was happy and back with him. James broke down again. He was glad she was happy, but hearing the news that the baby wasn't his was still upsetting as he'd planned futures in his head, prepared himself mentally for it now to be snatched away. I explained how I knew that Jenny had given birth and told him the story of how I bumped into her whilst shopping and her waters broke, then mine and the rest was history.

"No way!" He cried. "Oh Lillian, I'm so sorry!" He covered his face again, but this time he was crying with laughter, uncontrollable laughter.

"It's not bloody funny! Well, I suppose it is now, looking back, but it wasn't at the time." I slapped his arm, but as I did, he grabbed it and held it, then grabbed the other and pulled me into his grasp, hugging me and smelling me. I didn't know quite what to do. I hadn't had a chance to take him in, to look at him properly. I hadn't seen him for an eternity or studied the scars of prison life. It wasn't long before I noticed, for as he held me close, kissing my head, I felt his strong, manly guns embrace me, which wasn't the only muscle that had grown. Was it wrong that I wanted to grab it?

"Ooooops, sorry, wasn't planning for that to happen!" He smiled, turning to readjust his groin area, then offered me a now probably lukewarm coffee.

"Shall we?" He asked, leading me back into the lounge. I followed like a lap dog, absorbing his smell, his clothes, his hair, his stature, everything. Sitting down next to him, I still couldn't believe James was here. James, who I'd worried and fretted over for such a long time. He looked well, fit, very fit, bigger, stronger, lean, defined. Fit! Did I say that already? We were engrossed in conversation, catching up on all things, Freddie, the girls and Florida, when my mobile rang again.

"Hadn't you better get that?" James asked. "Someone clearly wants to speak with you... urgently!"

The phone rang out as I tried to hide my crimson cheeks.

"Hang on a minute, it's flower guy, isn't it? Is he calling for an answer? Those flowers seem very fresh to me, Lillian, so come on, be honest, is he ringing for an answer?" I sank further and further into the chenille cushions, but even gravity couldn't save me from this. "Or... have you given him an answer? You have, haven't you? You've said yes!"

We were getting on so well, how could I admit that yes, it was true? Did I regret my reply to Rob? OMG, Rob! How would he feel if he was here? Tears appeared as I slowly whispered, "Yes!"

"Yes? Lillian, have you said yes?" James asked.

"Lillian, be honest with me, look at me!" He demanded, peeling away my fingers from my face with his strong hands. "Had you just said yes when I walked in?"

This wasn't going well for me and I couldn't worm my way out. I owed him the truth. "Yes," I whispered again. "But that's before I knew…"

It was too late. James was already on his feet, looking tall and lean. Strong, handsome, in control, and sexy.

"Before you knew what? That I existed? That I may want to see my child?" His voice was raised. "That I'd asked you to marry me? Which proposal came first, Lillian, mine or…" He was still holding the card from the flowers. "…Rob's?" He shouted.

"James, keep your voice down," I whispered looking towards the ceiling, "you'll wake Freddie," I continued. "It wasn't like that; they both came at the same time!" I exclaimed.

"But you had already made your mind up that you were going to marry Rob?" His voice was softer, desperate. "Lillian, you must have read my letters, you must have known how I felt." He placed his half-empty cold coffee cup on the mantelpiece, taking in each picture of Freddie in the process.

"He looks like you," I offered. "Don't you want to see him?"

James looked at me then back at the picture. He didn't reply and silence filled the room, I could feel the atmosphere changing.

"He does a little, but just to be sure I will need a DNA test, Lillian. This hasn't quite gone the way I'd planned it. I seem to have gone from being the father to two babies, then possibly the father and husband to a family, to having no involvement at all in anything that has kept me going whilst being stuck inside the darkest, most depressing place on earth. So, whilst you were strutting your stuff around Florida with…. Rob…" He thrust the flower card in front of my face. "I was planning our future, Lillian, our future with our son, so forgive me if this sounds a little harsh, but yes, I need clarification that he is actually mine before I have any more involvement with you." He headed for the door. "And you can sort this out, Lillian, YOU. I'll provide whatever you need, hair strand, spit, blood, whatever it takes, but I'm not going forward with anything until I know for sure that Freddie is my son!" Tears filled his eyes, tears of anger.

"James, wait, WAIT!" I shouted after him, despairing, "don't leave like this!"

"I think I've heard enough for one night. Go on, ring your precious Rob back. I'm sure he'll be ecstatic." He was already out of the door, slipping through my fingers.

"Wait! James, how do I contact you? I need your number!" I pleaded, tears flowing.

"It's under J for James on your mobile, Lillian. It's not rocket science!" And with those words, he left, disappeared again, leaving me with my mobile and a hundred missed calls from Rob.

My sleep was almost non-existent. I tossed and turned, distraught, fear rising in a froth of bile hovering at the top of my throat, ready to attack. I didn't speak to Rob again after James had left. How could I? The excitement and elation we'd both experienced had gone, and although I searched deep into my inner soul, it wasn't ready to surface. I couldn't believe what had happened. Why did these things keep happening to me? Was I cursed? Did I do something in my past life that was so terrible, so unforgivable? Would it always be like that? Was it even worth me trying to put things right? Where would I start? Who would I start with? But my anguish turned to anger. How dare he treat me this way. I was the victim here, not him. I went through pregnancy, birth and raising Freddie *alone*. He couldn't just waltz in, claiming to be the casualty. Playing the evening over and over again in my head tormented me and I couldn't settle my brain. I got up, ran downstairs and returned with my old friend, Harvey. If all else fails, Harveys Bristol Cream does the trick!

THIRTY-FOUR

One thing I never thought I would be doing was sitting in the waiting area of a private path lab with Sally, both waiting to receive DNA results of our (unborn and born) children. After the crazy events of the past months, especially my little episode with James, Sally suggested maybe we went together and try for a 'buy one get one free' test. So here we were, together, awaiting our dreaded fate. We were the only ones in the unwelcoming waiting room with uncomfortable chairs and a few out-of-date magazines laying limp on the 1970's coffee table next to our individual envelopes, waiting to be opened.

It had been weeks since my surprise visit from James and my excited acceptance of Rob's proposal. For a few days after, my memory was hazy, having to convince myself that those events had really happened. After a while, I accepted that a DNA test would be a good thing. I knew James was the father and, although only an innocent fumble with another, it couldn't hurt to be certain and have the truth there in black and white. Of course, I had to tell a few white lies to Rob as to why I hadn't taken his calls, but I needed time to digest. I didn't blame James for leaving the way he did, and of course he deserved the truth. I accepted all responsibility for parading my wedding proposals in such a way, but also harboured some anger at his self-righteousness, as though he was blameless in it all. I hadn't stopped thinking about that dreadful night and how our first meeting went frightfully wrong. He knew me so well. I couldn't hide the fact that I'd just accepted Rob's hand in marriage, but what I could do was keep the whole evening away from Rob. No point creating unnecessary angst for no reason. I'd told Rob I would marry him and that's what I planned to do. The girls were right, if Freddie hadn't been around, I wouldn't have thought twice about James. We would both have moved on with no ties. I was content with Rob before I'd heard from James. I would have thought about him occasionally, but generally I had moved on and was ready for more stability, to settle, to commit. But, out of respect for James, (and Freddie), I was humiliating myself in a path lab searching for a DNA match.

Sally and I counted to three before opening both our envelopes. Within seconds, Sally burst into tears as soon as she saw the '99.9% related to Lloyd'. I burst into tears for another reason, as mine said '99.9% unrelated to…'

"OMG, Sally, James isn't the father! How can that be?" I exclaimed.

"What do you mean?" She gasped. "So, who's the daddy then?"

"I have no bloody idea! I simply have no idea who it could be! Oh god, Sally, what am I going to do? Poor

James! What is he going to think?"

"Never mind James! What about Freddie? He's going to grow up not knowing who his father is. Lillian, that's far worse!" She was holding my arm as she softly pointed out this obvious fact.

"This can't be right, Sal, it just can't be. I may have joked around saying that I hoped he was the father because I'd fooled around with a few others when we broke up, but it didn't get that far, and I think I would know who the god damn father of my own child is! I'm not that much of a hussy!"

"Give it here, let me see!" Sally grabbed the letter from my trembling fingers and scoured the text, looking for errors. Thank god for her patient, accurate mind, because she found some.

"Lillian, look! It's not even addressed to you! There's James' details, which look right, but that isn't you and if that's Freddie's date of birth then he's not even born yet, so James wouldn't be the father!"

"Oh shit, they send a copy to James!" I cried.

"Not if you stop it now. Go on, get someone's attention!"

So that's exactly what I did. Luckily, it was a terrible error on their behalf and I was refunded my £256.

It took a further agonising ten days for the results to arrive, but at least the truth was there for all to see, '99.9% related to' printed in black and white. To think Freddie may never have known his father had been eating away at me. I pictured him bullied at school and visioning the years of searching that would lay ahead of him. James had to be involved so that Freddie had an equally close relationship with his dad as he would with me. It was quite the wake-up call.

James rang me the minute he received his letter and, although a little distant, he was most appreciative of my agreement to do it. Sally's wonderful news would put her and Lloyd's world back in sync, but I wasn't quite sure what the future held for me. James was keen to put something in place so he could officially become Freddie's father. And I would have to confide to Rob that James had returned and was now playing an active role in Freddie's life. I wasn't looking forward to that part and all these changes were confusing my world. Emotions ran high and I was battling with my affections for James. "So, you're still going ahead and marrying Rob?" Asked Jess as she helped take the feast of crisps, crackers and peanuts into the lounge. We were having a small DNA party to help celebrate Sally's good news, and of course mine!

"What was that?" Said Sally. "I thought you *were* definitely marrying Rob?"

"What? Are you not getting married now? Poor Rob!" Piped up Lou.

"Poor James, more like!" Said Sam.

"Stop!" I shouted. "I didn't say I wasn't going to marry Rob!"

"But...?" prompted Sam.

"There's no 'but'..." I let them relax for a second. "...however, although I do want to marry Rob, I do feel a bit *weird* about James! Oh god, I'm never going to heaven!" I slumped into the cushions, hiding my face while confessing my struggle with it all. "If it wasn't for those stupid letters, I wouldn't have thought about James!" I cried. "And it doesn't help that he's amazing, gorgeous, and sexy!"

"Sorry, that's my fault. I should have hidden them!" Apologised Sally.

"And you…" I pointed at Sam. "…you pointed out that if it wasn't for James turning up, I would have said yes to Rob, making it sound romantic and wonderful. I just got carried away so as soon as you'd gone, I picked up the phone, excitement took hold and I screamed 'Yes, I'll marry you' down the phone!"

All the girls looked at Sam as if it was her fault.

"Sorry for making it sound so good and making you ring Rob to say yes you'd marry him!" Said Sam sarcastically.

"And…" added Sally, "…sorry I'm all smug now that I know that Lloyd is the father to my unborn baby." She leant over, offering an endearing squeeze. "Lillian, nothing has changed for you, not really. The good news is that at least you know that James is the father and he can be involved with Freddie and you've got a great chap in Rob, who incidentally wants to marry you!"

"So why can't I stop thinking about James?" I made a dramatic gesture of throwing my arm to my brow. "He's got the most amazing guns, they're huge. He held me close and got a hard on!"

"You didn't tell me that!" Exclaimed Sally, pushing me away.

"Ssshhhh, let her carry on!" Interjected Sam. "Tell us everything!"

"There's nothing more to tell, it's just a mess. I've said yes to Rob but I could have quite easily said yes to James!"

"Yes, we know you got two proposals, yes, very good, very clever, but look where it's got you!" Said Jess.

"So, help me then. What shall I do?" I begged. "What would you do?"

"Awww, it's just like old times! We're all back together again with a problem to sort!" Said Sam as she sneaked off to get the sherry from the kitchen.

"Marry Rob," offered Jess. "It's a no-brainer!"

"Yep, marry Rob for definite!" Added Sally.

"Wait for me, wait for me…!" Sam was shouting from the kitchen. "After a few of these, you won't care who you marry! Cheers, girls, here's to DNA!"

"To DNA!" We all cheered.

Rob was arriving in nine days. He planned on moving in with me until we were married. I hadn't thought that far ahead, I had only pictured me *getting* married: dress, ring and church. I'd gone from holiday/ work fling to fiancé, having an ex in jail so far away that I didn't have to worry about, to him collecting Freddie at weekends and sharing the responsibility; from living alone and having the girls on tap to living as a couple, a real couple, all in the space of what seemed like five minutes.

A feeling of nausea enveloped me as I sat pondering my situation, so I reached for my Rescue Remedy before a full-blown panic attack took over. Rob had been so sweet and understanding. I told him all about James and Freddie and he took it all in his stride. They would meet eventually, that was inevitable, but I wasn't sure I wanted that to happen. It was all too soon for James, and for Freddie, and most definitely for me. Freddie had gone from it being just the two of us, to three family members and then to four. I couldn't keep up myself! I'd lost count how many times I'd plagued the girls for reassurance so to raise my spirits, they'd planned a wedding dress shopping trip. That helped lift my mood.

THIRTY-FIVE

The dust settled, even mine. Sally and Lloyd were happier than ever and moving in the right direction. They'd rebooked their wedding, decorated the baby's room and planned a romantic trip away to reconnect before their family grew. Jess was wearing her engagement ring again and living with Thomas, and Sam was dating the doctor/porter chap. Rob had moved in, which wasn't as bad as I'd initially thought as our jobs kept us busy, especially Rob, who was hardly ever home. Not that I'm saying that's a good thing for a relationship, but it certainly helped for a gradual merger. I was secretly pleased as there's only so much trapped wind a girl can suffer. I hadn't been with him long enough to fart and my stomach was aching from holding in those morning smellies. To top it all, it was costing me a fortune in Gaviscon! (hmmm... not been with him long enough to fart but long enough to get married!)

We had set a date for the wedding, which was almost upon us. When we discussed a date, it just slipped out, 'the sooner the better!' I wasn't ecstatic, but content. I had to move on. I'd spent forever waiting for James, waiting to hear from him, waiting to see if we had a future together, and it was exhausting. I couldn't do any more waiting, and although Mum wasn't too pleased as she thought it too soon, we had arranged to tie the knot in two months' time. Hey, what girl doesn't want a wedding?

It did, however, mean there was a lot to pack in that time as, not only was I the Bride-to-be, I was also *The Wedding Planner*. I secretly loved that part, with my organised binders and colour co-ordinated labels, although it felt like I was planning someone else's special day. I still had my doubts and was frequently faced with the uncertainty of my place in this love triangle. It was becoming increasingly difficult to be in the same room as James, which was especially problematic as he was spending more and more time with Freddie. There was a routine in place that, although weird at first, soon became the norm.

After those short few minutes in the DNA lab of thinking that Freddie didn't have a father, it certainly brought home the enormity of what that could have signified, so to have James there was a godsend. But the chemistry still existed between us, I could feel it. He looked *different* somehow. Trendy, confident, leaner, happier? Was *not* being with me making him happy? He'd changed his look and his clothes – had he always been that hot? Every time our eyes met, I'd lose my balance. Just being in the same room brought goose-bumps to the surface, confusing me. I was marrying Rob, but was it James I should be standing next to?

Fortunately, I had the girls to keep me on track.

"Don't be fooled by clothes and cologne. Remember those cowboy boots and Levis. He's just trying to impress you. I bet the minute he's home he's straight back in his ranch clothes!" Sam sniggered.

"But he is Freddie's father!" I would point out. "Who *did* ask me to marry him!"

"Yes, yes, he did, but when you're away from home, trapped in a prison, getting shagged by smelly inmates, of course you're going to wish for a wedding with the last girl you left at home. Anyway, how do you know he wasn't writing to the gorgeous Jenny Ward?" Sam's eyebrows raised in jest.

"Fine, fine, I'll marry Rob then!"

"Good girl!"

But of course, you can't have a wedding without a hen party, so a girly weekend was just the medicine to blow any doubts away. Sexy, sassy and sophistication were probably words left in the dictionary as veils, vermouth and vomiting would better describe the experience. Old friends, new friends, work friends, we danced all night and drank until dawn with castle and dungeon excursions thrown in for good measure. I pitied the allocated tour guide with his historic enthusiasm displayed through gritted teeth. I doubt Edinburgh would welcome our return.

Although our heads were throbbing, there was just one obstacle to endure before heading home as Sam delivered, enthusiastically, news of one final surprise.

"High ropes?" I questioned, not quite sure what this meant.

"High and ropes in the same sentence? I'm out!" Screamed Jess, looking horrified as we were greeted by the thrill-seeking sound of the zip wire in Queen Elizabeth Forest Park. The last thing we needed was to swing from the trees, but as Sam had gone to all this trouble, we agreed to take part…. well most of us!

"I can't do it; I really don't think I can do it!" Jess shrieked as the warden clipped her harness into place.

We were each kitted out in a Bear Grylls ensemble. Heading for the steps on the very first tree, we ignored Jess' protests and began to climb, placing Jess in the middle to encourage from one end and shove from the other. It was all going well until we were faced with some metal-barrelled tunnels.

"No way, I'm not going through them!" She squealed. "No, no, no, not doing it!" Clinging on for sheer life, Jess foolishly looked down.

"Don't look down!" Sam demanded, "you'll feel worse… too easy to think about falling and plunging to your death!" Although pleased with herself, her words weren't received well.

"Sam!" I cried. "Be quiet!"

But it was too late. Jess clung to a tree and wouldn't let go. No one could pass, so a queue soon formed with every other participant trying to coax her, but unfortunately it didn't work. Kids were staring and asking their daddies if *that* lady was ok. I really didn't know if she was.

Eventually, help arrived, lowering Jess to the ground, followed by me and a very apologetic Sam.

"What?" She asked. "I was only joking!"

So that was the hen party!

THIRTY-SIX

THE EVE OF THE WEDDING ...

The eve of my wedding was rather solemn: high tea in the parlour, drinks in the bar and an early night had by all. I'd wanted to involve Sally, who had missed the Hen party as she was uncomfortably pregnant. But it all worked fine as the girls were happy to save their stamina for a good knees up at the wedding. After the usual hugs and farewell wishes to my remaining hours as a singleton, I headed back to the bridal suite alone. James had offered to have Freddie during the ceremony and, although I took his wedding pleasantries in good faith, there was no hiding the spark between us.

With PJs on and chocolates in hand, I surfed the channels for an interesting watch, but nothing could soothe the building anxiety. Was I doing the right thing? Maybe we had hurtled just a tad! Messages from Rob – 'Can't wait to be married to you', 'sleep well, love you' – only fed my collywobbles. At least texts from the girls – 'You better turn up or I'll kill you!' (Sam), 'Knock 'em dead, girlfriend,' (Jess) and a long, sweet message from a heavily pregnant Sal made me smile. However, as movies failed to grip my troubled mind, I was bored senseless, regretting this so-called *quiet night*. After all, it was the night before my wedding!

Saved by the bell, I realised that my wedding shoes and bag were in Lou's room, so maybe there would be more going on there. Not wanting to be seen in my PJs (a fluffy koala bear onesie), nor could I be bothered with getting dressed, I slipped out of my room with key in hand, creeping slowly down the corridor to the lift.

But I was clearly in the way as she rehearsed her reading, so with shoes and bag now in my possession, I crept back to the lift, hoping no one would see me. Not expecting the elevator to have people in it, although that is what it's designed for, it was full of people who thought my attire highly amusing. Thankfully, they trundled off at the next floor.

However, as the door was closing, a very handsome, very blond, semi-smart, familiar male jumped into the lift. My brain searched for a connection. Surely, I'd remember those piercing blue eyes? Until, there it was: Jess and her electric blue Lycra in a heap on the floor; buying pregnancy tests at the chemist; crying for chocolate in the shop; him barefoot, carrying a surfboard. The cogs were turning, and I suddenly remembered that the last time I'd seen him I was a blubbering mess with a smelly, crying baby. I hoped he didn't remember. We exchanged eye contact, and his were lingering. He was gorgeous! Oh, why was I still in my PJs?

"Don't I know you?" Asked his sexy Aussie tones.

"I don't know, I think I recognise you from somewhere but not quite sure where!" I lied as the lift arrived on my level, although I didn't wish to leave. What should I do? "Bye then!" I said, looking back, trying not to appear desperate to engage more. What was wrong with me? This was the night before my wedding! I took the slowest steps, hoping he would continue our conversation.

"Yeah, bye," he shouted back, his voice faint behind the closing lift doors.

Disappointed, and still taking baby steps towards my room, I heard the lift doors open again.

"I do know you! Your friend, she fell? Blue shiny outfit and an ambulance came?" He questioned.

I turned and pretended to think. Of course I knew! I looked down; he had no shoes on.

"You were barefoot?" I gestured towards his feet. Would it be so wrong if I crouched down and sucked his toes? *Stop, Lillian, you're getting married in the morning, well, afternoon!* "and... were you carrying a door?" I added, although I obviously knew it was a surfboard!

"Surfboard!" He corrected

"Oh yeah, I remember. Yes, my friend, she fainted!"

"Did she recover ok?" He asked, clearly wanting to drag out this brief meeting, which suited me fine, as so did I.

"Yes, yes, she's all good now, thank you!"

I was treading on dangerous ground, so dangerous. *Maybe you should just walk away now, Lillian, step away from the sexy man.* But I couldn't. He was so cute and my room was so boring. *Oh dear god, help me, help me!*

I carried on walking until his distinctive Aussie

twang reached out, "There's a party going on, er room 401 if you're interested? Come as you are, no-one will care. A few friends are over from Australia, so it's cool, chilled, they'll love your outfit!" He nodded to my koala onesie.

Was he waiting for an answer? Could I go? I wanted to go. *Stop it, Lillian, STOP IT – WALK AWAY FROM THE SEXY MAN!* I'd been silent too long, he thought I wasn't interested.

"I'll leave it with you, see you later." The doors closed.

Noooooooooo! I stood frozen to the spot, my mental cogs spinning until they opened once again.

"I really would like you to come, as my guest?" He stood, waiting for a response. "Come on… it's fate, what with my being Aussie and all, and your stunning pyjamas!"

I bit my lip, thinking, *I shouldn't go, no, nope I'm not going it wouldn't be right….*

"Yes" I replied, maybe a little too eager. "Thank you! I've got a long day tomorrow, so a party might not be a good idea… but…"

"Me too, got some suave function to go to myself," he interrupted, "a distant relative somewhere down the line, some British chap I've only met a few times, but I don't want to bore you with that." He paused for a moment. "So…?" He coaxed.

"Maybe just one drink?" I hesitated.

"That'll do for me!" He saluted, then winked just as the elevator closed. "Room 401!" His voice already distant.

Of course, I was only flirting. And of course, I wasn't going to go and have a sneaky drink with a sexy Aussie the night before my wedding. I mean, how awful would that be? What sort of girl do you think I am? However, back in my room, as much as I tried to lose myself in a chick-lit film and channel hopping until my thumbs were sore, my mind kept drifting to the sexy Aussie and room 401. I had just been invited to a party on the eve of my wedding. Don't they say the *Hen* is allowed to have that last fling? Not that I was thinking of *flinging,* even though he was so scrummy. My mind returned to that first meeting when he came to our rescue in bare feet carrying a surfboard. There had definitely been electricity between us, I had felt it, an attraction, the intensity of eye contact. I could still feel it. The party consumed my brain. Room 401. Was it 401? Or 411? I wondered how far away it was. It had to be at the other side of the hotel. Maybe I could still get there without having to pass reception. Maybe I could wander over and take a cheeky look, no one would see me. I'd just blend into the background with all the other people dressed in PJs! No, no, I couldn't go, that would be terrible.

It was no good, I just couldn't stop thinking about it. Maybe if I rang Sam, she would advise me what to do. No, she would talk me out of it, of course she would. I didn't want to be talked out of it. She could come with me? It was 9.40pm, she was probably getting her beauty sleep. I should be getting mine!

Twenty-five minutes later I was on the fourth floor. OMG, what was I thinking? I was in my PJs, but I was on Floor 4 looking for 401. It wasn't far from the lift so I 'door hopped', hiding behind each plant in the hope of not being seen.

"Hey, you made it!" Came that familiar Aussie voice. "You can't get out of it, just admit you wanted to see me again!" He teased, messing with his blond curly locks.

I hadn't expected to get wobbly knees every time he spoke. It was the night before my wedding and I was in a hotel corridor with another bloke – not even James, which may have been forgiveable. I didn't even know this chap's name, but he was making me weak and I wasn't tired. I still wanted to go but as yet hadn't crossed the threshold to the party, so I was doing nothing wrong. Yikes! This was wrong on so many levels, but there again, I would be married tomorrow. This was my last chance to have some fun. It wasn't that Rob and I didn't have fun, just a different kind of fun, and I was in the mood to let my hair down. I had no Freddie, I didn't have to be up too early in the morning as the wedding was after lunch... or was it? My mind had gone blank; I couldn't even remember what time I was getting married! Oh dear!

We crossed the threshold of room 401.

"Here! Cheers!" Handing me a beer, his eyes lingered. What a way to start your marriage! I reassured myself I'd only have one then I'd head back to my room!

After my third beer I could feel the effects, aware I was leaning in closer.

"So, what are you doing at an Aussie party with a strange Aussie fella?" He asked. "What are you really doing here? At the hotel, I mean?"

"I'm going to a wedding," I answered. Well, it wasn't a total lie.

"A wedding? Wow, not yours I hope!" He giggled then hollered over to one of his friends to 'shout him another beer and a wine for the lady!'

I was about to decline, but as the wedding subject dropped with no further questions, I relaxed into the ambience and, despite knowing on every level that this was so wrong, I eagerly took the wine. It soon went to my head as all I had eaten since four that afternoon was a handful of chocolates and a few bags of crisps. But wine wasn't the only drug I didn't refuse as I took a few puffs on a joint, turning my legs to dust as I flopped into a sitting position on the floor. I felt liberated, excited and in control; alive, giddy, and happy. Aussie heaved me up, plonking me down on his lap.

"Are you alright? I don't even know your name. What do I call you? Can I call you? He asked. Timing!

"Phew, I'm not used to smoking, or drinking at the same time!" I replied, trying not to think about the fact that I was sat on another man's knee and also trying to avoid giving out my name or number!

"Lillian, you can call me Lillian!" I offered foolishly, his knee still taking my weight.

"Ok, Lillian,' he replied with his magnetic smile, making it hard to pull away. The spliff concoction with wine and beer turned my forthcoming nuptials into a hazy whirl; I was in too deep. I was also in no fit state to return to my room; I didn't think I would even find it.

"So where is the wedding? It must be close by, seeing as though you are staying in this very swanky hotel?" Aussie viewed me curiously, waiting for an answer. "I'm Brad, by the way, very pleased to meet you, Ms Lillian!"

He took my hand, raising it to his lips, where he softly brushed them against the back of my hand, leaving those soft tiny hairs standing to attention. Our eyes met. I knew I should break away. This was my cue to go but I just couldn't. Would I get this moment back? We had something, a look, a connection, something that brought us together. There could only have been an inch between our lips, if that, as they moved closer and closer. Then it happened, they touched and I could feel the volcano erupting inside. Nothing was going to stop it. We were kissing, really kissing. It was amazing, electrifying, circuit breaking, wonderful, yet innocent. But it wasn't innocent, was it? I was engaged to someone else, but this still didn't make me pull away, although I could feel myself swaying.

"Everything ok, Lillian? Maybe you've had too much. Can I get you a coffee, water….?" Before he could finish, someone put two spirits in front of us – vodka and tonic. I took one, I bloody took one without even thinking of the consequences.

"Cheers!" We both said together, our eyes holding the gaze. I wanted him, there and then, to rip my onesie off. Who would know? OMG, did I really think that? That wasn't Lillian White talking, maybe it was the wine, maybe it was the joint. I had to get in his knickers, then I remembered I wasn't wearing any!

"Is there somewhere we can go?" I couldn't believe I asked the question.

He stood, holding my hand, and led me to his room a few doors down. We didn't speak; we stripped naked, got into his bed and then it happened. Earthquake. I didn't feel guilty. I wanted more. I checked my watch. 11:50pm. We were in the shower together when it happened again, another earthquake, but I wanted more and more. Something had snapped in me, maybe the box had been opened (literally!) but I suddenly felt alive. Brad opened the mini bar, so we sat naked, eating the nuts and chocolate and devouring the contents of each tiny bottle. I couldn't stand, I was so pissed, so it happened again, right by the mini bar, surrounded by tiny little bottles of pleasure whilst I got mine. I didn't pull away or attempt to leave. I was there in the moment. I searched for the guilt to rescue me, but it couldn't be found. I was a terrible, horrible person who would rot in hell for what I was doing, but even that didn't pull me away from his embrace.

"We need more booze!" Brad said. "Shall we go back to your room?"

I found myself agreeing and taking him back to the honeymoon suite. What was wrong with me? I was that drunk I didn't even care who I bumped into on the way. We were even holding hands and must have stunk of sex – great, satisfying sex. We arrived at the door, but Brad failed to notice the 'Honeymoon Suite' plaque staring back at him, or if he did, he wasn't fazed. The door closed behind us and we were naked again on the floor, on the bed, in the bed, on the bathroom floor, against the bathroom door; in fact, every inch of the honeymoon suite was touched by our naked, desiring bodies. At one point, we were wrapped in my veil, but even that didn't deter us. The mini bar opened, I remember that much, but then it just became a blur, a cloud and I lost sight of everything...

THIRTY-SEVEN

MORNING OF THE WEDDING

His hand is still on my thigh. Why haven't I moved it? I know I should want to move it, but I don't. I just want his fingers to stroke it again. Oh shit, what the fuck am I doing? It's my wedding day! I want to die. Today is my wedding day but I have just had the best sex I have ever had with a blond stranger and I'm due to get married in less than four hours. Forgive me, vicar, for I have sinned, and I am a horrible, disgusting person. What's even worse is that I have a huge grin on my face and I still haven't moved his hand!

We slide back under the duvet, falling naturally into a close embrace, still half asleep, neither of us ready to move, but where do we go from here? He smells divine, he looks divine, I could just eat him all up – oh god, maybe I already have. Please forgive me, please, please, please forgive me. I realise I'm covered in sticky DNA – it's not mine. What a filthy whore! My head feels like it's being squeezed in a vice, my throat is burning and my mouth dry. I couldn't tell you my name, where I am or even really who I'm with as the ability to think has disappeared. Flashbacks: his tongue teasing, erupting in intense pleasure, caressing my breasts, hands travelling down my body, rush of excitement, teeth tugging my clothes. Fuck!

But as I sober, as my brain begins to function, I look up, mouth open, remembering who this is. Is this why I'm not moving, why I'm treasuring every moment, not wanting it to end? I want to stay here forever wrapped in his safe, toned arms, drowning in his scent. Oh god, the confusion. What the fuck am a doing? I am so overwhelmed, my emotions unbalanced: happy, sad, guilty, giddy. The tears start falling, dribbling onto my chin and resting on my chest. I can't believe what has just happened – it's bad, really, really bad. This should have been a missed opportunity. I should have walked away, so why didn't I? I am ridiculously hung over and feel like death. I feel guilty, excited and riddled with anxiety. The bile rises in my throat. I can't stop crying. He kisses every salty tear then kisses my lips. He's gentle, it's meaningful and the intensity builds again. His hand is now rising up my thigh...

We lie in silence, each lost in our own thoughts. This changes everything. If it hadn't happened, then maybe I would have woken in a different place in my head. Maybe I'd have a clear space for my wedding to Rob, for my thoughts to dance around and gel with my new found overwhelming warmth and security. Space for my marriage and future with my husband. But it did happen, the proof is lying right next to me. It's done and can't be changed. I'm in complete and utter shit.

It's 11.27. I'm still in bed. We're still in bed. His hand is no longer on my thigh and, although this disappoints me, I have a sudden urgency to push forward. I hate to admit it, but I have that awful feeling in the pit of my stomach when a date you've loved comes to an end and you don't know if or when you'll see them again. You're desperate to ask but you wouldn't lower yourself, so it's never mentioned and, before you know it, he's gone. Why am I even bothered? I'm getting married in... OMG, less than two and a half hours!

Blond surf dude rises and heads for the bathroom. He doesn't speak, and I wonder if he's feeling that same nervousness. I check him out. Great arse, fabulous legs and a humongous bulge. OMG, he's gorgeous! What do I do? Should I display manners and see him out or stay put. I'm suddenly bashful, even though I'm guessing he's already seen me in all my glory. I try to move but I'm frozen to the bed. In fact, when I think of what just happened in the bed, I may actually be stuck to it! Even though it's my wedding day, I quickly check myself out in the mirror before he returns, when really I should be thinking that my husband (to-be) hasn't even used that bathroom yet! I hear the lock; he's coming and he's looking straight at me. His eyes lock on mine. He gets dressed. Oh god, I remember everything. He heads straight for me and doesn't stop until he's kissing me in the most endearing embrace. His lips graze my cheek as he pulls away and, on leaving the room, he pauses at my wedding dress which hangs before him. He brushes the material with his fingers, looks directly at me, smiles, then closes the door behind him. That feeling right there, it's horrid.

I have to stop myself from passing out and pinch my skin to check this is real. Did that really happen? Am I the lowest of the low? Do I have no respect for Rob at all? Oh god, Rob! I can't get my head to focus on him or the wedding. My heart tells me not to go through with it and to chase the surfer down the corridor screaming STOP! But the few brain cells that have managed to escape are saying I have to go through with it. I know I have to. There's no alternative, there is no way out unless I ruin not only Rob's life but my own and everyone else's within it. I feel sick and rush to the bathroom, emptying the contents of my stomach, the burning bile heating my throat.

I manage to stand and stumble out, leaning against the door frame. Looking at my room, the events unfold in my mind. It's trashed. The mini bar is open, the remnants scattered, an aroma of stale alcohol remains. The contents of my dressing table decorate the carpet, as does my veil. My left wedding shoe is full of what I can only guess to be champagne. The sofa cushions are missing and the bridal welcome pack devoured. I throw up again, only just making it to the toilet in time. I discover my phone amongst the chaos with zillions of missed calls. Oh, dear god! I rush to the toilet and throw up again, and again and again. I just about manage to text Sam; she doesn't shock easily and is great in a crisis:

Sam, I've slept with someone! I need you NOW! Come alone, bring food and pain

```
killers! Hate myself!
```

Sam arrives within minutes.

"I told Lou you'd been for a swim and a sauna and you'd ring her when you're back in your room. She seemed to buy it. What the fuck…?" Her voice trails off as she enters my room, absorbing the unexpected devastation which lies before her. "My god, it's like the room from The Hangover in here. Should I expect to see a baby and a tiger?" We grin as she gives me a hug and gets to work.

I wilfully drink a sachet of magic hangover cure with two Paracetamols *and* two Ibuprofens, not in a fit state to question the dosage. She's brought cereal bars and chocolate and, within minutes, room service arrives with a variety of stodge from the breakfast menu. She'd pre-ordered the minute she received my text. I devour most of it. She runs a bath and plonks me in it then gets to work on clearing the room and stripping the bed. I hear her giving orders to some poor chap on the end of the phone, demanding that the bridal suite be urgently addressed and refreshed as the client has taken ill, but not to mention it to any of the bride's relatives.

Within an hour I feel considerably better, thanks to Sam, and my room is back in order. She's stuffed a dry flannel in my left wedding shoe and rescued my veil. My dress, thank god, appears untouched. We both admire the sheer beauty of it.

I had seen the dress in a TV drama, and it had caught my attention. After hours of surfing the net researching the program and finding the right episode, I eventually found a similar design; It was an ivory/silver full wedding spring gown with a strapless sweetheart neckline and ruched bodice. It has the most beautiful embroidery and beading on both the bodice and skirt, and a lace-up back and chapel length train – utterly stunning and out of this world.

"I don't know what came over me!" I stammer.

"Don't you mean *who*?" She giggles, not that Sam is digging for dirt.

"I don't even know him," I continue, "only in passing. There was always this *attraction* as if we both knew it would lead to something at some point, so when I bumped into him, it was…" Sam hushes me before the waterworks start, forcing more coffee upon me. "I'm just so confused, Sam. James is never far from my mind, my life is just one long whirlwind after another, then Rob, Florida, work. The waiting, it's all too much and I just needed to release, you know?"

She doesn't say a word, just pushes the coffee cup closer to my lips whilst flicking through some images on her phone, which she clearly wants me to see. When it dawns on me that it isn't her phone, it's mine, the colour drains from my face and I burst out laughing. Sam flicks through some rather indecent photos of me and *another*. A smirk warms her face as the image of a strange man wearing my koala onesie and wedding shoes, along with a slash of pink lipstick, stares back at me. I throw myself back on the fresh linen, holding my hands over my face and fall into a fit of giggles. Sam can't hold it back either. We're both in hysterics!

"I prefer this one, look!" She demands, teasing as

she flicks to an image of me half-naked, wearing a tie, suit jacket and heels. I'm on all fours! OMG, I don't even remember doing it but there's lots more to see and of course delete! Sam does the honours as she gently leans into my shoulders.

We hold hands and sit in silence for a few minutes before my phone rings. She squeezes my hand and jumps to attention, answering the phone and pointing to my chest at the same time, rolling her eyes. I look at her questioningly then check in the mirror. To my horror, there is a slight love bite just below my left boob! OMG! I can hear a frantic Lou, whose voice echoes vibrantly. It's as if she's standing in the room. She is right outside the door with her groupies: hairdressers, make-up and bridesmaids.

They all fall in, eager to pour champagne. I slowly sip in appreciation, digging deep for enthusiasm, complimenting the girls on their stunning attire and reassuring them that all is well and reminding them that we can't ignore the time as I'm getting married in ninety minutes!

Sam sneaks away, returning like a princess and of course with my phone, which she discreetly places on the side, winking to indicate it's safe for all to see.

By 1.30pm I have been transformed. My hair is a creation, held in a French plait with individual pearl clips, soft springy curls gently resting on my shoulders, my mother's diamond tiara the finishing touch. My make-up is spectacular, subtle but thick with cement in all the right places, clearly needed. False lashes and heavy, smoky eyes disguise my sins. And my dress, well, my dress is just beautiful. I study it one last time before climbing into it and I can't help but think that maybe it is wasted on this wedding, wasted on me. I feel guilty even looking at it, let alone wearing it, but as it's fitted and laced, I admire my reflection and my mood begins to lift.

"You look gorgeous, Lillian, really beautiful!" Sally catches her tears before tainting her immaculate make-up. Pregnancy does enhance the emotions. "I'm really proud of you, Lil, you really are doing the right thing, he's a great guy," she whispers.

Am I? Am I really doing the right thing? I think I might just throw up again. If only she knew! Sam sends a reassuring wink my way as well as four more pills, which I reluctantly wash down with champagne. What would I do without her? She's been amazing and, as recent events have proved, she's always got my back! She hasn't probed, poked or prodded, knowing quite well that all details will follow when I'm good and ready. Thank god she's great fun too, hilarious in fact. Any silences in the room filled with her hospital stories.

After a good breakfast, a few bucks fizz and an hour with the girls, I finally began to relax and convince myself that I must do this. I must forget about last night and put it behind me. This is my wedding day, I'm getting married to a great guy and I'm getting married in less than half an hour. Shit!

"Where's the car? It should have been here by now?" Jess asks Sam, as her Uncle Jack is the limo driver.

"He's here!" Cries Lou. "Show time!"

I feel sick. As we head downstairs, all eyes are on me. I must admit, I look amazing. But as I reach the last step I almost trip as a chamber maid catches my attention, offering an insincere smile. OMG, does she recognise me? Did she see me last night or am I being paranoid? Does she know my secret? Shit, I'm not sure if I can do this. I need to stop it, stop it now!

"Come on, Auntie Lillian, you can't be drunk already!" My niece, Sadie, catches my arm, helping me down the final steps.

"Thanks honey, I'm just a little nervous, that's all."

I see Freddie as we pull up outside the church, my handsome little pageboy waiting for his mummy. I feel physically sick. The deceit and guilt rise to the surface at the thought of jeopardising his future. What was I playing at? Did I not think of him at all? I'd brush myself down and make this right, for him, for Freddie. But although my intentions are good, the bilious reflux, combined with the tight bodice of the dress restricts my breathing. I take the precious warm hand of my little Freddie, kissing his cheek before sending him ahead with Sadie as she enters the church.

"Watch your dress!" Sadie warns.

"This is the one time I know there's no sticky fingers!" I respond as I take Dad's arm and steady myself, catching a glimpse of the congregation and an outline of Rob standing at the altar. My breath is shallow, my lungs restricted.

"You look stunning!" My father whispers. "Ready?"

I don't know if I am ready. Will I ever be ready? Is this *being ready* for me? The alternative crosses my mind: confessing, admitting, hiding, running, escaping, all the above, but my thoughts flash to Freddie, the aftermath, the devastation, my poor mum, Dad, the whole family, but most of all, Rob. What would this do to him? I couldn't humiliate him like that. No! I had to ride the storm and face up to it. What happened last night was just a drunken, crazy, last minute wild fling. It's over, finito, done.

"Ready!" I reply, smiling at Dad and winking at Freddie, who's turned back to look at me, then slowly, head down the aisle.

I'm here, I've made it. Rob and I stand together at the altar. He whispers to me that I'm gorgeous, just stunning, and squeezes my hand. Guilt riddles my very being. He doesn't deserve this. He looks so handsome and happy to be here. My head is battered and I can't focus, flicking back to the events of the previous night then back to Rob and I lose concentration. Panic overwhelms and I begin to sweat. Oh god, what have I done? What have I done? How could I do this to him? Oh god, I need air. I smile at Rob, taking in all that is him, with his groomed hair, pressed shirt and shiny shoes, then my brain finds an image of *him, blond surf dude,* in his suit with bare feet, and I have to blink it off to refocus. I think of James, is my heart really with him? Would that explain my behaviour? I try to look happy and interested, but I hate myself.

The ceremony begins. Here we go, oh bugger, no turning back now. Then I hear the word 'wife'. Oh my god, WIFE! Shit, shit, shit. The words of the vicar roll into one and I find myself drifting. My mind begins to contemplate how much the whole damn thing has cost and whether we would get a refund if I pulled out now? What would Rob say if he knew I'd had another man in my bed, *our* bed? I couldn't claim ownership of it. It is the bridal suite, so it is as much his as it is mine. If only last night hadn't happened. But it was magical, electrifying, exciting.

I hear the vicar ask if there was anyone who does not deem this wedding fit to go ahead and I start to panic, thinking that maybe someone will. Maybe I should speak up now and own up to God. He does seem to be staring at me from all angles. Oh god, oh shit, I'm so sorry to keep swearing in your house! The whole church falls silent and the vicar doesn't speak again for some time as if knowing that someone might come forward. Oh shit, I wonder if he knows, if he senses it. He begins again but I'm not listening until the penny drops that he's saying my name again and again. I feel sick. This is it, my time, my turn. I have to say my part and surrender to this marriage. I can't breathe. I CAN'T BREATHE!

"Lillian, do you take Robert Lomax to be your lawful wedded husband? Lillian?"

I realise where I am and came back to earth with a bang. "Sorry," I whisper, holding back the lump of bile stuck in my throat as the vicar repeats his question one more time.

Just as I am about to force the words "I do", the church door opens and footsteps echo around the room. Everyone turns to see who has interrupted the ceremony at such a delicate moment. You can almost hear one huge intake of breath as the whole congregation sighs in disgust. I can feel the heat rising within me, burning like a fire, my heart thumping through my ribcage, racing to get out. I turn slowly, as does Rob. OMG, the surfer, last night, this morning, he's here. I'm looking straight into his eyes. I notice the girls, my mum and dad and then Rob and then... I pass out!

"Lillian? Lillian love, wake up!" I can hear the faint sound of my mother's voice, but it isn't that clear. I'm tired, very tired, exhausted... need to rest... "Lillian, you're ok, love. It's all ok. Come on, wake up!"

What does she mean I'm ok? I know I'm ok. I'm just sleeping, leave me alone. My head hurts, I feel sick. Am I shaking? Am I speaking, shouting or dreaming? Either way, I'm awake and try to sit up. Whoa, not so fast, take it easy now, lie back down!

What the fu...? I open my eyes slowly and focus on what appears to be people sat upside down with their feet in the air. Eh? Then I feel the comfort of my mother's warm hand stroking mine and, as I regain consciousness, I discover I am lying on the floor next to the altar!

"Why am I on the floor?" I whisper.

"You fainted, love. Are you ok?" Then she gets closer and whispers, "You're not pregnant, are you, Lillian?" Typical of my mother. "Come on, let's get you up and continue with your wedding!"

Arghh, wedding! I passed out! My mother heaves me into a sitting position, my back to the congregation, whose burning stares pierce through my bodice. Slowly, not so elegantly, I scramble to my feet, brushing down my dress. Both Rob and the vicar begin fussing over me but it's so damned annoying I force them out of my personal zone. As I indicate for them to back off, I'm suddenly aware of my audience: friends, family, and James, who looks at me endearingly with concern. Where did he come from? Oh god, now I'm more confused! I see Rob's family. Oh god, Rob's family! Pretty much everyone and anyone I know is watching me. I feel nauseous. Am I going to pass out again? I feel the bile rise and pray it stays in my throat, but as much as I try, I admit defeat as it travels from my stomach in a retched flow, projecting thick and fast! I hear that familiar gasp again as I vomit all down my dress, all over the floor, with the final speckles landing gracefully on the vicar's shoes. He takes a step back. I don't blame him, it stinks. Bacon, eggs, champagne, guilt. It won't let me hide; I can't escape it. Embarrassment doesn't cover it. I'm mortified, disgusted at myself, disappointed that I've ruined our day, my life, Freddie's!

I crouch down on the floor, just there where I am, in my sick, not caring any more. I'm done, it's done, I'm ruined. I have sick on my hands, in my hair, clearly on my dress and veil. There's no dignity here. It left, probably some time ago.

The congregation is shuffling, not sure what to do, where to go. Would you? They clearly want to watch the show but are overwhelmed about doing the right thing, not to mention the stench heading their way. The vicar asks them to sit and remain calm. There's no fire after all.

Not caring, with no inclination to move, I feel bodies around me, limbs lifting me as Sam and Jess each take an arm and lead me to the back of the church, to the vestry and out of the way. Lou is trying to save my dress from the puddles of sick on the floor. James offers a slight smile, reassuring, comforting. Does he know what I've done? They plonk me down on an old splintered pew, encouraging me to drink water, which I take gladly.

"So? What's going on? Have you eaten something? Are you ill? What happens now? There's another wedding in forty minutes, Lillian so I'm not quite sure where that leaves you! Do you feel well enough to continue?" Lou tries to show compassion, but her matron-like eagerness can't help but slip through. I know she is secretly panicking, and of course concerned. She would be left to explain to Mum and Dad. What would she tell them? She had already fought them off from entering the room.

Sam and Jess exchange glances but remain silent, cleaning around me, but I know they are all waiting patiently for me to speak. I sigh and take a very deep breath before I start.

"I slept with someone else last night in the honey-moon suite. I went to a party and got blind drunk, then shagged all night with a total stranger and had the best sex I ever had!" It felt so good to get it out. "I smoked a joint and drank the contents of the mini bar, I've been up all night and haven't slept."

Stunned silence.

"Are you friggin' kidding me, Lillian? What? Seriously?" Lou can't comprehend what's just come out of my mouth, she's not impressed and clearly in a state of shock.

Sam offers a smile, she already knows, she's already picked up some of the pieces. Who would pick up the rest? Lou is appalled, standing there, staring at me, watching my every move. I don't think she can quite believe how honest I've been.

"Was it James?" I shake my head. "No? Bloody hell, Lillian, what is wrong with you? So, what do I tell everyone? Do you still want to get married to Rob?"

I stare into space as I don't have the answers... to anything. "I don't know! No? Maybe? Do I still have that choice? I don't have the answers! Can I really go through with it, knowing what I've done? It's not fair on him!"

"How about if you tell him? He might forgive you. How do you know *he* wasn't up to no good last night? It was a night of freedom for both of you!" Shouts Lou as she marches off in temper.

Rob appears minutes later. "Lillian are you alright, love? I was worried but couldn't get near you." He offers Sam a stern look, clearly blaming her for his No Entry into the vestry. "What's going on? Are you sick?" He is almost within hugging distance but has a change of heart upon seeing the remnants of vomit.

"OMG, Lillian, look at you!" He covers his mouth slightly, trying to ignore the smell whilst telling me that we don't have long left of our ceremony 'slot' as there is another wedding at four. "Are you ready? Maybe try and clean yourself up a bit!" He gestures towards my sick-splattered dress, knowing he's stated the obvious. My wedding is now a *slot*!

Sam creeps away as she's caught sight of the vicar entering the room. She leads him back out again, shrugging her shoulders and leaving me to my own fate.

"Lillian? What's the matter? You're scaring me."

Rob has every right to be scared. I look a bugger, although deep down it isn't my appearance that frightens him; my hair has fallen out of its plait, my dress is ruined, and my tiara is knotted on one side of my head.

"Lillian, look at me!" He tries to grab my hands, but I pull away.

I don't know where my confidence has come from, but I find the courage to confess to Rob the events of the past twenty-four hours. I give him as much information as I can to aid fewer questions. It pours out, no graphics, no animation, just monotone text, no eye contact and no stopping for breath. There. It is out in the open like dirty laundry for all to see. I feel so much better, even some of the guilt lifts. I open a door in the vestry, which to my relief leads outside – fresh air at last. I lean against the frame, breathing in as much oxygenated air as I can.

"I'm so sorry Rob, I don't know what happened or what came over me, but it happened. Nothing you say will make me feel as bad as I do already. It's unforgivable, unthinkable and I shouldn't have let the wedding take place. I'm really, really sorry from the bottom of my heart." Tears are rolling down my face. Tears of sadness, tears of relief that the truth has come from *me*.

He gets to his feet and stands for a second, silent in thought as I watch the colour drain from his normally rosy cheeks. Then it comes...

"WHAT? Shit! What the fuck did you just say? OMG! Fuck, Lillian, are you kidding me? You're saying that you shouldn't have let the wedding take place? But you did, Lillian, it's taking place now! This is it, this is the memory you've left for our future! Thanks! Do you not think you should have said something? Did you *want* to humiliate me? In front of all our friends and family?" He paces up and down, fuming. He has every right to be. "Hang on, sorry, I may have misunderstood? Can you repeat what you've just said?" I'm just about to speak when he interrupts me. "QUIET!" He is so loud it must have vibrated through the church! "OH MY GOD, I've only just heard it, wait! I think I've got it... last night, before our wedding, whilst in your pyjamas, you were invited to a party by some stranger in a lift, who you've never met before?" I was going to interrupt and explain that he wasn't entirely a stranger, but I thought it might make things worse so kept quiet. "...you went to the party, got blind drunk on the whole contents of the mini bar and slept with him?" He looked me straight in the eye. "Whose mini bar was it, Lillian, our mini bar?"

Oh god, I think I'm going to be sick again. I can't do with these questions. I should have been more specific!

The silence is deafening.

"WAS IT OUR MINI BAR?" He roars. It is deeply upsetting listening to him repeat what I'd done, absolutely shocking to the core, as if he is talking about someone else, someone I wouldn't know. "ANSWER ME!" He demands, even though he clearly knows.

But I can't respond as the bile begins to rise again and the final dregs of my stomach make an appearance. I'm doubled over outside, trying to vomit as far away from the vestry as possible, when I notice another person has come to join the party.

"Are you ok, Lillian? OMG, that was far out, what happened in there. I had no idea this was *your* wedding, I swear. I absolutely swear, but…"

"Brad Johnson?" Rob asks. "Is that you? What an earth are you doing here?" Rob looks at Brad then straight at me, not giving him a chance to reply. "Wait…" I can hear the cogs of Rob's brain struggling to turn. "Was it you? Are you the secret shagger that drank the contents of my mini bar?"

They clearly know each other, so it soon becomes obvious to me that this was Brad's long-lost family member. I debate introducing them but think better of it! Brad looks up, sighing, not quite believing what mess he's got himself into.

"Look mate…" he offers.

"You're clearly not my mate…"

Rob starts shouting and pushing at Brad, who tries to calm him down, but it is too late. Rob takes a swing, knocking Brad to the floor. I gasp in horror, as do Sam, Jess and Lou, who had come flying outside after hearing the scrap.

"Rob, calm down, I didn't know she was your bride, dude…!" Brad tries to squirm his way out of it as I realise I was just some bird he'd had fun with. Brad tries to hold Rob back, but he is too strong, his anger too fierce, as he challenges Brad, sending him flying once more.

"Boys, stop it!" Shouts Lou. "Stop it!"

But it is too late. Rob is chasing Brad around the churchyard, with not only my guests watching the show, but the 4pm wedding guests too! They end up back inside the vestry, brawling around on the floor. Rob eventually gets to his feet.

"You're not bloody worth it, any of you. James, you're welcome to her, fill your boots!"

"My name's Brad, actually!" Brad shouts as he scrambles to his feet, "but who the hell is James?"

"I am!" James replies, as the whole of the vestry turns to see James leaning against the door, cool as a cucumber. "What do we have here then?"

"YOU, you're another one who's welcome to her. In fact, I should bloody hit you as well!"

Rob, still furious, flings himself in James' direction, hurling his fists. James ducks, grabbing Rob around his waist and wrestling him to the floor, keeping him there with the aid of Brad. At this point, Sally enters, looking on in astonishment at the commotion presenting itself in front of her. She stops dead in her tracks, looking directly below her to the floor. We all follow her eyes and gasp upon seeing that the poor girl's waters have broken.

"Boys, stop!" I shout. "Enough! Sally!"

The boys all stop, shocked as they too notice Sally squelching through her waters which have soaked her dress, bag and shoes. Rob gets to his feet, brushes himself down and nods at Sally as he leaves. Brad looks at me, then shrugs at James and also leaves the room. James runs to get the wedding car as we all fuss over Sally to calm her. Could today get any more eventful? Sam and Jess slowly but surely get Sally into the back of the Jag then jump in themselves, but stop me as I am about to follow.

"Lillian, your dress!" Sam states. "You'll have to take it off!" She is right, it is still covered in dried sick, not good for a woman in labour. "HURRY!"

I turn to James and ask him to unlace my dress, just before our eyes lock. I feel a shiver as his hands brush my neck, then smile as he indicates the awful aroma coming from my finery.

"Wait a second!" He runs back into the vestry as I shuffle out of my dress. "You know what a vestry is, don't you?" He hands me some sort of cloak. "It's a cupboard for church clothes!"

James helps me into a dusty cloak, attempting to ignore my undergarments, despite having seen it all before, then slots me into the car. Pleased at the distraction, we encourage Sally to take deep breaths as James closes the door, hitting the roof, indicating for Jack to go. Laughter fills the car as we zoom off at speed to the hospital. Sally's contractions are coming thick and fast!

Swaddled in the church cloak, ignoring the stares from hospital staff, I exit the labour ward, leaving Sally and Lloyd with their new bundle of joy, a baby girl. As I look up, I come face to face with James and Freddie.

"Mamma!" Freddie shuffles towards me, throwing his warm, cuddly arms around my legs.

I pick him up, holding him close, when the tears begin falling. James pats the seat next to him, which I gladly take, still clinging on to Freddie. I shed mountains of tears until my ducts are dry. James takes my hand as I sink deeper into both of them until the last tear falls. We all sit huddled together in silence.

"Nice cloak!" Says James. "Suits you!" He gets to his feet, scooping Freddie in his arms, then reaches his hand out for me, holding my eyes in question. It doesn't take long for me to take his hand in both of mine. He pulls me to my feet, holding me close, kissing my temple. He doesn't let go as he leads us both out of the hospital. "Let's go home."

ACKNOWLEDGEMENTS

First of all, I'd like to thank my family and friends for their support and reassurance that publishing this book was the right thing to do. My husband Dave, my rock, and my amazing mum in supporting me on this journey and never doubting for one second that my goal could be achieved. A special thanks also goes to my illustrator, Mark Wilcox, who not only designed the stunning front cover, but who also became more of a mentor as my wobbles frequently rose to the surface. And to Sian-Elin Flint-Freel my Copy-Editor, for all her support and knowledge that helped bring this novel to life.

Thank you

KAREN KELLY

Karen lives with her husband Dave, children Charlie and Maggie and their devoted collie, Baxter.
A successful Blogger, Volunteer Radio Presenter, Mum and Homemaker. She began writing over 20 years ago as a hobby alongside her chosen career path as cabin crew. If she's not running around like a headless chicken, she can be found with a large G&T and a bucket load of crisps!

KAREN KELLY Author can be found on Facebook or you can follow her on Twitter @karenlindakelly